D'

Divine

Ecstasy

Other Titles by Setta Jay:

The Guardians of the Realms Series:

Hidden Ecstasy

Ecstasy Unbound

Ecstasy Claimed

Denying Ecstasy

Tempting Ecstasy

Piercing Ecstasy

Binding Ecstasy

Searing Ecstasy

Divine Ecstasy

Setta Jay

A Guardians of the Realms Novel

Copyright:

Disclaimer:

This book is a work of fiction. Any resemblance to any person living or dead is purely coincidental. The characters and places are products of the author's imagination and used fictitiously.

Warning: Sexually explicit content, dirty language and Gods behaving badly.

Contributors:

Editor: BookBlinders

Proofreader: Pauline Nolet

Acknowledgements:

As always, a huge thank you to my editor and proofreader, Lindy and Pauline, for helping make these books the best they can be.

Tons of love to my husband for just being amazing throughout the process.

Thank you to all the Book Bloggers who have given me immeasurable support and guidance. Sending out big hugs to you all!

I also want to thank those of you in the Setta's Sexies fan groups on Facebook and Goodreads. You make me smile every day! I love you all! I want to send a special shout out to Lee, Kumiko and Suzanne for being awesome Admins.

Thank you to all who post, engage or just watch the craziness from the sidelines in all my social media outlets.

And lastly, a MASSIVE thank you to all of the fans for reading. I wouldn't be able to do what I love without your support.

Divine Ecstasy – Book Eight (The Guardians of the Realms)

The slave of demented Gods, Sacha knew only a life of anguish and suffering until she was reborn as a Guardian of the Realms. Gifted with immense strength and rare abilities, she has spent thousands of years battling to protect the four Realms with her Guardian family. Time has allowed her to construct the perfect mask of calm and control so none can see the past shame and immense pain buried in the darkest recesses of her mind. Now, an encounter with a new and powerful enemy has left Sacha the victim of a poison induced coma that all are unable to heal. The last thing anyone imagines waking her is a God with the strength and potential to unravel her entire world.

As the most powerful of the Gods, Hades was awakened from the Creators' enforced sleep to help the Guardians in their quest to find his heinous brother, Apollo. After a brutal battle with an unknown Goddess leaves him in need of healing he finds himself powerfully drawn into the room of a sleeping seductress. Her soul calls to him relentlessly, but if he surrenders himself to that connection and gives her the strength to heal, life as he knows it will end.

With their worlds unraveling and new threats at every turn will Sacha's past destroy them? Or will she bring a God to his knees and lead them both into Divine Ecstasy.

Prologue

Apollo's Palace, Earth Realm – Millennia Ago

A gony threatened to split Sacha's mind in two.

The painful rending nearly forced a cry from her lips and came with a wave of emotion so powerful and heartbreaking she was forced to brace a shaking hand against the smooth stone wall. She drew her hand to her side, heart tightening as she glanced down the long hall, making sure there were no witnesses to her agony.

Her sister was dead.

The second she could move, she shifted her long mass of ebony hair back over her shoulders and slipped quickly through the candlelit space. Her slippers were silent against the marble floors, they had to be. She could not afford to call attention to herself, and there was no time to waste.

The onslaught of confusion and pain running inside her mind fed her urgency. She swallowed past the constriction in her throat. Mourning wasn't possible.

Not now.

Not ever.

She allowed herself one last shaky breath before she closed off all emotion and willed her heartbeat to steady. Too many of the guards were Lykos or Ailouros, and the wolves and felines existing inside those Immortals made hiding all emotion necessary.

It was not only her pain attempting to rip her apart, she was also subject to the agony and disorientation of the small boy who needed her now. Her blood. Her sister's only child and the son she would claim and protect as her own as she had promised. She forced calm into her mind, blocking most of his pain, as she followed the mental link to him.

Her last few minutes with her sister replayed in her mind as she slipped through the dimly lit tunnel.

"There is not much time. Apollo will be expecting me soon." Phedra's words were low as they both darted glances down the tunnel. *"He plans to send me to gather information on Ares and Artemis."*

"He cannot," Sacha ground out, her mind was reeling with her sister's words. Others of their race had been sent on similar tasks through the years, never to return. A glimpse of the golden serpents circling both their wrists reminded Sacha just how powerless they were. Those bands not only drained Immortal strength and power, they severed family bonds and kept them all from rising up against the corrupt Gods.

They were slaves.

"He can, and he will," Phedra said with added force.

This could be a death sentence, or worse, if the stories of Ares

12

and Artemis were true. Sacha could only hope that those tales had been fabricated by Apollo to keep them in fear of the other Gods, but too many had been lost after leaving the island.

Already her mind was working to find a way to save her sister.

The low cadence of Phedra's voice slipped through Sacha's thoughts. "I need you to do something for me."

The dim look in her sister's eyes made Sacha's bones ache.

"I need this. I wouldn't ask it otherwise." Strength and determination combined with urgency told Sacha just how real this was. How little time they might have.

Her heart stilled, but she nodded. "Anything."

"I need to mentally link you to Sebastian." Phedra's son, her only child, who'd been taken at birth to be raised in the warrior camps. The boy had been thrust into the fate of all Immortal young. An existence both she and Phedra knew well.

Sacha wouldn't hesitate to protect her sister's child with her life. But she didn't want to, she wanted Phedra to come back.

"You will return..." The attempt at reassurance was bitter on Sacha's lips.

The very real fear that Phedra wouldn't be able to complete her task settled inside Sacha's stomach. She barely heard her sister's voice as she blindly nodded.

She could take her sister's place, but Apollo would never consider it. She was a failure in the God's eyes, which had been her exact intentions in hiding some of her talents. Even her secret ability *wouldn't be enough to allow her to take Phedra's place.*

The only skill Phedra had managed to conceal from Apollo and Hermes was her power in forming mental links. It was something that no Immortal should have been capable of, not after all the Gods had done to control and imprison them. Phedra had linked them mentally long ago, having felt the echoes of their true family bond the moment they'd met. They couldn't communicate through it, but the connection allowed them to feel the other's emotion and track each other's location. With all the intrigue in the palace, it had been a lifeline they had often used... Their one true comfort.

"Thank you. I would not ask this of you if there were any other way." Her sister closed her eyes. "I should never have reinforced my bond with him after he was taken, but I could not stop..." Phedra sucked in a shuddering breath. "I had to know he was safe. I had to have that small connection to him even if he never understood. Never knew I was there. It was selfish, but I cannot help that now."

Phedra's dark eyes were hard when she gripped Sacha's hands in hers. "If my bond with him breaks, he won't understand. And you know what it is like in the warrior camps." The urgency in her sister's tone said it all. They'd both been raised there. A yawning void opened inside her.

Sacha nodded. "I know." Any show of emotion was dangerous in that place. Only aggressive emotions and acts were allowed. Anything else meant the mental training had failed. Failure equaled death for the very young... Their bodies were but instruments in creating the Deity's perfect army.

Apollo had used beasts in the first Immortals to make them stronger. They were nothing more than weapons, breeders or servants. That was the reason the God tore families apart and mentally conditioned them as children. Their only value was in serving him or protecting his island.

"You'll come back." Sacha infused her tone with conviction.

When her sister shook her head and tightened her hold, Sacha held her hard gaze. "You have to come back." She didn't want her sister going into the task already defeated. "You will. But I promise you that Sebastian will be protected if something happens. On my life, I swear it."

Or Sacha would die trying. "Now promise me that you will do anything you have to in order to gain sanctuary with Hades, Athena or Aphrodite, or return here."

Her sister's bronze shoulders straightened. "I promise I will do everything possible to make it back." Phedra brought her in for a tight embrace. Sacha soaked in the warmth and sweet scent of her sister. She held her emotions intact even as her heart was breaking.

"I'll be waiting," Sacha whispered. "Now do it."

Her sister's shoulders eased, but she still maintained their tight embrace.

Sacha sucked in a breath when she felt her sister inside her mind. It was comforting, warm, but when the new sliver of light slid from her sister out to her, Sacha was forced to hold onto her sister's arm. The connection was incredibly pure, so brilliant and light that she never wanted to see it dim. The second it locked into place, she searched her sister's eyes and felt the breaking of both their hearts. Neither could say anything for a moment. They would pretend for the moment that Phedra was coming back and the child hadn't just become Sacha's.

"Thank you," her sister said with a hitch in her voice. "I must go." The finality in her tone was as harsh as the booted steps echoing from down the hall. "Take care of him." Phedra squeezed tight once more before adding with a slight hitch, "When he is old enough to understand, tell him I loved him more than life. And that the greatest gift I could give him was you."

Sacha forced tears away as she tried to be strong for both of them. "I love you... He will know." With a last hug, both swallowed. Phedra turned and was gone.

Sacha came out of her memories, forcing away the anguish all over again. She had a promise to keep and a child that needed her, but after that she vowed to find some way, any way possible to destroy Apollo and Hermes.

Her mind racing, she turned down another hallway, alert to any movement in the silent tunnel.

Not only would she wield the power she'd managed to hide from the Gods, she was going to enter the one place forbidden by all but a select few of the highest-ranking guards.

And she had to succeed.

Outwardly she was calm, her breathing steady and her features soft. Nothing in her appearance would betray her emotions. She slid her dark cloak back to show her bare shoulders and the sheer white of her dress. She'd be at the entrance soon and she only had one opportunity to get close. Her body was one of the few advantages allowed her, and she would use it without thought. She relaxed into the seductive glide she knew would show the sentry what she was offering.

Sacha lowered her lashes and lifted her lips in invitation when she grew near the Lykos.

The big male raised a dark brow. "You shouldn't be down here, female."

"I thought you would like the company." The sultry affectation slid from her without thought.

The male lifted his nose to the air, and she was careful not to allow anything in her scent or demeanor to betray her. She was used to dealing with the animal breeds. She focused her mind and body to exude pure sexual intent. Male Immortals were base creatures who needed and wanted all the time. Sex and the Earth's energies were fuel for their bodies. She was grateful for that weakness.

His amber eyes clouded with caution and a hint of desire. "I am on duty now," he growled.

She just needed to get a little closer. She slid her fingers over her bottom lip before whispering, "We can be fast... Quiet..."

When he lowered his hand away from the blade at his side and looked behind her, she knew she had him. Moving in close, she lifted to her toes and slid her hands over his chest. He didn't pull her in, but he didn't push her away either when she drew his head down to whisper in his ear, "What's the harm in a few moments of play?"

His lips curved. "Quickly, then," he agreed.

The big male pulled her lips to his, and the second their breaths mingled, she loosed the full force of her power to paralyze the hulking male. To jolt his mind with the air she breathed through his lips. He groaned and stilled, caught in time. She'd have to see the promise through later, but for now she had only a little time to get to Sebastian and back while he was caught in the moment. She hoped there weren't many others. She already felt the drain of her energy at having used the powerful ability.

The guard's eyes were focused on nothing as she slipped through the doorway behind him and into the dangers beyond.

Chapter 1

Guardian Manor, Tetartos Realm – Present Day

Compulsion and need were riding Hades unmercifully. The first sight of the stunning figure sleeping in the small cavern room beneath the Guardian manor was tearing him open, but the sound of her soul was unhinging him completely. It was dragging him in, pulling at his own soul, something until this very moment he would have argued he didn't have. It was demanding and intoxicating in a way that wrecked him. The dim memory of his nephew Draken at the doorway barely entered his mind.

He dug his fingers through his dark hair. Every muscle in his body had pulled tight from the moment he entered the room. All he could do was fight the pull and stare at her prone figure lying alone there in the darkened space. Her bronze skin and features were perfection, from the high cheekbones down to the soft slope of her nose, but it wasn't just his cock reacting to the lust that came from being near a beautiful female. His entire being ached for this female.

His wings flexed and violently unfurled, taking up the space around him. Ebony feathers twitched as he concentrated on what this meant.

He knew who the exquisite female was. His son, Pothos, had informed him of who all the Guardians were when Hades had been awoken from the Creators' enforced sleep. He'd seen her image when Pothos had telepathically shared his memories of all the centuries he'd lain in stasis, but he'd never before seen the beauty in real life.

Sacha.

Even the sound of her name called to him. He imagined how it would sound on his lips when he slid inside her.

He growled in frustration. A deep primal part of him disliked seeing her lying so still in the bed. Harmed. Poisoned by some unknown beast, according to his son. Why hadn't the healer already taken care of her? He growled, knowing it meant Sirena hadn't been able to. He'd always had a weakness for females, but never had he felt this harsh, pulse-pounding need to care for one.

He gripped his long hair and tied it back in frustration and in need of doing something with his hands. He wanted them on her body, but he was standing on a ledge. If he stepped off, his life was forever altered. She would be his to protect for eternity.

Ares and Artemis were still locked away, unable to target her as they'd done with his son and sisters, but it didn't make any of this easier.

"Fuck!" Drake snarled from his spot at the door, and Hades ignored it, too lost in his own battle to deal with his nephew. The blond dragon leader of the Guardians could wait for whatever he wanted.

Hadn't he envied his sisters, Athena and Aphrodite, for their soul bonds with their males? It had only given him more beings to keep safe all those millennia ago, but his sisters had been so damned happy. Aphrodite had always teased and taunted him about all the pleasures he'd never know without having a soul bond. As deep as he hungered for that pleasure now, there was no doubt in his mind that things would be different for him.

He was the strongest of the Gods, so he'd never need the added power an Immortal could give him through the soul bonding. But that didn't matter... this small female needed him. She needed his strength to heal, and his flesh crawled at the sight of her lying there with poison running in her veins.

He growled again. Time seemed to have stilled.

The soft cadence of her breathing pulled him closer as her soul continued its song, drawing him near like a Siren's voice.

It was making him lose his mind. His reality singled down to one key point.

She belonged to him. Fate had made the choice for them both. For eternity. He forced his body to calm as he attempted to see the advantage. The Guardians would never band together and attempt to force him back into the Creators' sleeping unit if he was bonded to one of their own. They could never go back on their word to allow him freedom after he found Apollo and locked the escaped God away.

The Guardians obviously needed him more than they cared to admit to themselves, to his continued exasperation.

But it was his son who needed him most, and he could be ruthless in his intent to make sure the boy was safe.

He gazed down at her and mentally cursed because none of that mattered as much as it should when her soul's call was so damned incredible. Long dark lashes rested against smooth bronzed skin, so beautiful and so in need of his strength.

"Hades, listen to me," Drake growled as he moved into the room, stalking closer to Hades' side. The thrumming of her call almost completely drowned out the sound of his nephew's words. He only spared a quick glare into the emerald eyes of the dragon, the male took up nearly as much space as Hades, which meant the room was too damned full.

He ignored the male as he gazed down at the bed, flexing his wings.

After the battle days ago with a Goddess of Thule, he'd been forced to refuel his energies down below the Guardians' manor. The entire time, he'd been on edge, and now he understood why. He was a God; he didn't get agitated. But being close to *this* female had affected him to the point that he'd been led to her side.

He growled as he moved closer and steeled himself for what he was about to do. What he fucking needed to do.

"You can't touch her." His nephew's growled words were enough to distract him. The dragon had made it to his side.

Hades' eyes shot to him as power licked out at the male in warning. His wings unfurled even further, curling in to touch the bed as he spoke. "Do. Not. Presume to tell me what to do, nephew."

His eyes landed back on his female and he changed the course of his life in the blink of an eye. His muscles tensed and then power unleashed, sliding out to fill her up so full it felt like his whole being was inside hers, causing Sacha's unconscious body to shudder. His groan was deep and animalistic as he connected them fully, infusing her with his strength. The intensity was enough to bow his back in pure pleasure. It was erotic to the point that his cock felt ready to explode before even touching her skin.

The sheer intimacy of the soul bond hit him like a blow. This was the secret ambrosia his sisters had spoken of, the treasure he'd never fully understood. Never thought he'd have the chance to know.

He glimpsed her supple back bow under the blankets, lifting full breasts toward him in sweet offering. The soft moan that slipped from her sexy bow lips called to him. It was the last he heard as he waited to see her eyes.

Draken's body and power lashed out against him before he could pull her into his arms. Breaking them both apart as the dragon ported Hades away from his prize.

Chapter 2

Outside the Guardian Manor, Tetartos Realm

When Hades reformed, his eyes flickered in the sunlit wooded area by the manor. He grabbed Drake by the throat and lifted him in the cool mountain air. His blue gaze tinted toward crimson as fury reigned. He'd been cheated out of the sight of his female waking for him because his nephew had teleported him from her side.

Everything felt out of control. His need, the intensity of his fury were all stronger in the moment.

And his iron control was stretched near breaking.

Draken fought the hold as Hades readied to drop him to the ground. Before he could dispose of his burden and teleport back to his female, his son was there. His son, Pothos, slammed his unique ability into the mix. Numbness filled Hades' limbs, but nothing could dissipate the fury of his own child using power against him.

"Hades, you need to calm the fuck down before I knock you on your ass," Draken snarled as the dragon grabbed his arm and fully broke Hades' grip while putting out a telekinetic hold, preventing Hades from teleporting to his female. It seemed that Draken hadn't been as affected by Pothos' power, or his son was directing the majority of it at him. That thought made him more than fucking furious as he glared over at the boy.

"What the hell is going on?" Pothos snapped.

He ignored his son's question and directed his anger at his nephew as his wings flared out behind him. Hades was a benevolent God, but a God nonetheless and not one to be challenged. He'd known the responsibility of the Realms since before they were even born.

Yet, since he'd been awakened to help the Guardians find his brother, they had been challenging him at every turn. And because their collective power and abilities were strong enough to put him back in his sleeping unit, he'd been forced to compromise at every turn.

His anger resurged as he let his power free, knowing it was the need to get back to his female fueling his anger. He pushed against his own son's power to let Draken feel his rage; his ability gripped the male's soul and squeezed, attempting to loosen the male's telekinetic hold.

The dragon grunted and his thick shoulders tensed before he narrowed his emerald eyes. His nephew withstood the assault before launching into him. Hades sailed back into something hard and he heard the sound of wood snapping. More wood cracked from the force of impact as Hades powered Drake into nearby trees in return, but he still couldn't port. It was like fighting through rubber as Pothos' power pulled at him, every muscle in his body strained as he battled through it.

"Son of a bitch, would you two stop being assholes."

Pothos growled as a female reformed next to him.

Hades was telekinetically ripped away from the dragon with a force that pushed the air from his lungs. Power constricted around him, holding him a few feet in the air. His narrowed eyes met the glittering gold of Drake's mate, Era, once known as Delia. The small female's black-cherry hair lifted in wild waves around her with the sheer power she unleashed on him. Fire licked at his flesh, and he fought the need to show her what it meant to challenge a God.

Pothos regarded them with a shake of his head. "I thought we'd already done this fucking pissing-contest shit. Did you two really think Era wouldn't know you two were going at it? The whole place is shaking with the power from your damned temper tantrum."

Drake whispered soothingly to Era, who looked all too happy to let her fire have him. New skin worked double time to regenerate the singed flesh. When it eased, he pushed against her telekinesis and watched her body jerk as he ripped free of the hold, but he was still prevented from porting by Draken.

He needed to get back to his female. He had no time to deal with whatever Draken's petty issues were now.

"Enough," Pothos commanded.

Hades narrowed his eyes at his son. Bright sapphire eyes assessed him back. Pride and anger fought for dominance in his mind. He loved his son, but this constant distrust was grating. It didn't matter that he'd hidden things about his son's mother and that she'd been a priestess of Thule. In the end he'd been on his way to Pothos' home to discuss it when he'd been drawn to Sacha's room.

"Release your hold," he commanded with a push of power in warning. Thoughts of Thule and the Goddess Kara, who'd come through days ago, had a minimal calming effect on his cock. As of that morning, the Goddess was still unconscious. A quick check on his link with Apollo confirmed the missing asshole was still nowhere to be found. He'd been doing the same thing from the moment his nephew had told him the bastard was loose and that they needed his help in finding the God.

His skin itched with the need to get to his female. To see her whole and healthy and greedy for him to consummate the bond. He needed to feel her skin, her pouty little lips on his body.

His muscles twitched at the thought of all the ways he wanted her.

He growled as his glance hit Pothos. His son should be on his side. It had been a source of discord between the two since he'd been awoken. Pothos had been chosen as a Guardian when Hades was sent to sleep. The Creators had chosen wisely, his son was meant to lead. But now Pothos was duty bound to keep watch over the sleeping Gods, even him, while also ensuring humanity had the ability to evolve, which was why the Immortals were confined in Tetartos Realm, away from the fragile mortals of Earth.

He understood his son's duty, but Pothos was Hades' fucking son. It was right there in his features. The only differences were in hair and body adornments. His son had his black hair cut short, whereas Hades' was long. His child also had black things in his ears and markings all over his arms. His child even had his wings. Though Hades would never understand why Pothos preferred to keep them retracted and wear shirts.

His son growled, "Someone tell me what the hell this is about." It was obvious to Hades that Pothos was meant to command, yet he kept to the shadows instead, allowing Draken to lead. He shook his head. Need beat at him, and annoyance wasn't helping. Rational thought was a flimsy concept at the moment, but force wouldn't help him now. He could get free, but they would only come for him in greater numbers and they'd only go through this same damned thing all over again. He drew a deep breath. Never had he dealt with anything like this.

"Why did you take me from her?" He commanded the dragon to speak.

His nephew snarled, "I was saving your ass from doing something fucking stupid."

Hades' eyes flashed and narrowed at the dragon as he snapped, "From healing her? The Guardian you were incapable of helping?"

"Somebody needs to make sense. You healed Sacha?" Pothos' brows lifted and he seemed surprised and pleased by that, but also confused. Hades mentally growled; he'd been doing nothing but fixing Guardian issues since they'd woken him. His healing Sacha shouldn't come as any surprise.

"He's *mated* to Sacha," the dragon bit out as if this was bad news.

Hades growled, "This should make you all happy."

"Oh, fuck." His son ran a hand over his short hair. "How the hell... What..." The boy appeared lost for words.

"Exactly," Drake bit out.

Hades met the dragon's gaze. "I need to get to her. So speak and let me fucking loose." His words had the power to shake the ground beneath them.

The hold eased slightly, but he was still being prevented from teleporting away.

His son's next words were tinted with resignation. "What'd he do?" As if Hades were some errant child?

"I helped her. As opposed to letting her stay in a poison-induced sleep."

His son ignored his words to ask another question. "She's awake?"

Drake answered this as more Guardians and their mates started filling the wooded area. "She is... Sirena is with her, attempting to explain what the hell's going on. Trying to explain him!" Drake threw a hand up in Hades' direction.

Frustration lifted smoke from the dragon's lips, but Hades was even more irritated.

"Did you touch her?" his son demanded. He was getting really tired of the constant challenges in this new world from all the damned Guardians and their mates. Even his own son.

Why did it matter if he touched the female? She was *his*. He growled, tired of all their ridiculous rules, like no wings in the human Realm? Ridiculous. He'd apparently made some other infractions, and though he knew he needed to deal with the Guardians like this, he hated it. His body was strung tight with want. With need.

"I did not touch her," he growled. "Not that it's any of your concern. Now, just tell me what petty rule I've stepped on and be done with it." He was done talking. He instinctually pulled at his bonds, wishing he could just teleport to her side. Drake and Era jolted with the force of his power, but managed to continue pinning him.

"You think you broke a fucking rule?" Drake snarled.

29

His gaze fell on Drake's mate. She was shaking her head as if Hades should know what the hell they were talking about. The shimmering gold of her eyes was unique and completely otherworldly, showing her odd power. He nearly growled in frustration. He had been the one to relieve her of the beasts forced on her by experiments done by Apollo's now dead son. Hades had been the one who'd made their mating possible, and now they were banding against him?

"Listen to me, Hades. I'm attempting to do you a fucking favor," Drake snapped, smoke slipping from the dragon's lips showing his annoyance as he continued, "Sacha's been unconscious for weeks. She doesn't even know I've released you from stasis to help locate Apollo. You would have confused the shit out of her, not to mention pissed her off along with every other Guardian here by not allowing her the freedom to accept your touch. By not giving her the freedom to choose your ass as her mate."

The dragon paced in front of him as more smoke lifted to the sky.

What the hell was he talking about? "Choose?" He shook his head in exasperation. Either there was a soul connection or there wasn't. There was no choice. It was fate.

Sacha was born in Apollo's labs, his son added telepathically. *You do not touch her without her consent.*

He growled. "She's mine. Of course she wants me to touch her." She'd want his touch beyond anything, and they were keeping him from doing exactly that.

I get that you think that. But she will hate you for taking her choices. She was born a slave, Pothos said. Shaking his head, he spoke the next words aloud. "Tread carefully, Father. It may take actual effort to win her. But at the very least give her a second to figure out what the hell is going on right now."

He was Hades. Females flocked to him, begged for his touch. What made this different? They were all daft.

He flexed his wings. They were protective. That was what they were.

"Point made. Release me."

He heard a chuckle to his left and saw Vane and his twin brother, Erik, Athena's sons. Wonderful. More nephews. Vane was mated to one of his ex-warriors, Brianne, though the female was not at his side. He glared at Vane, who was grinning widely. It was a veritable family reunion, Hades thought drolly. Vane, light to his brother's dark, was the one who spoke. "I never thought I'd see the day."

Hades didn't have time for any more of this and cocked a brow at Draken to make that point.

The dragon just shook his head as he crossed his arms and watched. The male's long blond hair whipped in the wind still surging around them as Hades attempted to keep his temper under control.

When Vane spoke again, the words pricked at Hades' barely leashed irritation. "I don't even have to threaten or torment you, Hades. Brianne will literally pluck you like a fucking chicken if you fuck up with Sacha." The amusement in the male's bright blue eyes annoyed the fuck out of Hades. "I gotta say, I feel a little cheated. Sacha, Sirena and Brianne have been closer than sisters for years, so they'll get first dibs when you fuck this up."

Vane's grin widened. "I kind of feel sorry for you."

He felt his muscles contract, pulling against the invisible bonds holding him in place. Lucky for Vane. He knew the male was still ruffled because Hades had amused himself with making him jealous by flirting with Brianne.

He vaguely appreciated the concept of them banding together for their female warrior, but it was overkill and ridiculous not to want one of their own "mated" to him.

"I would never harm my female, so your fears are unwarranted. We're done here," he commanded.

At that moment Bastian and his female arrived. The Kairos, he knew from his son's memories, was Sacha's adopted son. Which would have made the male's dark look endearing if Hades had not already been dealing with his own nephew's issues.

The male stepped directly in front of Hades, and his tone was low and even as he issued his own warning. "Do not think you can continue as you have. If you think you can treat her as you do other females... don't. It won't go well for you. She deserves respect."

Pothos' voice slipped into Hades' mind. *That means if you can't keep your dick in your pants, you may as well walk away now. Don't even try to win her, Father, if you can't do that. She is one of three females we hold dear. We're a damned family and that's her son. Don't fuck up, because it will end very badly if you hurt her,* his son sent through their telepathic link.

We... you and I, are family, he reminded his son with a bite of reprimand. He wasn't even listening to it anymore.

We are. And that is why I'm trying to help you see that your

32

actions in this will have serious repercussions.

"Are you done?" he snapped as more power lifted from him. He glared at Draken. "You say I must let her choose, yet you keep me here so that she can't."

Draken nodded. "Wait until Sirena is finished talking to her."

He growled in annoyance. The damned healer didn't like him. And not one Guardian had left the wooded area. If anything, he was now faced with the majority of the bastards and their females as he crossed his arms and gritted his teeth in irritation.

He heard Jax snickering before the cat spoke. "So Bastian and P are going to be brothers? Damn, I feel cheated, I want to call Hades daddy."

Hades sent a blast of power that slammed the cat into a tree. He was rewarded with the sound of the male's harsh grunt before the snapping of wood. His lips curved when the tree fell with a ground-shaking thud. He cocked a brow at the male as he dusted off the wood chips with a growl.

Drake and Era were holding him there, but he was never truly powerless. And he was in no mood for more of their humor.

Chapter 3

Guardian Manor, Tetartos Realm

Sensation flooded through Sacha's body in hot waves. Undiluted pleasure filled every cell to the point that her flesh ached with it. Even her skin was sensitive. The softest touch would probably make her come, but the desire kept flowing deep inside.

She lifted her lids to see an empty cavern room.

Alone.

But she hadn't been. Power that wasn't hers was licking over the walls, flowing inside her. There was also a faintly intoxicating scent in the room that she couldn't place.

Dizziness hit as the warmth inside her seemed to move. Anger and frustration filled her as her body broke apart in a scattering of cells. She forced them to reform, breathing hard and gripping the soft bedding as if it would keep her grounded. Her heart rate spiked as she racked her mind for memories that were out of reach. She couldn't focus enough to find answers as to why she was there. Why her powers were out of control.

Sirena, she called out to her sister Guardian. The healer would know what was happening to her, even though she had a feeling what the answer might be.

Sacha slipped from the bed, and the caress of the soft material over her bare legs was its own torture. She was wet and confused. She knew she was below the Guardians' manor, more specifically in one of the subterranean rooms with stone walls and a few soft lights filtering in from the hall beyond. These rooms had been set up for her and her brethren to refuel their energies below ground, where the Earth's strength could replenish their own. A place to gain Immortal sustenance. And it was where they went to heal if they were injured.

I'm on my way, Sirena said, and Sacha's muscles relaxed. Good.

Her body started to break apart, and again she forced it back under control. Need. Emotions that weren't her own and the unrelenting desire to port somewhere could only be pointing in one direction.

Her heart beat faster as she searched her mind. She gripped the edge of the bed when she found a bright and shining thread that hadn't been there before. Sacha sucked in a ragged breath and stilled as she built a mental block to keep her own emotions and thoughts from seeping out to the unknown.

It seemed she somehow had a mate. She knew from the other Guardians that the first stages of a mating frenzy left your mind open and vulnerable, and she had no idea who was on the other side of that thread.

What the hell was going on? Why couldn't she remember anything about a male, not one touch, not a face?

Her brethren had been falling to the mating frenzy one by one in the past months. Even her son, Sebastian, had found his other half in Tasha, but... her? She never imagined she'd be next, because in reality there were no truly compatible males for her to mate with. Immortal females were in a sense cursed to only mate or desire males more powerful than them. Sirena had once said it was likely a byproduct of the small amount of beast blood Apollo infused into the races with his twisted experiments all those millennia ago. As a Guardian, one of the most powerful beings left in the world, that left only her brethren as options, and those males were her family.

So, who? How?

She lifted her hands to push the long mass of dark hair away from her face and squared her shoulders.

"I'm here," Sirena said as she rushed into the room with a smile that beamed with relief and joy. The blonde healer's faelike features lit up as she spoke. "It's so good that you're finally awake." Her sister Guardian gripped her hands, and Sacha felt warm healing power sliding through her body, assessing it.

"What happened?" Sacha asked and noticed Sirena's intake of breath. What was her friend bracing for?

Sirena eyed her seriously for too long before speaking again. "There's a lot you need to know."

The urgency in her friend's tone and mannerisms instantly put Sacha on guard. "Tell me."

"What's the last thing you remember?"

Before she could speak, images of a battle flickered in her mind. "I remember fighting kilt-wearing warriors with golden staffs outside a country house in Earth Realm. We'd found Apollo and were about to take him when the air charged and warriors came out of shimmering-looking air." Apollo had been loose in the Realms

36

because one of the Guardians' now dead enemies, Elizabeth, had found and freed the God. She closed her eyes, trying to remember more.

She felt the beginning flicker of her cells trying to break apart again. Each time the heat boiling inside her ramped up even more.

"What are you feeling now?" Sirena was being too cagey.

"Like I'm mated. How?"

"Yes, I think you are. Do you feel a link?"

Sacha nodded. "I can see the connection. I just don't know who it leads to."

Her heart was racing. She'd always been able to lock down emotion, an engrained skill she'd lived with all the centuries of her life, but it felt like a dam had broken inside her and she was fast losing all the control she prized so highly.

"Drake intervened before he touched you," Sirena said. "Or at least he thinks he did. Are you feeling the frenzy? Pain?"

She shook her head. "Desire. But no pain. What do you mean Drake intervened? What aren't you telling me?"

"It's going to be okay," Sirena said, infusing her voice with Siren healing power. It both calmed and unnerved her all at the same time. If the healer felt the need to use her ability, it had to be bad. Was she mated to one of those unknown warriors who'd come through trying to take Apollo? She searched her memories, but they were still so fuzzy.

"Am I mated to one of the warriors?" she asked, holding her

breath, hoping that wasn't the case. She felt new power flowing in her veins, but she was disoriented, and her cells kept trying to break apart against her will. Not to mention the odd emotions floating inside her were all making it hard to form thoughts. "And why can't I remember?"

The desire wasn't getting any better as the time passed. But at least no pain. If you didn't feed a mating frenzy with sex, it sent compulsive desire and sharp pangs of pain until you succumbed to the demands. Fate's way of forcing a pair to complete all the bonds. Right now it was a dull ache making her nipples hard and body wet.

Sirena eyed her. "You were poisoned by a beast that came through the portal. You've been unconscious." The healer softly added, "I'll need to take blood to make sure it's all gone now."

She'd been poisoned? "Sirena, not telling me is only making this harder," she pointed out before gritting out, "Who is my mate?"

Instead of answering outright, Sirena began pacing and continued. "I need to start at the beginning for it to make sense... Apollo was taken by the warriors you remember fighting. They left no clues behind and even their dead disappeared along with the portal they came through."

Her heart stopped at the word "dead." "Bastian?" Had something happened to her son? She'd instinctually checked his telepathic location when she'd awoken, hadn't she? Her mind felt too hazy. She wasn't sure if that had to do with the poison or the mating.

She saw it now. Bastian was close, near that other connection to her mate. So many other Guardians were also there. What the hell was going on? Bright lights flickered in her mind's eye. They were in a grouping not far from her location.

"He's fine. Everyone's fine," Sirena assured her.

As if her thoughts conjured him, Bastian spoke. *I'm on my way to you.*

No. She softened her tone before adding, *Don't. I'm fine. Sirena is filling me in.* Awkward didn't seem a strong enough word to describe the thought of having him here when her body felt so out of control. Her cells flickered again, and each time her power fluctuated trying to teleport to the unknown male, it sent a hint of anxiety and frustration through her. But she needed to give her son more of an answer so he wouldn't worry. *I need to shake off the fatigue from being still so long. I'll come to you soon, Sebastian.*

He paused for a long moment. He knew who her mate was, she could feel it, and though she wanted information, she'd rather hear it from Sirena. When he spoke, she could sense his unease. *I'm happy you're awake. I'm here for whatever you need.*

His words were enough to make her heart ache. She felt the hint of love he sent through the mental link and shared some of her own.

She refocused on her friend, her sister. "I need answers, Sirena."

"I know. I'm getting to them." Sirena nodded, but her eyes were hard when she moved on. "Because the warriors took Apollo and we had *no* clues to finding him, Drake awakened Hades."

Sacha's entire being stilled. "What? Why? Now we have two Gods out of stasis?" She was aware that Hades had been known as one of the three good Gods, but he'd still been sent to sleep with the rest of the Deities. Hadn't the Creators deemed all Gods too powerful to exist alongside humanity? That meant the Guardians now had one horrible God somewhere loose and another God they'd need to watch closely. She felt a dull ache behind her eyes.

Sirena nodded. "Hades has a sibling link to Apollo. Drake hopes to use it to find the bastard God."

Brianne rushed in at that moment, a mass of fiery hair and attitude tempered with a bright excited smile in Sacha's direction. "Oh, damn, am I happy to see you standing."

Her sister pulled her into a tight but abbreviated hug, and Sacha relaxed a little while in Brianne's warmth. Neither were known for displays of affection, so it was obvious to Sacha just how worried her sister had been. For centuries she and Brianne had partnered while patrolling the Realms, and just the sight of her eased Sacha. Partners had shifted around after the first matings started, but she was closest to the Geraki. Brianne's race was half bird of prey. "It's about time your ass woke up."

Sacha's lips twitched of their own accord at Brianne's words. "How long was I out?" For this much worry, she had to have been out longer than just a day or so.

"Weeks." Brianne's tone was hard.

Sacha's stomach clenched. Weeks would definitely explain her sister's worry.

The redhead turned to Sirena. "You haven't told her?"

"No," Sirena bit out.

"Tell me." She knew she would appear outwardly calm, but she wasn't. Her pulse was pounding in her ears, and desire was still burning under her skin no matter how much she pushed it away and focused on her sisters.

Sacha watched as Sirena sucked in a deep breath and nodded.

"Hades is your mate."

Sacha's entire world stopped as she stared at her two sister Guardians. She felt everything inside her shutting down, her heart rate slowing, her breathing evening out. Old habits moving into play because she couldn't think and she *had* to. Fate had to be joking.

A God? Everything inside her rebelled. It didn't matter if he had been one of the few good ones. She'd spent the first several decades of her life as a slave to Gods. Memories, ancient nightmares of a time long gone, came rushing over her as if only days had passed. Her dead sister. A constant fight for freedom and survival, doing things that shamed her and made her feel like no more than an animal in a cage. Fighting to protect her son.

She breathed through those thoughts. That part of her was gone.

Dead.

When the Creators had freed the Immortals of their slave bracelets and deemed her a Guardian of the Realms, she'd been given a new life. She'd been given power and purpose, and she hadn't even thought of that time for centuries.

She barely heard Brianne. "This'll be okay. You know I like Hades. And Vane volunteered to chat with Hades when Drake told me and Sirena what happened."

Two sets of sharp eyes were staring at her, assessing her. She knew her features were even and her breathing was sound. Beneath all the shock, she felt sickening numbness trying to take over; old traits had seemingly resurrected themselves along with the memories. She fought it back because that was not her. She was a Guardian. No God could ever make her feel powerless again.

She worked to manage her thoughts.

This was why she'd felt stronger when she'd woken. She had a God's power sliding inside her veins, and that realization forced her to battle back old demons that were making no logical sense. Because this wasn't about a God controlling her. If anything, it was her taking his power, her becoming his equal. That was how matings worked.

It would be fine.

She forced her mind to bring up what she knew of Hades. Brianne had been one of his warriors before she was lured and caged by Apollo and Hermes. Sacha remembered her sister Guardian being sure that Hades would find a way to free the Immortals and take down Apollo and Hermes. He hadn't. It had been Drake and Pothos who had eventually tracked down an artifact that called the Creators back to contain the Deities. Her sister Guardian had been mistaken in that, but Brianne would never have fought at the side of a God she hadn't deemed worthy of her sword.

Brianne had only been on the island a few years before the Creators had come back. She'd been spared a portion of the horrors, because all new Immortals spent the first year undergoing transformations when they were infused with animal DNA.

She and Brianne had bonded all those millennia ago. Sacha had lost Phedra decades before, but she'd gained Brianne and had always been thankful that the Geraki hadn't gone through all the hell Sacha had lived through.

"Tell us what you're thinking, Sacha," Sirena started softly.

"I just need to know what happens now," Sacha said calmly.

Both sisters narrowed their eyes at her. "What do you want to happen? Drake found Hades here and teleported him away. They have him contained in the clearing to the north."

"Contained?" She wanted to fight. Wanted to rebel against everything, but she wasn't ignorant, she was realistic. Resisting wouldn't do any good. Matings were permanent; they were for eternity. They required sex and connection even after the initial frenzy was fed. It started with wild need, vows, blood bonding and then the final connection, soul bonding after a long night of consummation. These were centuries-old traditions encouraged and needed to forge the deepest connection. She sucked in a deep breath and forced those nerve-racking thoughts away.

"He really is a good guy," Brianne said, blowing out a breath as she pushed the wild mass of red curls over her shoulder.

She'd been happy for the other Guardians, for her son, to find matches that fit them seemingly perfectly. Partners. How could she have anything like that with a God?

She mentally shook her head, knowing she'd somehow deal with Hades. Deal with being tied to him for eternity. Why had she thought the other bonds looked so beautiful? Maybe it was due to the fact that she'd never truly considered the possibility of it happening to her. Because in reality she felt trapped by fate. The thought of blood bonding during the mating ceremonies, which meant the sharing of memories, actually turned her stomach. She balled her fists, because it didn't mean she wouldn't see it through.

"Drake is keeping him there while we see what you want us to do with him."

Drake was protecting her. She felt her heart clench, and a slight smile tilted her lips at the thought of the Guardian leader containing a God so she at least had the illusion of choice along with the upper hand.

Drake had always cared, though he would never admit it. The dragon had spent the millennia consumed by his duty to the Realms, to them, working harder and longer hours than any other.

Aside from maybe Sirena.

The last time she'd seen Drake, he'd been tormented and losing control of his dragon half, because his destined mate had been tortured and experimented on, making it impossible to claim her.

"Is Drake okay?" She guessed he was still holding on to control if he'd leashed a God for her.

"Sacha, you know you can talk to us about this." Brianne eyed her.

Sacha drew a breath and nodded. "I know." But what was there to say? A mating was permanent. Eternity bound to a male she didn't know. Had never *wanted* to know. No Immortal had control of it, nor did they have a choice. It didn't matter that the others seemed to fit so well. If there was even a shred of silver lining, it was the power she was already gaining from the bond and the fact that it would give her brethren a way to keep track of the Deity while he helped get Apollo back. She'd just have to look at it as one more duty.

One that would involve having a sex life. Her heart thudded inside her chest, thinking of her millennia-long abstinence. With that she was forced to consider even more. The possibility of children? As a mated female, she may actually end up pregnant for the first time in her life. Her stomach clenched. After a spell cast in the last year of the Gods reign on Earth, no Immortal had been able to conceive unless it was with a true mate. She'd never conceived, not even those years prior to the spell. No matter how many hideous times they'd tried, she hadn't been able. Her hand went to her stomach.

She swallowed, not sure how to feel. Birth rates were still incredibly low, usually starting a decade after the bonding, but Gregoire, her brother Guardian, had managed to get his female with child on their mating night.

She shook it all off, because it was irrelevant at this point. There was no Immortal birth control, and fate had already had its say. "I'll deal with it. For now I need to know what all I've missed." She was a Guardian first and foremost.

She kept a mental eye on the link to Hades so she'd know when he was coming for her. It was a given he would at some point. The desire needed to be fed eventually.

Sirena nodded. "Okay, well, Drake and Delia completed their mating."

Sacha stilled, surprised. "How?" She was happy for the dragon, but how had they done the impossible?

"Hades released Delia's beasts."

Sacha opened her mouth and closed it again. The God had helped them? By taking her beast halves?

Brianne seemed to understand her confusion and hint of horror because her amber eyes tracked Sacha's face before she spoke. "You know Hades has power over souls. He said Delia's animals hadn't bonded to her, so he released them." Brianne shook her head after a second. "He said it was possible only with her situation, so it's not like he can just free any Immortal's animal half." That was a horrifying

45

thought.

She sure as hell hoped not. Those with a true animal would go mad if their beast was taken away.

"I know. It's still scary as shit," Brianne admitted. "Hades has always been powerful, but I can truly vouch for his not being an asshole. I've seen him battle and I've seen him with his ranks. He's never been cruel. Don't get me wrong, he's a badass, but he's a lover not a fighter."

Sirena groaned before snapping, "Brianne."

Brianne sighed and threw her hands up. "I'm being honest. Also, he's a fucking God. Arrogance is a given."

Sirena cleared her throat before changing the subject, for which Sacha was grateful. "One thing you should know about Delia is that she's completely different now." The female had been tormented and experimented on by Apollo's son, Cyril. It seemed the apple didn't fall far from that tree. Cyril's attempt to find a way to take any female as his mate had nearly destroyed Delia.

Sirena smiled softly. "And she goes by the name Era now. She wanted Delia to stay dead to the world." Sacha completely understood needing a new beginning.

Era deserved a happy ending as much as Drake did. "Drake's in control again?"

Brianne nodded with a bright smile. "Oh yeah, he is. And Era's perfect for him. If not a little scary powerful."

Sacha tilted her head. "Scary?"

Before anyone could answer, she had to fight another pull to teleport. Emotion hit. Anger and frustration.

"Are you okay?" Sirena asked.

"I think I'm feeling Hades' emotion," she said. It was a side effect of their mating. She closed her eyes, knowing she was stalling under the guise that she needed to learn everything that had happened while she'd been unconscious.

"Shit." The healer shook her head and started for the doorway. "I know you want to know what's happened, but I need blood samples. I'll be right back."

Sacha nodded at Sirena's retreating form, happy for a reprieve that didn't make her feel cowardly.

Brianne assessed her. "Hades might take some work, but right now the others are on his ass."

Sacha cringed. "Bastian's there?"

"Warning him to be respectful, according to Vane," Brianne added, obviously telepathically communicating with her own mate. Brianne paused before adding, "Okay, here's the good and the bad of it... Hades has a soft spot for females."

"I'm sure." She'd heard about the God's appetites long ago. It had never seemed to matter that he was known for his love of orgies and females. She didn't want to hear that, because she sure as hell wasn't going to be joining any orgies. And the thought of having a mate that wasn't faithful grated.

Fate couldn't be that horrible to her.

Brianne continued, "I'd recommend bringing his arrogance down at least a dozen pegs before succumbing to his charms... That might be because we'd all find it amusing. Do what you feel." The redhead stared off for a while, smiling. Her next words made it clear she'd been mentally talking to Vane again. "I fucking love that cat. He's tormenting and threatening Hades on my behalf. And Vane says Hades isn't taking any of it well. He's apparently unable to process the fact that you might not want him as a mate." She chuckled and her smile grew into something mischievous.

Sacha shook her head, eyeing her sister Guardian. "I'll deal with Hades when the time comes. Right now I need to know the rest of what I missed." She remembered being poisoned now.

"The poison from that creature knocked you out, but didn't seem to do any permanent damage," Sirena said as she reentered the room with a syringe. The blonde kept speaking even as she started prepping Sacha for the blood draw. "It was a lot like Hell beast venom."

"And Hades hasn't been able to find Apollo?" She wanted the bastard back in his box for all eternity.

Sirena shook her head. "No, he hasn't. He's getting nothing, but he had an idea." Sirena distractedly spoke as she took the vial of Sacha's blood and set it aside. "The short version—Hades, Athena and Aphrodite had a secret allegiance with another God all those centuries ago. A God from Thule, another world that had been populated by a different set of Creators. Hades tried to contact his old ally Agnarr, but another God, Kara, came through instead and attempted to take Hades, which ended in a battle. She's locked up and unconscious at the moment, but in the process she admitted that Apollo was in her world."

Brianna spoke. "I can give you a telepathic rundown."

Sacha nodded slowly. She'd missed a lot and that would be quicker. "I think that's best." A second later she was seeing flashes of meetings and information. Drake telling the other Guardians of new Gods. Of them learning that P's mother was a priestess of Thule. P being forced to stay away from the battle because Hades felt sure his son could be in danger from the Gods of the other world.

More images filled Sacha's head, filtered from Brianne's thoughts. It was mind splitting how much Sacha had missed.

She was caught by images of Hades, of him with her brethren. Of him helping free Delia of the two beasts. He truly was a sexual creature. She sucked in a breath at his beauty. She'd known, but seeing him wield his power, the way his midnight wings lifted and took up the space around him. It was a sight. And there wasn't a doubt in Sacha's mind that he knew just how attractive he was.

Another flash told of Nastia and Sander's mating. The Phoenix finally got his happy ending with a female who couldn't be more perfect for him. That made Sacha smile.

More flashes showed Hades again. Beautifully shirtless with wings outstretched in battle against an unknown female. She knew from the accompanying thoughts it was the Goddess Kara from Thule, their female prisoner.

She was surprised she could feel such intense attraction just at the sight of his muscle-packed form. She was a little nervous to have sex after all this time, but the fates were ensuring she'd want it.

"You get it?" Brianne asked, her amber eyes boring into Sacha's.

"Yes." She nodded, though in reality she was still processing

49

details.

How do you want me to handle this, Sacha? Drake asked.

She closed her eyes and took a deep breath. Better to get it over with then dwell on how it would work. Fate needed to put in some extra effort and ease the way because she wasn't sure what she was doing. It was just sex, beings did it all the time for the pure pleasure of it. She could do this. *Let him come to me.*

I'll be there when you meet, he commanded.

No. She had no desire to deal with the arousal in front of anyone. *Alone.*

You're sure? Drake bit out.

He has no intention of harming me, she pointed out realistically.

No.

I'll be fine.

I'll be here at the manor. Her lips lifted a hint. That was just one reason they followed the dragon. He didn't manage them unless he had to, but he would always be there if needed. But in this, the last thing she needed was witnesses.

She felt the second he was there. Power, wild pheromones and need filled the room. It was hard to breathe through the strength of it, and she was grateful that fate listened to her.

"Leave us," he commanded of Brianne and Sirena, who'd closed ranks in front of her.

Sacha spoke before either could rip him apart. "I'll be fine."

Brianne glanced back at her. "Call."

Sacha nodded. This would be fine. She'd done far worse and lived through it.

Brianne's voice was clear. "Hades, do not make me regret telling her you were okay. I like you, but fuck this up and I will rip off all your pretty feathers, shove them up your ass, and then use you as a feather duster."

Sirena choked as she said something more to him before both females exited.

His eyes were on her not her sister Guardians. The brilliant blue bored into her and she felt all that heat and intensity deep inside her soul.

Chapter 4

Guardian Manor, Tetartos Realm

Sacha's breath caught in her throat when the God's undiluted pheromones hit her. His wings took up the majority of the space in the darkened cavern room. They were a brilliant ebony and only added to his easily seven-foot height. He was bare to the waist and packed full of sculpted muscle leading to a perfect vee that hid beneath his low-riding black slacks. His body was a thing of beauty, not that she'd thought it would be otherwise.

Her eyes shifted back up along his hard jaw to the small indent in his chin. His long dark hair was pulled back so she couldn't see it all, and honestly she didn't care, it was the brilliant sapphire of his gaze pulling her in. There was something beyond heat in his eyes, it was incredibly intense, like he was staring into her soul. She realized with his power something like that might actually be possible, and it left her even more on edge.

"How are you feeling?" His deep voice slid over her flesh, the smooth seductive cadence promising wicked, dirty pleasure. When he added a hint of a sexy smile, her mind short-circuited. That quirk of his lips changed his appearance so drastically that she was caught up in its thrall for long seconds.

And his scent. It wasn't just intoxicating, it was consuming, it didn't matter that her senses weren't as attuned as some of the shifting races. His pheromones still rocked her enough that she couldn't help but take in measured breaths. If she wasn't careful, she would become addicted to his smell alone.

She licked her suddenly dry lips before answering, "I'm awake." Because she wasn't sure how she truly felt. She felt strong. It couldn't be a coincidence that after his presence she'd suddenly awakened after weeks of unconsciousness.

He prowled toward her, full of catlike grace, as she attempted to will away the need curling around her, while another part of her pulled it in. Desire and logic jerked her in one direction as uncertainty tried to undo what fate had set into motion. She wasn't consciously fighting it, but something in her subconscious was. Falling into a God's arms wasn't as simple as it had seemed. Not for her.

His power was so much stronger than she'd imagined. It licked over the walls and caressed her skin, and she had a moment where it was almost too jarring.

"You needed the strength to heal." It was obvious he was equally affected by her. His muscled shoulders twitched and his wings flexed as his gaze heated with every second that passed. Every step he took toward her.

Each one of her senses had flared to life in his presence, but it was that seductive grin of his that seemed to affect her most, so she focused on it. It was cocky, but charming and sinful. Definitely wicked and full of promise. A temptation as opposed to an order. She forced back some of her trepidation and focused on how he made her feel. Eager and aroused, while their mental connection seemed to be kindling some kind of sexy warmth that was filling her entire body. It felt like quicksand, one step and it would swallow her whole. She just needed to force the movement?

In the blink of an eye he was a breath away, staring down at her, searching her eyes as if seeing everything she'd ever hidden. He growled as his nostrils flared. "Your scent. There's nothing like it," he said with a hint of awe and definite hunger in his tone. She didn't back away or teleport; she allowed him to invade her space. A part of her curious, but she realized that a part of her was searching for something corrupt in him.

He wasn't his brothers. She knew this... and hated that her mind even conjured the comparison when she knew it had no logical basis. She forced it all away and focused on the male in front of her. She wanted his touch, her nipples ached, and she could almost feel his fingers on her heated skin and she allowed herself to want them there. She was thankful her face wouldn't show her weakness, her inner turmoil.

She watched as his heated gaze tracked over her face and down to the soft green cotton hospital gown she wore. The back was open and she felt the air against her exposed skin, but she didn't care. It was just a body. And he'd see her naked soon enough.

Her emotions were all over the place, drugged in desire one moment and the next she was hit with a pang of anxiety that she had to push back.

Impossibly his power felt as if it were strengthening, flowing in waves over her body... slowly gliding inside her. She shivered and was forced to hold back a moan. Good. Pleasure. She needed more of that to take away her nerves. He rasped, "I need to taste you." How was it possible for words alone to be filled with enough heat to burn her up? She heard him growl, "Sacha."

Her name on his lips drugged her nearly as much as the sensation of his hand tunneling in her hair, or the other rough hand clenched at her hip, pulling her into him as his lips descended. That first touch was electric; lightning speared through her body as his kiss destroyed the nerves. His cock was so hot and hard against her, and she lifted higher on her toes to get him to where she ached. She was so damned wet and getting more so with every plundering thrust of his tongue. He was feverish, a little wild, but she felt him actually holding back. His touch was firm yet gentle, questing and tempting as his fingers moved along her nape, massaging her hair. The mix of sheer need and care along with his barely leashed hunger was intoxicating.

Sacha set her fingers free to explore the tense tendons of his neck, down to his straining shoulders, reveling in every shuddering muscle. His body's response emboldened her. Even his wings were moving and pulling around them until she felt the soft feathers caressing her arms. She moaned and slid her hands back up to his cheeks. The stubble there was rough on her skin, but she loved the feel of his jaw working as he kissed her and pulled her hips tighter. She'd never felt anything like it; he kept her from sliding into the abyss alone.

With one hand he lifted her, and she wrapped her legs around his waist, lost in sensation, the seductive tangling of their tongues as his cock throbbed between them. A second later he broke the kiss on a deep groan that fueled her desire.

"Incredible." His lips moved to her throat and her head fell back into the feathers that cushioned her.

Yes. This is ambrosia. His growled words slid through her mind as her fingers slid back to the packed muscles of his shoulders. His skin was burning under her touch and she could feel his restraint slipping. Something about being confined in his hold and his lack of control sent a stab of cold through her body.

But then his lips trailed over her sensitive flesh; the pleasure pulled her back in. His warm breath and trailing lips felt incredible to the point she could barely breathe as more nerve endings sang to life. Her dress eased down her shoulder, his teeth and tongue roving to her swollen breasts, making her moan as goose bumps rose over her skin.

His hand hitched her leg higher and his fingers ripped away her underwear, and then he was caressing her between her thighs. She gasped when he slid a finger inside her wetness. *That's it, thisavre mou, get me all wet.*

His treasure.

Everything inside her chest stilled and started going cold at the idea of being a God's possession. It didn't stop her body's heated reaction, but she felt her breathing hitch. He shifted, and when she felt the head of his cock at her wet entrance, old numbness began to work its way inside her and made her stomach hitch. It was the only reaction she'd ever had during sex and was something she hadn't felt in thousands of years.

She tried to shake off the chill and grasp the mindless pleasure she'd fallen into, but she couldn't get ahold of it. When she felt his power sink inside her soul, she knew it was meant to feel good. It should have been a beautiful rarity, but she felt caged and trapped as the icy cold numbness hit her with the force of a skyscraper.

It all turned on her so fast she couldn't process it or fight it back. Her wrists suddenly ached with the memory of her shackles and her power being snuffed out, suffocated. She felt how mindless he was, how full of need, and she felt herself shutting down.

She teleported from his arms. Disoriented. And the numbness was making her physically ill. She didn't leave the room, refusing to retreat without saying a word, knowing he'd only follow. She just needed to fight for her mental calm, but she rubbed her wrists while willing the sickness of her past to go back where it belonged.

"Give me a minute." She was shaking inside, but she knew he wasn't seeing most of it. He looked like he was fighting the haziness, the frenzy of his arousal. His eyes were still glassy with lust as he ran his hands over his head, but he didn't reach for her, and that was good.

"What happened? Did I hurt you?" he bit out, still struggling to focus, to understand. It wasn't accusation, there was true concern there; she felt it in their bond.

That knowledge and no amount of logic could stop her muscles from tensing, waiting for some angry tirade. You didn't pull away from a God.

She rubbed her cold wrists one more time before stilling the movement. The disorientation and need were nothing compared to the sheer anxiety chilling her bones.

She pushed her hair back but didn't answer him. She wasn't fully certain what to say. She only knew she needed air and time to gain control, to stop this sickening numbness.

His brows were knitted, but he didn't demand she return to him.

He stood there looking beautifully concerned and a little wild as his hands tunneled into his now freed hair. The scent of sex in the room was too strong to withstand with everything else.

She hadn't expected the reaction that was twisting inside her, turning what should have been something beautiful, or at the very least pleasurable, into something ugly.

"I need air," she said and hated that she needed it so desperately, because her lungs wouldn't fill.

With a thought she ported away.

Chapter 5

Sacha's Paris Home, Earth Realm

Sacha reformed amid the potted plants of her roof garden. The clean scent of rain helped as she panted for breath, shocked and embarrassed, but in the end just violently ill. She lifted her head to the downpour, sucking in the much-needed oxygen before gazing out to the busy Paris streets below. She was high enough that the rushing humans couldn't see her peering down at them. She'd always loved watching mortals live their lives, seeming to revel in the small joy to be had in their short existences. To see them bustling around with packages for their families, lovers.

She blew out a breath, aware the moment he reformed behind her. His presence at her back made her spine tingle, but she breathed through it. She needed to be around him without the constant twitching of her muscles. He wouldn't attempt to harm her. To do so would be to harm himself. They were connected.

She wondered if her reactions were solely stemming from the fact that she hadn't been with a male since Apollo's palace. She never thought this would happen. She hadn't even thought of her time in the palace for eons. For it to have an effect on her now infuriated her. She ran a hand over the soft cotton of the hospital gown and turned to him.

"Where is the back of your dress?" he demanded with a pained look on his beautiful face. No doubt her sisters would find his reaction to the hospital gown amusing. Just the thought of them eased her some. She wasn't the female she'd been. She was strong, even stronger now that his power flowed inside her.

Drops of water slid down her cheeks, but only for a moment. A glance told her that the rain had ceased only around her. She felt his power. Hades was shielding her as he stared at her. He seemed cautious as he assessed her closely.

What would happen if she wasn't able to have real pleasure in sex, in their bond?

She stilled. Something else wasn't right about this, aside from her sickening reaction.

Why wasn't she in pain from not finishing the frenzy? Delaying it was reported to be excruciating.

It wasn't that she didn't want him. The desire simmering beneath her fear and the slick throbbing from his fingers inside her told her this wasn't over.

"Why doesn't this feel like the mating frenzy?" she asked, sliding her hand to her stomach.

He ported directly in front of her then, his gaze searching hers, seeking answers in her expression. Answers he wouldn't find. His eyes narrowed, and she swore she felt too much concern. She couldn't handle his pity.

That was before he cocked a dark brow. "This isn't frenzied, Sacha?" he asked, gently lifting her hand and placing it against his throbbing cock. His eyes were still bright with want, but she felt his confusion. And something inside her felt like he was trying to ease her mood more than screw her.

She stifled a groan and forced her hand away, still feeling his heat against her palm. Could she finish it now? Did she dare try to risk more panic and humiliation? She wanted to, but she felt like she needed more time. Time to be alone to find some semblance of herself and find the answer to how she was going to do this.

She wasn't sure what to do as he spoke. "Our souls are already connected, *thisavre mou.*"

She didn't have the harsh reaction to the endearment this time and she was thankful.

She narrowed her eyes. "What are you saying?" She was still half waiting for him to pounce on her, and hated that she couldn't get a handle on the small pangs of unease.

He stared at her as if speaking were difficult. "That the bond is complete." She felt confusion and controlled intensity coming from their bond that jacked her nerves up to new levels.

"We don't need to blood bond now?" Could she truly hope that she'd been given one reprieve in this mating? That he'd used his soul power to skip all the steps a normal mated pair would have to go through? Blood bonding was the section of the ceremonies nearly every Immortal dreaded, as it showed each mate the most poignant memories of their partner's past.

"Those ceremonies don't pertain to us. Now, tell me what happened." That confirmation eased her some, but that should have completely dissolved it. It hadn't; she was still on edge, barely holding on. The desire was sizzling under her skin, but the anxiety felt like it would jump out at any moment, making her muscles ache.

"I need some time to process this. I'm not fighting this. But I can't finish it now. I need you to go." So she could figure out exactly how it went wrong and figure out a way through this. A muscle at his jaw ticked and she felt his immense shock in the bond, though it didn't show.

Even though she was getting snippets of his emotion through their bond, a part of her still half expected a Godlike tantrum at her words.

All she felt from him was need and genuine worry, but she was thankful he hadn't tried to touch her, tempt her back into his arms, because she was treading a thin line and that would have sent her over the edge.

*****

Hades wasn't sure what the hell was going on. Sacha looked utterly beautiful and completely calm, yet he was feeling emotions so deep in her soul he couldn't begin to understand. Panic, desire, distress, fear, need, anxiety. And so much more, but she refused to explain why, and her range of emotions made it impossible for him to push for fear of making it worse. She seemed so fragile one second and a force of strength the next. He was at a fucking loss.

She wanted time. Wanted him to leave so she had time? Shock held him still.

His cock was rock hard and she was confusing him at every turn. He wasn't sure what direction was up at this point. Never had a female reacted like that to his touch. And having one ask him to leave?

She was his female. The soul bond should add something

62

intense and wild and perfect. Not this.

His jaw had locked into place from the moment he saw the curve of her bare back and the temptation of her perfect ass. From there he'd experienced every emotion imaginable and so had she.

When it started in the room, he'd been too far gone attempting to control the frenzied need created by her touch. He'd managed to force it under, some, but by then he'd lost her somehow. When the first hint of her fear invaded his mind, he'd finally been able to beat back all the blinding desire only to have to port after her like a pup.

In his experience females didn't burn hot and then flee. They stayed and enjoyed all the pleasures he had to offer. And when he grinned at one, they sure as hell didn't ask for him to leave. He was aghast. And... worried. Which was new. He hated the emotions coming from her, and it didn't help that she'd closed him off, he could feel it like a steel trap. She'd drawn away. And the fear she felt made his stomach turn.

This was his female, he'd never tasted anything like the sweetness of her skin, and he hadn't even had a fraction of the time he needed to sample it all, to give them both the release they needed.

He hissed out a breath. He needed to speak to his son. Pothos would tell him about his female and give him a damned clue what the hell was hurting her, because her emotions were driving him mad. He couldn't fix things if he didn't know what caused them, and the need to care for her was ingrained so deep inside his soul it felt like he was tearing apart. He'd never felt such a driving need.

The only time he'd felt the same intensity was the moment he'd set eyes on Pothos for the first time. The infant had slayed him. And now his female was.

"How long?" He attempted to conceal his exasperation. If he hadn't felt her sincere fear, he would have... Fuck. What the hell could he have done? Demanded she bend over the balcony so he could see her ass again? Her entire body had stiffened, and he could see as well as feel how much she didn't want his touch.

"I'm not sure. Maybe a day. I will call to you." She confirmed with a slight nod of her beautiful head.

He didn't see the relief in her beautiful eyes, but he felt it.

Fucking hell.

Pothos, meet me at your home. He needed to figure it all out. He growled, because he also needed a home of his own. He hadn't had time, but he needed to rectify that soon. His female needed space and greenery, it seemed, considering that the last thing he'd seen before porting away were hundreds of potted plants. When she finally came to him, she would be comfortable. Fuck.

When he reformed, he stood in a room full of females. He growled in annoyance, having forgotten they were even there. They were enjoying each other, naked, and the scent of female arousal hit him hard.

The second it did, he stilled. His mind reeled as his entire world shifted around him. A part of him had known, but confirmation after his female had denied him was a harsh jolt. Looking out at the sea of beautiful female flesh writhing together, their moans echoing in the room, he realized one thing was blatantly certain, he had no interest in joining them. His usually more than eager cock was less than enticed at the idea of anyone's smooth flesh but his female's.

DIVINE ECSTASY

The room felt like it was spinning in a wide arc around him.

For the first time in his life, the sight of females, his true joy in existence, held no appeal. Even one of the bronzed beauties beckoning to him did absolutely nothing for him. It didn't matter how similar her coloring, she wasn't his female.

Females moved to him, soft hands met his bare chest, and his muscles jerked in distaste. He just stood there staring at them all, his jaw hard. He didn't speak when he felt his son reform at his side. He didn't hear any words; not even the sounds of wet flesh and throaty calls made it through the buzzing in his ears.

The second another pair of hands slid to the zipper of his pants, he actually felt a little ill. He lifted the hands away in a kind of blind stupor before teleporting to a mountaintop without having said a single word. If his female denied him for good, it seemed he'd never feel the joy and pleasures in a female's hands.

Snow fell all around him as he processed what just happened. His hands fisted at his sides. He thought back to the sight of Sacha's pert ass, and his cock started growing, more than interested. He felt the harsh need rebuilding at a single mental image.

The bastard was definitely hers.

Where are you? his son said a moment later.

He couldn't mentally speak.

Suddenly the reason for his sisters' loyalty to their consorts was confirmed in harsh light. Aphrodite had always taunted him with how much hotter and perfect her life was with Ladon. How he'd never know true pleasure until he had a female to soul bond. She hadn't admitted to this part.

His wings flexed and twitched.

He rubbed the bridge of his nose, and an ache had set up in his head. He couldn't do anything without knowing what the hell went wrong.

Send Sirena to check on my female, Hades demanded before snapping, *And send the females back to their own homes before coming to me.*

He released a breath as he sent his son a visual of where he was.

Her emotions eased back from him when he'd left her, so there was that, he thought derisively. Now all he could think of was that he'd have one female for eternity. It kept playing in his mind. He needed to find a way to get her to accept him or it was going to be one long fucking eternity.

Pothos responded within seconds, concerned, *Is Sacha okay?*

A moment later his son reformed at his side.

"What happened?" His son's tone was one of castigation, and Hades was in no mood. He glared at the boy before demanding, "Tell me about my female."

Pothos stared at him for long moments before shaking his head. "I told you... Now start from the beginning."

Hades bit out the entire thing, not leaving out any details.

Pothos groaned and ran both hands over his head. "Damn it. Why can't you comprehend the concept of too much fucking information? Don't tell me that shit. Fuck me, this is awkward." His son took a deep breath and Hades shook his head.

"I'll never understand your issues with sex."

Pothos growled. "If I have any issues, it's the fact that my father has no problem whipping his dick out at the slightest breeze. I don't need to imagine any of that going on with Sacha. Sacha is like a sister to me, and now I'm hearing about you almost fucking her and what she smells like and shit."

"Issues," he gritted out as his son bit out more expletives. Sex was beautiful. Females were intoxicating, or they always had been. He closed his eyes as he rolled his tense shoulders. The need was getting stronger, and his actual soul fucking thrummed as if he needed to get closer to her now. None of that could be good, and he didn't have the ability to even question his sister, to see what would happen if this wasn't fed. His female said she wasn't denying it, but he wasn't so sure.

The last thing he had time for was dealing with why his son had something against pleasure.

"Wait. You soul bonded her when she was fucking asleep?"

"Yes," he bit out. Did everyone forget he was a God? His wings flexed in the wind and he tried to control the need.

"We asked if you touched her."

He growled. "And I hadn't." His son wasn't helping. He ran his hands through his hair again, wanting the long mass gone. It irritated him.

His son just stood there with his arms crossed over his chest. "Shit." A beat passed. "Okay, give me a second." Another moment slid by until Pothos finally added, "Sacha is logical. That's where you're lucky. But, fuck, I told you she was born in Apollo and Hermes' labs."

Hades nodded in agitation. His son had said that, but it had been while Hades was concerned with getting to Sacha. He hadn't considered what that meant.

He was now... And his breathing sawed out as tension filled the space between them.

P waited a beat before speaking. "Okay, this is not going to be pretty since I don't think you know what being born in the labs means." Hades felt tension pull every muscle tight. Need slowly morphed into something else, something ugly, as Pothos spoke. "Sacha was born a slave. I think she was there for at least several decades. I don't know details of what she went through there and that's her fucking story. I do know what the general order of things were. Young were taken at birth and raised in warrior camps after their family telepathic links were severed. When you reached your majority at twenty years old, you were sectioned into groups based on skills—servants, warriors, guards—but they were all required to submit themselves for breeding. The females started with Apollo and Hermes before being passed to the guards."

Hades' vision burned crimson as fury ripped through him. Knowing of his brother's methods for building his army in theory was one thing, having it painted like that while imagining Sacha was too much. His wings flexed wide as tension and a blinding need to kill filled him. Wind tore around them in gusts that matched his rage.

He barely heard his son's soft words through the rage. "The only Gods she had any experience with were them. You may have triggered old memories."

He remembered her rubbing her wrists after she'd teleported

68

from his arms. Her beautiful features hadn't shown any fear or hurt... but she'd felt the echoes of shackles. He felt physically ill.

Hades growled low, deadly. He'd fucking hated his brothers before, but this... hate was too tame a word. It was blinding. All he wanted, all he could imagine was his brother's blood running through his fingers. Death was too good for Hermes and Apollo both. He imagined their hands on Sacha's smooth skin, and the ground beneath his feet shook. He searched the mental link to Apollo and it was still silent, as it had been. He would find him and he would shackle the male and bleed him dry as he ripped gaping holes in the male's soul just to hear his screams.

And then he'd do it again.

Had she imagined their hands when he'd been touching her? His stomach tightened as the roar of an avalanche rent the air. The skies darkened, lit only by the lightning strikes all around them. The uncontrollable need for blood lifted his wings into the winds. But he had no target, no outlet to ease the sickness and violence inside him.

"I'm sorry." He heard the sympathy from his son.

"Come on. We're going to kill some Hell beasts, Father."

Kill.

He growled low as he faced his son. "Get me a blade."

Blood.

Chapter 6

Hell Realm

*I*othos was mentally kicking his own ass. He'd only seen his father like this one other time, and fuck, he never wanted to see him like this again. Looking back at all the battles they'd fought when the Gods ruled the Earth, Hades had always been controlled and precise.

What he was doing to the Hell creatures was like what he'd unleashed on Ares and Artemis the only time they'd personally attempted to breach the palace, trying to get to P. He'd been maybe ten, but the sheer fury his father unleashed had rained Gods' blood all over the palace keep.

These beasts didn't stand a chance.

P had taken Drake here when his dragon needed to rage over being denied his mate. Had it been a month ago? Two? It didn't fucking matter. It seemed he was destined to spend his days in Hell.

Literally.

But his father needed this. Though if P thought Drake's killing rages were bad, this was fucking epic.

The geographic setup was the same in all Realms, but Hell rarely saw a storm like the one that followed them there. Lightning strikes wrought their own havoc on the land below.

After getting his father a blade, he had a split second where they both gazed out from a rise above packs of dozens, maybe hundreds of Hell creatures before his father's battle cry echoed throughout the Realm. It was deadly and frightening enough that it felt like the entire world quieted in fear.

From that moment on it had been a bloodbath. There were so many Hell creatures it almost looked like they were drawn to the spot. To his father.

P'd stayed at his father's side from the second Hades took flight. Fury rarely worked well in battle. It generally made a warrior careless, but not his father. Another dark battle cry rent the skies, shaking the ground beneath them as rare black Hell dragons soared in and were dropping to the trees in rending crashes of wood and fire. P admitted just how scary his father was when he unleashed his rage.

Blood flowed over the ground; the scent of sulphur and flames from the beasts filled his nose. His father's eyes glowed with power and fury. Thick muscled shoulders bunched and stretched as he let blade and power lay waste to Hell beasts, and death cries and screeches filled the air around them.

It felt good to fly free, but not like this. Something about this wasn't right. He wasn't sure if it was the sheer wildness in his father or the power the God was unleashing, which seemed stronger than ever before.

P understood his father's pain and fury. He had a feeling there was guilt there too. That Hades hadn't helped Sacha all those centuries ago. It wouldn't matter that Hades hadn't known her then. Drake went through the same thing when he realized that his mate had been tortured and experimented on and the dragon hadn't somehow known and protected her. Hades would only be thinking about the time she'd suffered and the acts forced on her. Of all the decades that his female had been a slave to the twisted depravity of his brothers. P couldn't imagine what it would feel like.

His father was arrogant, but he'd always been fair. His warriors followed him by choice. Hades had never abused his power and made his people suffer like most of the other Gods had. The females had always flocked to his father's charms and bed. And, if P was honest, he'd admit that Hades had been a good father. Boundaries had always been a fucking issue, however, since his father and sex were synonymous.

He and his father had actually been close. Hades had doted on him in his youth. It wasn't until Ares and Artemis had birthed their incestuous demon-spawn triplets, the Tria, who'd started a brutal reign of carnage in the world, that he and his father had been at odds. P'd been furious and fucking disappointed that his father had refused to look for the artifact that would call the Creators back to deal with how out of control and insane the other Deities were. If Ares and Artemis had been feeding off the death and pain they'd forced upon the human race, it was nothing in comparison to what their purely evil triplets had done in the world.

Then there were Apollo and Hermes holed up on their island, abducting and experimenting on all the Immortals they could find, creating an army.

Hades and Aphrodite had gotten some Immortals off of the island. Athena was less active, preferring to stay hidden with her family as she built her own army, while Aphrodite and Hades had employed Dorian, P's brother Guardian. The Nereid had managed to escape Apollo in the early years and had eagerly used his water ability to infiltrate the island to get some Immortals free. That had worked until Apollo and Hermes found a way to lock the island down completely.

P hadn't been able to let go of the fury that his father hadn't been doing more. But Hades kept saying that he would take care of the other Gods. P'd always thought his father had arrogantly assumed that he and his sisters could combat the other *nine* fucking Gods. Plus the Tria. His father was powerful, but that would have been ridiculous odds.

So he and Drake had actively worked with others to find the fucking artifact themselves. It had taken decades, but he'd eventually found it.

P'd had no idea that his father really did have a plan. In fact, P still needed details about that, about the other world. Thule. P wanted to learn more of his mother, whose identity Hades had hidden from him until days ago. His father was supposed to have met him tonight to explain, but now, with Sacha...

Fuck.

P sighed. Sacha deserved happiness and he knew his father was capable of giving it to her, so he'd wait to drill his father with questions until after his fury finally settled. Still, it killed him not to know the specifics as to why Hades wanted him away from Thule and everything about the other world. Especially since the Goddess they currently held had admitted that Apollo was there. She was still unconscious from her battle with Hades, and that left P with nothing. And he wanted answers.

More hordes of beasts trampled through the meadow below. P frowned at the sight. His father's rage hadn't eased, but that was the largest swarm P had ever seen in Hell Realm.

He wasn't sure how long his father was going to be at this. He didn't seem to be tiring. P could see the Hell beast blood simmering all over Hades' bare skin. The flesh seemed to regenerate before the acidic blood ate through.

He stared down at the herds before sending Drake the mental image of what was happening.

Do you have any idea why they're swarming? the dragon growled.

No. Unless Hades' presence in Hell is pissing off the Tria. The triplets had been imprisoned in the Realm before the Creators had been called back. It took the combined forces of Hades, Aphrodite, Athena and their consorts as well as Drake and P to imprison them. And it had come at a fucking cost. The Tria were just too damned powerful. They existed beneath the ground there, and just because the bastards couldn't leave didn't mean they couldn't cause problems. They created havoc by sending Hell beasts to Tetartos and Heaven Realms and demon souls to possess evil humans in Earth Realm.

Keep me updated, Drake bit out.

P mentally nodded. It wasn't as if the bastards could get free of their prison, and if Deimos, Than and Phobos wanted to sacrifice their beasts in some kind of tantrum, so be it. It meant less swarms being released into the other Realms.

Drake growled, *I'm guessing things didn't go well for Hades with Sacha.*

Yeah, not exactly. I think he triggered old memories.

Fuck.

She sent him away. Told him to come back later. I was the lucky one who got to explain some of her past and what she likely went through with Apollo and Hermes.

P was happy about one thing. He'd seen the shocked and pained look on his father's face when the other females had laid hands on him. P had never imagined his father brought completely to heel by one female. His brother Guardians would love to have seen the look on his face. He wouldn't share it, but he was happy. Sacha deserved a male whose focus was completely on her.

Do you need me there? Drake understood more than most what P's father was likely going through. The dragon harbored his own guilt at the fact that his mate, Era, had been taken by their enemy and tormented.

No. It's better that no one's near him. He wasn't sure anyone would be spared from Hades' fury at the moment; only P was truly safe from his father's wrath at this point. *How is the interrogation going?* Drake had been trying to get the warriors from Thule to speak.

Nothing. And Kara's still out. Hades had done some serious damage for another God to be unconscious this long. She'd gotten her own licks in during their battle, which was why Hades had spent days recovering himself.

P gritted his teeth at the reminder that he hadn't been at the fight. He fucking hated having been benched.

Have you heard from Sirena? P asked. He'd asked her to check on Sacha when his father had demanded it. He mentally groaned at all his father's commands and demands since being awakened from stasis.

Just checked. Sacha told Sirena that she was fine and showering. I'm not sure what that means.

Sacha had always been private. She was closest to the other female Guardians, but he doubted even they knew the extent of what she'd survived during her time in Apollo's palace. Brianne had been there only for a short time, and Sirena had been secreted away at birth.

He kept a close eye on his father and picked off any beast Hades may have missed.

Drake growled, *We can only hope to hell Hades is wearing out the Tria over there. I'm so tired of those fuckers.*

P agreed. There'd been a surge of evil humans being possessed in the mortal Realm in the last few days, and demon-possessed were the biggest pain in the ass for a Guardian to deal with. Since the assholes were technically human with demon souls, Guardians couldn't harm them without feeling the same pain times ten, thanks to the Creators' curse.

Hades' wrath finally seemed to ease. His father swooped down and landed on a mountain rise, and P settled to his feet beside him.

Moments passed as they gazed down at the carnage, but one look at his father's eyes said he had something else on his mind, and then the Deity was fucking gone.

Son of a bitch. What the hell was he up to now?

Chapter 7

City of Efcharistisi, Tetartos Realm

Hades reformed inside the palace in Efcharistisi. The Immortals milling around, laughing, stilled. "Bring me Zandra," he commanded. One scampered off to do his bidding.

"Leave," he growled at the rest. He was in no mood to deal with others.

He'd only stopped once, at his son's home to cleanse himself of the Hell creature blood. It had taken time to get his rage under control and he still wanted blood, but not from beasts. Only his brother's would do at this point.

Until he could have that or his female called him to her side, he planned to clear up past misdeeds. When he'd been awoken, he'd been forced to search old books and information on the Realms in search of the stone that called to Thule. It had been in his palace when the Creators had come back to the world, but it had been missing from his things when the Guardians awakened him.

Hades narrowed his eyes. He'd wasted days of his time only to find a frivolous book on this palace with an image of the stone set in a chandelier.

He would deal with the thief now. And he planned to attain a home for himself at the same time.

Now that the hardest bite of his rage was gone, his need for Sacha was swelling back to life. His cock was getting more demanding with every passing second. He needed distraction and he wanted a home of his own. One that would be suitable for his female and where he was free to allow his wings out. The Guardians made him promise to keep his wings hidden in Earth Realm, so he would choose a home in the Immortal Realm.

He stifled another growl of sheer frustration. This was the only place he'd come across that seemed pleasing and suitable for a God and someone of his size while equally appealing to his female, who liked trees. There were several gardens and atriums in this place.

He flexed his wings.

He heard footsteps rapidly clicking on stone, and then Zandra, the Aletheia who owned the palace, came gliding around a corner. The beautiful female smiled brightly. She'd lived in his palace millennia ago. Her hair was different now, short to her chin with streaks of black and red. She was in a long gown and at her side was a dark-haired male the book had also photoed.

"Zandra," he acknowledged.

"Hades," she said, her eyes lit with pleasure. "Welcome to our home. This is my mate, Damon."

The male smiled, friendly but watchful. Hades was in no mood for pleasantries. "Explain to me how something of mine ended up here." He wouldn't like to think that a female who'd once enjoyed the protection of his palace had stolen from him.

Zandra and Damon both stilled, their mouths dropping open.

"What? Hades, I assure you I'd never have taken from you. You took me in when I escaped Apollo's island."

He eyed her before nodding at the genuine horror and offense in her tone. He assessed them both. "Then tell me where you acquired the chandelier," he said and pointed at the crystal above them.

Zandra sucked in a horrified breath before answering, "I had it made in town."

"By who?" His tone was deadly. His wings flexed as the pair looked at each other.

"Pietr made it."

He felt her sending him and image of a shop. "Good." He nodded before glancing around. "There are hotels and resorts in Tetartos?"

She frowned. "Yes."

"Good. I require this palace until mine is built. My son will give you whatever you require so that I may use it."

Neither spoke, just gaped at him, but he was already porting away.

*****

Put him down, P gritted out to his father the second he reformed and saw what the hell was going on. Hades was livid. And P wasn't much happier, he'd been trailing the Deity only to find him holding up an Immortal Geraki, half bird of prey, by the throat. It seemed the large expensive shop was vacant of anyone else, but a

79

glance at the windows showed that they did have witnesses.

This was going to be a diplomatic joke. The Guardians had told those in the cities that they'd woken Hades and were responsible for him. And now it would spread that the God had lost his mind if P didn't contain the issue. The last thing they needed was the Realm up in a panic that the Guardians couldn't control a God.

He'd known shit was going to get worse after the battle in Hell Realm. His father had looked too damned contained at the end of that bloodbath. He'd thought he'd get a reprieve. That had been his mistake.

I'm serious. You need to put him down and tell me what's going on, P demanded through their mental link.

No, Hades bit out.

"Now tell me, Pietr, how long did you serve me?" His father's voice was quiet as he turned his attention back to the Immortal. And calm. Too damned calm. The God's wings flexed and twitched as Hades' power made the massive chandelier-filled room jingle. The place was too delicate to withstand a pissed-off Deity.

The male currently dangling by his feet sputtered, "I served happily for years."

"And when did you decide to steal. From. Me?"

The last thing P wanted to do was have to unleash his hidden power on his father. Pietr would feel it, and P wasn't overly sympathetic to the Geraki's plight at the moment. He'd let his father vent a little longer since he wasn't killing the male.

His thoughts turned to something else, making him frown. *How*

80

are you hurting him and not feeling the effects?

I was only cursed against harming humans.

P stared at him before adding, *Apollo was cursed with harming Immortals and humans alike.* The Guardians had learned that after Apollo escaped, along with the fact that the Creators had given Apollo a self-defense out when dealing with Immortals. The Guardians had been under the impression that all of the Gods were cursed like that before the Creators put them in stasis.

I'm aware of that, his father growled.

How?

Hades turned to him and gave him a hard look. *The Creators told me.*

Why weren't you cursed the same way?

I am not my brothers. Hades growled and turned his attention back to the Geraki. P wondered if his father was thinking about Sacha with that comment.

Pietr sputtered, "I didn't steal from you. The Creators were already here. We all felt what was happening. Their voices filled the air and we knew that they were containing the Gods." The male's amber eyes were wide and his face was red. The Geraki kept shooting looks in his direction and P nodded for him to tell Hades what he wanted to hear.

And then it took a shittier turn.

"*My* things would have gone to my heir. So are you saying you stole from my son?" If anything, his father's words had gotten colder.

P breathed out. It was impossible for the Geraki's eyes to get any bigger when he looked at P.

"What else did you take?" his father demanded.

"Nothing." Damn it, the idiot was asking for punishment now. P could feel the lie just as easily as his father. The crashing of broken crystal and glass filled the room.

Drake ported in at P's side. *What's this? Word is out that Hades is losing his fucking mind.*

Pietr was the one who stole the stone from my father's palace all those centuries ago.

"I didn't intend to steal from your son, I swear it," Pietr sputtered.

Hades looked off for a second, like something else caught his attention, before turning back to Pietr, looking vaguely disgusted but not angry. Hades tossed the male into a wall; more glass shattered around them as his father bit out, "Pothos, find out what else he took."

P didn't have a second to speak. His father was already gone.

Son of a bitch.

Go find him. I'll deal with this, Drake growled.

Where the hell are you? he demanded of his father and hoped to hell he'd actually answer him this time.

P got an image of the mountaintop they'd been to earlier. He ported away, leaving Drake.

When he reformed beside his father, he could tell it wasn't good.

"Tell me more about her," Hades asked. His anger was gone, but he seemed distracted.

P considered what he could say that he hadn't already said. "Like I said, she's logical. Calm. She's been partners with Brianne for centuries. She and Bastian do some of the diplomatic stuff in the cities of Tetartos Realm because only they have the patience to deal with any of their issues."

"What issues?"

"Issues like when a God demands someone leave their fucking home so he can move in, or trashes a store," P bit out.

Hades glared down at him. "Would you rather I move you out of *your* home until I have one of my own built?"

"No, but we do have other homes." Hades had been staying with him so P could keep an eye on him. "And Sacha has homes," he pointed out. "And my bet is that she's not going to be happy with your new place and how you got it."

P could almost hear Hades' teeth grinding. "What would she be happy with?"

"Ask her," P said, shaking his head. "We don't have time to deal with the shit demands Zandra and Damon have. If you want something of your own, you can have the Guardian island that Dorian and Rain just moved from until shit calms down. We need to find Apollo and figure out about Thule." He sent his father a visual of the island. He'd need to tell Drake about it when he was done babysitting.

"When Kara wakes, I will find out all there is to know," Hades growled. "Apollo is mine."

What the hell did he say to that? There was a line, and according to the Creators, they couldn't kill any of the Gods. That didn't mean Apollo didn't deserve to bleed for all he'd done before they got him back in his box. He wouldn't even ask if his father was getting through to Apollo. P had a feeling they'd all know when that happened because Hades would lose his mind.

P narrowed his eyes at his father. "You can't kill him. You know that, right?"

"Yes. And I have no intention of killing him." Hades' tone seethed, and P knew that meant Apollo was going to be made to suffer.

"Inform Zandra I no longer have need of their palace," Hades gritted out.

P nodded and they stood looking out for a while. One issue averted.

"Apollo couldn't be unconscious this long," his father snarled. Hades had been hit with the same energy when the Goddess and he had battled and it wiped him out, but only for days, Apollo was taken well past that timeframe.

"I agree." Something was obviously blocking his mental connection to Hades.

"I want his blood."

"As long as you don't kill him."

84

Hades nodded absently.

"Sacha will be okay, and when she's ready, she'll call to you. She was unconscious for weeks and hit with all this. It makes sense she needs time to process things."

Hades growled, "And once she does, how do I make up for decades of torment she suffered from my own brothers."

"You don't. You get to know her, be patient. Sacha's smart but contained. She was strong enough to deal with all that she was faced with and come out of it a Guardian. But her only experience with Gods wasn't good. I'd minimize some of your Godly shit."

Hades turned his head and stared at him, with clenched teeth. "You're saying to pretend I'm not a God?"

"I'm saying you need to show her a male who gives a shit about what she wants and needs. And don't make her feel caged. Once she sees you're a good male, she'll be fine."

Hades glanced back at him, a smile touching his lips. "Am I a good male?"

Hades' brow creased a second later and P wondered if Sacha was communicating with him.

"You have your moments," P said, shaking his head. He'd been sincere, his father was good, loving, but he wasn't sure how bad Sacha's memories of Apollo and Hermes were. He had a feeling Hades was going to need all the help he could get. The question was how P could help him. He could get the information to Brianne and see if she could do anything to ease Sacha.

Sweet fuck, now he was a matchmaker. After all the babysitting and this, he might as well turn in his male card.

Chapter 8

Sacha's Paris Home, Earth Realm

Sacha curled up on a couch in one of the seating areas nestled between potted trees in her living room. Water gurgled quietly in the shallow koi ponds that weaved throughout the large open space, but she barely heard it. She'd changed into loose pants and a tank top and crossed her legs on the soft cushion and leaned her head back to gaze up at darkened skies beyond the skylight, trying to find calm through the storm of her emotions.

It was nearly impossible with all the emotional spikes she'd felt coming from Hades. It had been hours since he'd left, and his surges of feeling seemed to be coming in more succinctly, more like true thoughts than emotions. She knew he wasn't any more pleased by being so open than she was, because she'd felt him trying to build blocks against it. She'd tried as well, but apparently fate didn't feel that they needed emotional privacy.

She shook her head in frustration and fought for quiet while a slow burn of arousal slid under her skin, reminding her of what they hadn't yet done. The desire to have him was there, but with it was the anxiety of reliving her past.

It all felt like a cosmic "screw you."

First she'd been hit with his rage, so deep and pained that it affected her own emotions. She'd mentally tracked his location through the bond to find him next to P's telepathic signature. His emotions had been so damned clear that she'd known exactly what happened. There was no doubt in her mind that his son had told him what she'd gone through with his brothers. Or at least a general version, as she'd never shared the details. She wasn't angry at her brother P, it was better that Hades understood her past if they were linked for all eternity, but she'd been swept away in his guilt and fury.

And she hadn't been sure how to process it. Each wave since had pulled her in, making her concentrate harder in an attempt to understand the male she was tied to.

When one blast of anger hit her hard, she'd been compelled to mentally touch the link. The moment she did, his anger had dissipated, leaving them both uneasy. She had power over the God. At least enough to ease him with a single mental touch. It was empowering, but unsettling.

But she hadn't called him to her yet.

She'd told him that she wouldn't fight this, and she had no intention of doing so, but she'd needed some time. She deserved it. They weren't in the frenzy, so being apart wouldn't hurt either of them. But in the end she didn't feel alone, not with the link to him growing stronger with each passing moment.

Was this how mating with a God was? Being constantly open? With a constant hum of need just under her skin? His seemed even more intense, and that was likely because he was male. Immortal males burned hot. Not that she'd ever been concerned by it. Not since no male had ever been capable of interesting her in that way.

She felt the exact moment when Brianne and Sirena ported

through the wards of her home.

"Are we crashing your party?" Brianne asked, reforming with a smile. "If so, too bad. You were unconscious for too long and scared the shit out of us. And since you're not fucking Hades sideways, we figured that meant girls' night."

Sacha's lips twitched, she hadn't wanted to see anyone when Sirena contacted her earlier, but now they were here, she could at least learn more about her mate. Maybe simply knowing more about Hades would be enough to stop her past from coming back to haunt her when she was with him.

Her sister had duties, though, ones she should be getting back to soon.

She cocked a brow in the healer's direction. "You're actually taking time off?"

Sirena nodded. "Yeah, and I'm not sure I know how to do that anymore." She was in her usual retro-style pencil skirt, and her platinum hair was down and curled into shiny waves. The healer slipped off her pumps and sat on the nearest love seat, with her feet tucked under her. Her delicate beauty didn't hide the tension in her smaller frame.

Sacha's heart clenched at the sight of her exhausted sister. How long had Sirena spent trying to find a way to remove the poison from Sacha's blood? Sirena needed this break.

"And you don't have patrols?" Sacha confirmed with Brianne, who'd already gone into the kitchen and was opening bottles of wine.

The redhead shifted the long waves of her hair over one

shoulder as she spoke. "Vane is taking Erik. They need a little twin bonding time." When the female started moving back to the seating area, she eyed her. "You're not getting rid of us. Besides, we have juicy gossip."

Sacha shook her head in vague amusement. She'd been trying to wrap her mind around how her life had changed. Her words to Sebastian when he'd found his mate were coming back to bite her. She'd told him that she liked to believe only the good found mates. She mentally cringed at how she'd always been so happy for her brothers and Brianne when they'd found theirs.

Brianne handed her a glass and sat in front of her.

"You don't have to tell us anything you don't want to," Brianne started, "but I will tell you that after you made Hades leave, he told P to send all his God groupies home."

"God groupies," Sacha muttered. Of course he'd have females all over him the moment he'd woken up; he was said to be a grand lover. She felt her grasp on her wineglass tighten and forced the hold to relax.

A gentle touch against their bond jolted her. He didn't speak, but he slid his mind over the link and she eased just as he had.

She sat processing that.

"P said he can't stand the touch of another female."

"He went from here directly to other females?" she asked calmly, while beneath it all she seethed.

I did NOT go to other females. His deep tone in her mind intensified the arousal sliding under the surface and stilled her. She

90

barely heard Brianne explaining that P had told her that Hades had apparently forgotten an entire house full of females. She clenched her teeth.

This hadn't even been something Sacha'd had time to consider, but now that it was in her head, he was fortunate that he hadn't screwed one of them. She wouldn't share her mate.

After hours catching up on patrols and all that Brianne had mentally shown her earlier, Sacha finally calmed. And it seemed Hades had as well. When Brianne mentioned there had been surges in demon-possessed and Hell beast attacks again, Sacha felt a pang of guilt that she wasn't already back to work patrolling.

"Don't feel guilty."

Sacha narrowed her eyes at Brianne.

"I've been your friend for centuries. I know that look."

Sacha felt her lips twitch.

"We have more help than ever. It's covered."

"Bastian and Natasha?" she asked of her son. She'd check on him once Sirena and Brianne left.

Sirena answered, "They're good."

Brianne turned her questions back to Hades at every chance, and this time Sacha paid attention. Anytime her sister Guardian had mentioned the God through the years, Sacha had admittedly tuned her out.

Even Sirena added, "I remember him doting on P whenever he

came to Aphrodite's palace. And he loves his sister. They were close," the healer said, smiling. "And he is vaguely amusing."

"Give him a chance," Brianne finally said.

"I'm not fighting it," she said. "I just needed time."

Her sisters eyed her.

She took a long drink of wine. The need wouldn't go away, and prolonging the unknown wasn't going to help her or make any of this more comfortable. And if she refused to share him, then she'd better take him and have some faith in the fates that she could get through it all without losing her mind.

Because this was permanent.

Chapter 9

Sacha's Paris Home, Earth Realm

Sacha closed her eyes as she slipped out of her steam-filled bath.

After having been connected to the God for over twenty-four hours, she'd finally realized that she couldn't do it anymore. The need was too constant; she wasn't even sure if it was his or hers since she felt so much emotion from him in the last hours. This wasn't a painful surge punishing her for not feeding a frenzy, it was a relentless erotic caress. The only thing to do was feed it.

She'd spent the entire night writhing and wild in her empty bed. Her dreams had been a more vivid version of their first touch. In them he'd entered her. He'd taken her like he'd been so close to doing. She hadn't felt memories or numbness; all that came was pure unending pleasure that felt hollow the moment she'd awoken.

All day she'd concentrated on every emotion to get to know him better and did mundane things in her home to avoid the inevitable until she was certain she could control her own memories of her past.

Throughout the day, she'd felt soft caresses on their bond, him attempting to ease her. And it had worked.

All she knew now was that she couldn't do anything until they finished this. She couldn't go see her son or anyone else, fighting some constant burn of arousal. She'd be mortified seeing her brethren with their enhanced senses, knowing they were likely scenting just how wet she was.

At least she'd spoken to Bastian last night after seeing Sirena and Brianne. Her son was worried, but she'd assured him she would be fine and was looking forward to seeing him in a few days.

And as much as she rebelled at being so emotionally open, at least she felt like she knew him now, and at least they were both equally exposed.

She still felt anxious, but holding out longer just made her feel cowardly. She was a Guardian, she'd fought beasts for centuries, she could battle back an ancient past if it attempted to pull her back.

She took a deep breath to steel her nerves one last time and called to him, *Hades, come to me.*

You're sure, Sacha? She felt his blinding need surge through the bond, and she smiled that he'd even asked.

Yes, she breathed through the connection.

She dried quickly in the air currents and stayed nude. That was how she'd end up, so why bother dressing.

*****

Hades reformed inside Sacha's home and grunted when the scent and feel of her so close hit him. Soft lights flickered everywhere in the darkened space. He glanced over and saw bright lights shining through the windowed doors facing out to the city below. That was of no importance because at that moment all he cared about was seeing his female. He could feel her anxiety.

The muted sounds of gurgling water from the indoor ponds were the only noise he heard through the ringing in his ears. Moonlight shone as if he were outside, and the pale glow only added to the soft flickering of lights she had in the trees and plants around the room.

He felt their link pulling him in, getting stronger by the second, building along with the need to have her. He gritted his teeth as he flexed his shoulders, hating the slide of cloth over his chest. The shirt was even constricting his arms. In an effort to ease his female, he'd retracted his wings and borrowed the dress shirt from his son before she'd even called to him. He'd felt her emotions and known she would call to him.

After their fitful night of shared erotic torment, it had only been a matter of time. He'd paced the evening away at the island in Tetartos. His new home. It was small, but more importantly it had been empty so that he'd been able to suffer alone as he attempted to plan their next meeting.

He would be damned if he evoked memories of her horrors this time. All she would feel in his presence was the pleasure they both needed. He forced a tight hold on his own desires and focused on her.

He stilled the second he caught sight of her. Everything inside him seized at the image she made. Fucking incredible.

And completely nude. His cock jerked as he took her in, standing in a doorway that likely led to her bedroom. He growled low as he scanned every bronze curve of her body completely bared to him, her flesh supple and begging for his hands and mouth. Long ebony hair fell down her back as her dark eyes assessed him. The moonlight cast a light sheen over her, and he'd never seen a more perfect example of the female body. Her curves were a thing of pure beauty. He couldn't wait to taste every inch. His dick twitched just thinking of what he wanted to do with her heavy breasts, they deserved special attention, but her tiny waist and flared hips brought his mind back to the image of her pert, round ass when he'd seen it on the patio.

He bit back a curse and ran a hand over the back of his neck. Why hadn't she worn clothes? He felt her nerves, and that was the only thing keeping him from taking her up on her beautiful offer.

He breathed in, mentally bracing himself. Going slow and easy with her would be the hardest thing he'd ever faced. There wasn't a section of his aching flesh that wasn't on fire for her. She'd spoken of the frenzy that Immortals experienced with their matings. He had a bad fucking feeling that was exactly what he was going through. This wasn't anything like the mere desire he'd felt before for a warm, wet female. This was a craving, a compulsive need to consummate their soul bond. It was nothing like anything he'd ever imagined. And it wasn't just about sex. His soul was thrumming again like it had when he'd first seen her.

He growled as he worked to gain control of the need.

When he refocused, he realized that he'd ported directly in front of her without having willed the movement. The pull to touch her was too damned strong. Everything about this situation was out of his realm. He'd never had to seduce a female in his life, but he was about to.

"You are beautiful." He sighed as he lifted a hand to her soft cheek, just one touch. A gentle caress that he gave her plenty of time to back away from. Her skin was smooth and warm beneath his fingers. He held a breath while watching and feeling for any change in her emotion. Being this close to her scent was a torture all its own. She smelled of almonds and sweet wet female and fuck if that wasn't erotic.

He was looking at *his* female. The one that he'd have at his side for eternity and it was up to him to make her crave him the way he craved her or it would be an excruciating existence for them both.

He'd never wanted a female more.

Their bond was tightening even as he stared down at her, the emotions getting clearer than ever.

Sacha stared up at him as he fought for sanity in the face of her nude body.

He'd had the entire night and day to come to terms with the fact that she was feeling him on a level he'd never have allowed anyone to know. Neither had liked being this open, but there was no way for him to shield from her. Nor her from him. He gritted his teeth, knowing just how much fate was leading them.

He felt her need and eased some. She wanted him. But it was with a sense of determination that wasn't right. And the hints of anxiety mixed in kept him from pulling her into his arms.

Fucking hell. He needed to get out of there. Needed to cover her up. "Come with me," he said with a slight curve to his lips meant to ease her while ensuring his words were that of an invitation as opposed to a demand.

He moved into her space and lifted her hand in his. He set his lips to her warm palm while watching and feeling her every reaction to the simple touch. "Outside."

Hades wasn't willing to wait a second more to find her damned clothes. He released the buttons from his shirt and slipped it off and over her while reassuring, "I hate covering your gorgeous skin, but it's night. And cold." He fucking hoped it was cold. Hell, he hoped for a damned blizzard of snow to pack around his aching dick.

He swore he caught sight of a twitch to her pouty lips and a hint of amusement through the link. He wasn't sure if that was good or bad at this point. His only relief came as she slipped her arms into the sleeves. He buttoned them hastily, hissing out a breath when he saw the finished result. He was fucked. Her nipples were still visible through the white material, and her skin looked so damned sexy against the stark color.

He gritted his teeth, feeling the vague sensation of being ripped limb from limb. He'd never in his life actually *covered* a female's body up.

He wanted to lift her into his arms, but instead slid her small palm in his, twining their fingers. Baby fucking steps were going to kill him. No big displays of power, no fast movements. And he wasn't even certain this was the right thing to do, but he knew he wouldn't survive her sending his ass away again. He needed to figure out a way to show her how much pleasure he could give her without tripping bad memories and shutting her down.

Chapter 10

Sacha's Paris Home, Earth Realm

Sacha's first glance at Hades had surprised her. He was beautiful with or without wings, but the difference was compelling. Because she knew the reasons behind it, she felt the sweet sense of logic deep inside. His emotions were coming through the bond even clearer now that he was so near. And they were in this together.

He fully intended on seducing her while she'd intentionally been naked so they could just get through this part and see what happened. She'd softened with this attempt at making her feel comfortable.

Her skin tingled with desire at the simple touch of his hand. They walked to the patio doors, both a little out of control and instinctually fighting to get it back.

She tried not to let her lips twitch when she realized he wasn't even going to teleport them, he was so worried about showing his power, as if she couldn't feel it. It almost made her wonder if he forgotten she was a Kairos? That porting was the main power of those of her race, not to mention she was a Guardian who held a wide array of other gifts given to her by the Creators.

He glanced down at her and cocked a brow. "I haven't forgotten,

Sacha." She couldn't find fault in his approach, because he was trying and that warmed her. Add his sexy tone to the gentle, seemingly innocent clasp of her hand and it was entrancing her. He slid his thumb over hers, sending tingles of pleasure all the way to her aching nipples.

Her anxiety still buzzed in the far recesses of her mind, but she felt better than she had.

He lifted her hand up to kiss it gently as he smiled down at her. "There's no need to rush."

He said the words, but the heat of desire coming from him and rolling through her was strong. Enough that every inch of her skin felt tight.

His power glided around them, but he tried to keep it from licking across her skin. She wasn't sure if the wildness of it was from their mating. She had a feeling that might only be part of it. There was no mistaking the immense strength of his ability; it was nearly lifting her hair.

She couldn't help tilting her head to see more of his beautiful face. A muscle kept twitching along his jaw.

Her lips curved when he gratefully sucked in the cold night air. She was Immortal and could handle the temperatures with ease, which made his excuse for putting her in the flimsy dress shirt amusing when she knew he'd been excited by the sight of her nude.

He gazed down at her as she stepped on the patio of the roof garden. It was a crystal-clear evening, with the lights of the city glowing around them.

She wondered just how long he planned to fight the need,

100

because she wasn't sure she could last now that his scent was in her lungs, and the sight of his half-naked body was driving her wild.

He guided her to sit beside him on the bench while a muscle in his jaw twitched. When his brilliant blue eyes gazed down at her, she swallowed at the intensity, the hunger there. It was in their bond. In her. And she was wet with the thought of what they'd be doing very soon.

He hissed out a breath. "I know you can feel it." His gaze bored into hers. "You know just how bad I want inside you. And I can feel your desire, too." He groaned. "But first I have to know what I shouldn't do."

She eyed him. Hades might have been trying to seem less intimidating, but his eyes were nearly glowing with power that was getting wilder as the seconds ticked by.

He was asking about her triggers. And no matter how wild the arousal, he was still keeping his touch on her hand gentle. That caress felt like it was on her clit and she knew they were both too far gone to take this slower. His thumb was making circles as she considered his valid question. The problem was that she didn't have a definitive answer.

She blew out a breath and made a decision for them both when she ported to straddle his lap, her knees sinking into the soft cushion at either side of his thighs. She knew he couldn't take much more and she wasn't sure she could either. His need was bleeding into hers, filling her with hot jolts of pleasure and anticipation. She answered through harsh intakes of air, "I won't know until we start." She squirmed in his lap. "I think I have a grasp on what happened before." She leaned in and took his lips in a kiss because she couldn't not. He was addictive, and when he took over to devour her mouth, his hands came up to grip her hips. She felt his arms shaking as their tongues tangled.

Desire pulsed through her in a blast that tore a groan from her. She broke the kiss; his desire was getting closer to pain at this point.

"Just let me lead the first time." She gasped as she pulled at his fly, ripping material to get to his cock. Shivers of ecstasy were ignited with his hands as they roved under the shirt he'd wrapped her in. Hades' palms slid over the bare skin of her thighs to grip her ass and grind her against his hard cock. His hot flesh against her wet pussy made them both moan.

When she gazed down, she saw just how heated and glowing his sapphire eyes were. His breathing sped with hers, and tremors racked his muscles as he glided her bare pussy along his shaft. She was slick and getting wetter by the second. He searched her eyes and she was caught by the sight of his throat. The tendons there were tight as he swallowed, and it was an incredibly sexy sight.

He leaned in to kiss her again and she gasped as sensation made her grind her pussy against his cock. Wild need and power swirled all around them, through them both until all the slight noise of the city below was completely drowned out by their rapid breathing and needy moans.

Ambrosia, whispered through their mental link as he lifted from her lips and moved to taste and nip at her collarbone. *Nothing tastes this good.*

Her ears were buzzing as she lifted up, but he stilled her, holding her hips gently as he took one last taste of her neck. He pulled her hips in and slowly slid them back so that she was just riding along his cock. She tilted and rolled against him, reveling in the pleasure. "Just like this to start. Get me wet and grind your little clit on me." He said the words through clenched teeth, and she whimpered as he lightly directed her movements.

"Feel what you do to me. You'll make me come with just the touch of your pussy." He was completely seducing her.

And she was caught up in his words. She felt the fever between them. Felt the slow ride along her clit, and suddenly she was close. Anxiety rose in the back of her mind.

Could she come?

"Nothing more than touch, *thisavre mou*. Let it feel good." One hand came up and caressed her cheek. "You have all the power here, Sacha." His words were filled with heat and strength. Enough that she felt able to let go. He wasn't just giving himself to her, he was hers. She felt it deep in her soul. In his.

She moaned, so caught up in the beauty and pleasure she couldn't stop her climax from taking her over. With complete surrender she rolled her hips and leaned down to kiss his lips, crying out against his mouth in pure joy and relief. She leaned back while her hips were still jolting and watched his neck fling back as a pained roar split his lips.

He was beautiful and completely open to her as hot jets of come painted his stomach and chest. Some hit her breast and she realized that she'd never felt so connected and completely vulnerable with another being in her life. Yet somehow it felt safe and right.

When his eyes settled back on hers, he grinned, and it made him so incredibly gorgeous. He lifted a hand to her face and searched her eyes. "Are you okay, *thisavre mou*?"

She hadn't originally liked being called a treasure, but not now. Now she felt almost cherished, the way a mated female should feel in her male's arms as she breathed out, "Yes." Her first reaction was to deny it, but she could feel the truth of the feelings in the bond. They were connected on a level that didn't allow for deception.

She felt his cock twitch between them and looked down at his come-covered stomach. She felt the tendrils of renewing desire and sucked in a breath.

He growled, "Are you ready for more, Sacha?"

It was just the beginning, and she was thankful that her past might not be the problem she'd feared.

"Yes," she whispered as she leaned in to kiss him before teleporting them from the garden.

Chapter 11

Sacha's Paris Home, Earth Realm

Sacha reformed with Hades in her bathroom and she allowed the shirt to fall away. His pants slipped to the ground and she tried to suppress her amusement as he stood in front of her sink with his pants around his ankles. He cocked a brow at her and toed off his shoes. The rest slipped away as he gazed down at her with a sexy grin. He was deadly with that look on his face. His grin only widened and she knew he'd interpreted her thoughts.

She breathed him in as she turned on the water and slipped a hand towel beneath it. Sacha found something so oddly sexy about the sight of his come running down the dips and valleys of his muscled chest and stomach. He'd hadn't fought the need to spill all over himself; he'd let go completely and reveled in the pleasure. In her touch. He hadn't held back or cared that he was a mess. She sucked in a breath at how well she felt she knew him in this short time.

He stilled her with a warm palm over her hand. When she looked up, that devilish grin was in place and a mischievous twinkle in his eye caught her. "This pleases you." He lifted her hand to his mouth and kissed it before running a hand carelessly through the seed on his stomach. "Leave it, *thisavre mou*. I guarantee more will join it when I get my mouth on you."

He leaned down and inhaled the soft sound that escaped her lips. Her body was a mass of aching need already. His gaze settled on her chest and heat flared in his eyes. "I think it looks better on you," he growled as he set his thumb to the evidence still marking her chest. He trailed it over her tightened nipple and groaned. "Beautiful."

She licked her lips and his attention fixed there as if mesmerized for a second before his thumb came up and caressed the lower one. When her tongue darted out for her first taste of him, he grunted his approval.

She didn't stop there; she stepped closer so that her stomach and aching breasts were flush against him, his come marking them both until his skin was on fire and his muscles were twitching against her. He growled low and she felt the wild punch of desire that shot through him. His eyes held that same feverish glow he'd gotten before, and his cock pushed against her stomach.

Was fate forcing the issue of consummation? Because she felt a little wild and greedy when she wasn't sure she should.

When he lifted her up and carried her to the bed, he didn't stop staring into her eyes, and all the hunger she saw there fed her own. The fireplace flared to life and set the room aglow with flickers of warm light. Her cloud of blankets slid out of the way before he laid her down.

His chest rumbled with need as he followed her down. "My turn, *thisavre mou*." He was watchful as he braced himself above her. "Is this going to be okay?" he hissed, and she knew he worried about being above her. She nodded, but his eyes hadn't left hers. Once he was assured all she felt was arousal and the pleasure of his warmth cradled between her thighs, he leaned in for another kiss. His hot weight was over her, but it wasn't enough, she squirmed beneath him. He moved to her ear and down her neck as gooseflesh rose over her skin. He was concerned for her, but she didn't feel trapped beneath him and she had no experience with where he was going. No male had ever used his mouth on her.

"Never?" He lifted up, growling, and she felt a mix of emotion she hadn't expected. He was happy and displeased all at once.

"No," she confirmed as she caressed his skin and dug her fingers in his hair.

His eyes tracked over her flushed skin as if mapping her body, and then he growled, "I want to taste everything at once."

She grabbed him by the neck to bring his lips down to hers, making his choice for him. She loved his mouth, he tasted so damned good, but it wasn't just that. His kisses were consuming; he owned every bit of her, devouring, tempting, teasing... seducing her with a slow tangling of their tongues. Her back arched, meshing their hot flesh together, and it was a jolt to her already overstimulated nerves.

He broke the kiss and groaned as her fingers trailed over his shoulders and back. She couldn't stop touching him.

His lips found her neck again and some sensitive spot behind her ear, making her cry out. She'd never felt pleasure, and it seemed each new touch was going to light her on fire. She couldn't believe the noises he wrenched from her lips.

He seemed pleased with each and every one as he traced his tongue over an aching nipple. Her neck bowed as he nipped and then sucked her nipple as she cried out to the ceiling. She squirmed, grabbed his head and pulled him tighter. She felt like she might come from that alone. She wouldn't wonder at how that was possible. He flicked his tongue over it and then nipped before moving to the other. Air slid over her wet aching breast as he rubbed his stubbled cheek against the other. "So fucking good." He groaned and she felt how much hotter he'd gotten. When he teased her other nipple while caressing the one he'd abandoned, she nearly came off the bed.

She needed more.

He moved to her stomach and she couldn't take any more. Having their combined desire pulsing inside her made waiting for his cock impossible.

In a flash she was above him, impaling herself on his cock. There was no sickening numbness, just intense blinding pleasure, and she breathed through it, relieved. It rocked them both.

He shouted, "Fuck," as his hands went to her hips. His body was vibrating with need, so much that she felt it all the way through his cock. So hot. His skin was burning; both of them were feverish. She slid up and then slammed back down, taking every massive inch. It stretched her, filled her, made her crave more as the frenzy took them. She crashed down over and over as she watched him battle for control. His massive chest was rising and falling with each hard jolt of her hips. His hands went up her sides to her aching nipples as she circled and rode him hard. She could almost feel his heartbeat syncing with hers.

She leaned forward and his hands slid down, one holding her hips while the other trailed between them. The new angle hit a spot that made her dizzy. His neck arched back as he cursed, "Fuck. Harder, beautiful."

She slammed back over and over until his hips were lifting her up every time she took him deeper.

He groaned and she felt the intensity in his next words. "Come, Sacha. Your pussy is clamping me so fucking tight... I'm going to fill you so fucking full."

She shuddered as her orgasm hit. It kept going, wild and unfocused and never ending as she rode it out.

He gripped her hips, pulling her down tight as he roared his own completion. She looked down at him and felt the connection between their souls rise. She didn't feel any flinch like she had that first time his soul glided over hers. Again, she felt intense relief.

She wasn't disturbed by the connection of the souls, not when he was rubbing her back and holding her against his chest. "It's just me, *thisavre mou*. Just another part of me wanting more of you. Wanting to make you feel good."

She breathed out and felt something ease free of her. The second she felt the last of her anxiety melt away, her own soul curled against his. The caress pulled a deep groan from him and she felt a sense of true power and satisfaction in that.

Exhaustion set in as she rolled to lie at his side. He curled her so her head rested against his chest. It felt like a boulder had been lifted from her chest. She was able to have him.

Mere seconds passed when she felt his warm come between her aching thighs, and that was when it hit.

Memories latched onto her without any warning. Of being left naked with the evidence of having been used.

She ported to the bathroom, shaking in shock as she

telekinetically tripped the water to hot so that she could beat the harsh cold and numbness away. She pushed the old thoughts back with force as she quickly stood beneath the water. She felt him behind her and closed her eyes at the fury and guilt he was forcing down. The same emotions she was experiencing, though hers had the addition of humiliation.

The water eased her, and she would have moved away if she hadn't felt his helplessness.

When she finally leaned back against him, letting him comfort her, she started to ease. When his arms circled her waist, she relaxed completely. He'd been just as affected, and her big God hadn't even been sure if touching her was what she'd needed, but he hadn't been able to leave her to battle it alone. She hated feeling broken, but there was no hiding that the beginning of her life had the ability to torment her thousands of years later.

"I've got you," he said, and all she could do was nod. She'd shut down and talking wasn't possible. She needed another moment to get it all back together

Neither moved.

She felt his breath against her wet head and then pressure. His lips or chin touching her as he held her.

She breathed in the steam and felt her heart start to match pace with his. She closed her eyes and wondered how often her past would come back to haunt her. Them.

She wasn't sure how long they stood in there, but at some point the water had cooled and she felt completely drained. Her legs ached, too tired to hold her up, not that they needed to, Hades hadn't let her go the entire time. They both washed quickly before landing in bed, making sure to use air currents so they were dry the second their bodies touched the soft material.

She wasn't sure where to go from there, but for now the anxiety was gone and she felt relaxed and exhausted. She only needed to rest a moment. And she knew he needed this calm almost more than she did.

*****

Hades lay staring up through the glass ceiling as Sacha's breathing evened out. She'd fallen asleep in his arms, but he couldn't clean away the remnants of that numbness and what it meant. He'd never get it out of his head. She'd been physically ill and he couldn't get beyond that.

He had an iron grip on his fury, but it was a battle not to let it free. If it wouldn't wake his female, he'd let it rage. He was caught between the need to kill and the compulsion to hold her, to protect her from the nightmares he worried were going to come next. His muscles hurt like hell from wrestling back his desire for blood while he'd held her in the shower. He wasn't sure he'd ever done anything more difficult, and he had a bad fucking feeling it would get worse before it got better.

Now he let the rage simmer, not enough to wake her, but enough to vow that Apollo would suffer. If he could get Drake to wake Hermes, he would make that brother suffer unspeakable horrors as well

Sacha shifted and curled tighter against his side, and he blew out a breath as her hand snaked up his side, pulling him tighter to her. He didn't want her out of his sight, he wanted her like this every fucking night of his life, and that was a new feeling. He'd never slept with a female. Ever. He'd fucked them, but sharing a bed to sleep was an entirely different experience.

Their connection was so strong that he felt like she was a part of him. His sister hadn't been lying about the incredible pleasure, but she hadn't said shit about the protective instincts that were turning him into a beast.

He felt for the link to Apollo, and it was still silent and leading nowhere. His teeth clamped down tight. Soon. The second Kara woke, he would get answers from her about where Apollo was. He wanted the bastard back and he wanted him in chains.

Chapter 12

Mountain Lake, Earth Realm

Snow flurries floated around P as he stared at the small mountain lake. The air was crisp and cool... silent. He looked out at the glassy water; it was still, like a painting. Why had his father needed to call to Thule from here? Why use a special stone to drop spelled liquid into this lake as a way to call to a God of Thule?

Drake hadn't even been able to figure out what the stone was and why it had gone liquid. Uri's mate, Alex, daughter of Athena, had a small ability to touch an object and feel the history, and she hadn't gotten anything from it. They had more questions than answers where Thule was concerned.

After the battle with the Goddess of Thule, his father had spent days recovering, growling every time P had questioned him about this place, saying he didn't know why he needed to use this particular lake. All the while demanding P stay out of it.

How the hell was he supposed to stay out of it? P had always kept himself apart from most of the other Guardians, and now he wondered if his special thrall came from having a priestess from another world as his mother. The power had always been difficult to leash. Sander had never been fazed by the effects, and that made partnering with the Phoenix easy. But other Guardians had always felt a hint of it pulling at them no matter how locked down he kept it.

He needed answers and he was getting a little more anxious with every day that passed. An emotion he'd never truly felt or appreciated until his father had been awakened.

He shook his head. He had shit to do, but he'd found himself detouring to this spot over and over again.

Enough.

He ported away and reformed on a balcony of the Guardian manor in Tetartos.

His muscles were tense as he stalked into the media room and down the hall to the war room.

Drake glanced up from staring over Conn's shoulder at something on the wolf's open laptop. His cousin assessed him for all of a second before growling, "What's Hades done now?"

P shook his head. "He's with Sacha, so we should have a damned reprieve as long as all goes well."

Drake crossed his arms over his chest and waited as Conn stopped tapping at the laptop. The wolf leaned back in the big desk chair, resting flannel-clad arms on the sides as he asked, "How long has he been over there?" The usually mellow and amused Lykos was serious as he assessed P with amber eyes.

"About an hour."

Both nodded and Drake said, "Good," before asking, "You got Hades set up at the island before he went over there?"

"Yes." P nodded his head.

Conn grinned. "Zandra was disappointed that Hades won't need her palace anymore. Now she won't get all her creative demands. I'm surprised she found time to draft so many before you averted that nightmare. It's all over the Realm that he demanded the use of her palace."

P growled, "He offered to pay." Or more accurately he'd said P would give her whatever the hell she wanted, according to Zandra. He was glad he hadn't had to fight his father to end that ridiculous demand, because there was no way in hell the Guardians had time to deal with that shit.

"Yeah. I got that part." The wolf's eyes lit with amusement.

P shook his head before asking, "Are Bastian and Tasha still out in the Realm, unruffling all the feathers because of it?"

Conn laughed. "Hell yeah. I'm sure they'll be on that for a while." The wolf added, "Hades was on a damned roll. We still don't know what to do with Pietr. The little weasel's locating the last of the small artifacts he swiped from Hades' palace all those fucking millennia ago."

P nodded, but Drake grunted in annoyance. He'd been the one to deal with the Pietr situation in Efcharistisi after P was forced to trail after his father.

He took a minute and mentally tracked his father's link. He was still at Sacha's.

"Do you have telepathic links to him now?" P asked. He did because Hades was his father, but now that Hades was mated to a Guardian, he should have a shared link through her to all the Guardians.

Drake nodded. "Yes."

"We couldn't have asked for a better way to keep Hades in line." Conn pointed out what P had been thinking. They'd already agreed to allow his father his freedom after Hades helped Drake and Era find a way through their seemingly impossible mating, but they hadn't been looking forward to keeping track of him. But if his father hadn't released the beasts Era had been forced to house by their old enemy, she could have either gone insane or died. And the Guardian could've lost Drake to the fury of his dragon. The Guardians had owed his father.

"You're not worried about Sacha?" P asked the two curiously. P wasn't worried, but he wondered how everyone else was taking the mating.

Drake was thoughtful, but Conn shook his head easily. "I'm not. Sacha's strong. It might not be easy at first. But don't forget that I've known your father since before you were born," the ancient wolf pointed out, raising a pierced brow. "He's a good male, he loves hard, and he's incredibly powerful. And he always had a weakness for females. Give him a mate and I'd be surprised if he didn't eventually try to give Sacha the world."

It was hard to remember that Conn was one of the original Immortals created fully formed to care for the Gods after the Creators had birthed the Deities.

He nodded as the Lykos added, "And it's a good damned thing he had you send those females home or he would've ended up getting his dick ripped off."

P mentally cringed at that visual. But he smiled.

P ran a hand over his head. "I'm just happy to be done playing

116

the part of his valet and babysitter."

Drake raised a brow. "We don't know that yet. He's only been at Sacha's for an hour."

"Don't kill this for me. I'm glad to have my home back."

Drake snorted his assent as P nodded in agreement. Though, in reality he'd be happier if he had answers to go with his empty home. The agitation wouldn't abate.

He turned to his cousin. "Anything new with the prisoners?" Drake would have already told him if the Goddess had awoken, but he was itching for information, and Drake had been working to get something out of the warriors.

Drake shook his head. "Nothing yet."

He nodded before gritting his teeth as he eyed the dragon. Wondering if he might hide something from him since he was benched from dealing with anything Thule related.

"I know it's driving you crazy not to be a part of this, but you have to let me handle it," Drake growled. When P's shoulders tensed, his cousin shook his head and added more calmly, "Hades wouldn't be so damned adamant if he didn't believe they posed a danger to you. Give me time to get answers."

P gritted his teeth. He'd never been impulsive, but the whole thing was setting his nerves on edge.

Conn eyed him. Watchful and sympathetic and he wasn't sure what part of that he liked less.

He changed the subject. "Where do I patrol?" He'd spent

months shadowing Drake to make sure the dragon didn't run wild, and after that he'd been regulated to watching his father's every move. This was the first time in over a month that he could do a normal patrol. And if he didn't do something, he'd keep going back to the lake or the place were Apollo had been taken.

Or worse. He could very well find himself finding a way to get answers from the prisoners no matter what anyone said. And that was exactly the reason Conn and Drake were eyeing him.

He gave them both a hard look before asking, "Is Sander out with Nastia?" The Phoenix had been P's partner for centuries, but now he was mated to a female warrior, so he was probably patrolling with her. That'd been what they'd been doing since even before their mating was completed.

"Yes, he is... I'll go patrol with you," Drake growled.

Chapter 13

Hroarr's Palace, World of Thule

Gefn stood frowning at the deep blue seas beyond her brother's palace, listening to the waves crashing into the rocks and floating ice several hundred feet below. Clouds rolled in quickly, obscuring the sunlight glittering off the frosted stone. Her irritation and impatience were calling the storms as she stood beside massive rock pillars holding up the high carved ceiling.

Icy winds whipped through her long golden hair, the clasps only containing a portion of the mass flowing down her back. Her boots didn't make a sound as she started pacing, though there was a chance she'd muttered a few ancient curse words. She didn't even feel the temperature change through the leather of her leggings or the matching sleeveless vest.

Spa and Velspar, her precious cats, sat regally at her side, watchful as the air cooled with the darkening skies. The animals nearly topped her shoulders when perched on their bobbed tails as they were. She knew their golden eyes scanned the area around them, ensuring she wasn't disturbed. Their presence normally calmed her. As a Goddess of Thule, she didn't need the beasts' protection, she only truly required their companionship. She ran her fingers through the silky black fur of their necks all the way to the pointed golden ears before staring out again.

She hadn't been able to wait in the great hall. She'd have killed her brother Dagur herself if she'd been forced to spend more time with him.

Instead she was forced to defend the fool from their ruling sibling, Hroarr, who was going to be even more furious with him.

The atmosphere around her changed and she turned.

She faced the shimmering air of the portal her brother had obviously opened for his return from the outer reaches of Thule. It was generally a draining endeavor for all but her warrior brother; he was completely unfazed as he strode through. The waves of his long midnight hair had been tied back in a knot at the back of his head, and he wore dark brown warrior leathers just like the elite guard stepping through the molten air behind him. Her head nearly reached his chest as he came abreast of her. The males behind were only slightly smaller.

Warriors were a large breed, and the seven stalking behind her and her brother were the best.

Hroarr's boots echoed on the marble ground, anger riding every hard line of his body. A glance up was all it took to see the hard gaze in his brilliant green eyes, and she could almost hear the grinding of his teeth. It took two steps to his one long stride, but she was used to it. Spa and Velspar kept pace at her back. With no more than a thought, the massive double doors slammed open as they approached the entrance to the great hall.

She firmed her lips. He'd obviously heard the news. It was information she'd hoped to share in person, which was why she'd specifically sent Laire to call him home. She sent a look back in her guard's direction. The large blond male shook his head as he stalked beside the other warriors. Hroarr had likely demanded to be told everything the minute Laire had given her brother the message that he must return.

"It took you longer to get back than I thought," she started, knowing Dagur had sent a messenger for him days ago.

"And it would have been longer yet, had you not sent Laire. I will need to go back," he growled. "But first I will deal with our brother."

Servants stepped back, feeling the heat of Hroarr's fury as he moved over the polished stone.

"You can't kill him." Gefn sighed as she kept pace with him.

If anything, her words only made the packed muscle of his shoulders pull tighter. "I'm aware of that, sister. That doesn't mean he won't bleed for every one of my warriors who died," he snarled.

Dagur was too impulsive. Had always been so. It was what had nearly demolished his own ranks, and now he'd used Hroarr's warriors without consideration.

He may have gotten what he wanted, what their world needed, but there had been a cost. A cost that hadn't been Dagur's to pay, and now they had a mess to clean up.

Once again she was forced to play peacekeeper between her siblings. And it wasn't that she didn't want to rip Dagur into tiny pieces, she did. He was a pain in the ass, but he'd unfortunately been the lesser evil of their siblings. And now they were stuck with him.

A dull ache started behind one eye as she kept pace with her fuming brother.

The second they stepped to the edge of the great hall, she saw Dagur surrounded by females. Her reckless brother's bright golden eyes shone up at them, and Gefn groaned at the sight of his arrogant smile. His hair was a shade somewhere between her blonde and the black locks of her furious green-eyed brother.

"Leave," Hroarr bellowed to the crowd below, his eyes on Dagur. Within a second the others rushed out, heeding their ruler. Even Hroarr's guards and Laire stepped back to the doors; Spa and Velspar didn't so much as twitch at her side.

"Brother," Dagur said as he crossed his thick arms over a bare chest, his leather kilt the only thing covering him. His smile had gone as he focused in Hroarr's direction. "It was well worth the sacrifice."

Power slid from Hroarr, and the male moved so fast even she could barely see him slice through the air. In less than a second Hroarr had Dagur by the throat.

He sputtered and growled as his feet dangled.

Hroarr's voice was deadly calm. "Tell me, *brother*," he bit out, "was it your sacrifice to make?"

She watched them, planning to intervene before Hroarr killed Dagur, wondering when her sister, Kara, would finally grace them with her presence.

"Put me down," Dagur snarled as his hands grasped at Hroarr's, trying to gain freedom. He sputtered, "Would you rather I do nothing?"

"I'd rather you had a brain," Hroarr snapped.

"Hroarr, look at the big picture. We have another God," Dagur tried, and it was the wrong tactic at the moment.

"At a cost *you* were not permitted to pay?"

Dagur sputtered, barely able to speak.

"How many of my warriors did you send to their deaths?" Gefn was sure Laire had told him it was dozens, but she knew her brother wanted Dagur to admit it out loud and suffer for it. Hroarr was a ruthless and harsh ruler if needed. He was also strongest and most powerful of them.

Dagur lowered his eyes and choked out, "I'm sorry, Hroarr. I didn't intend it."

"But you didn't prevent it!" Hroarr bellowed, and the walls echoed and shook with his rage. Flames in the giant hearth roared to violent life at the ruling God's fury.

They had too few left in their world. Gefn felt a harsh pang that Hroarr had lost dozens. They had lost dozens when birthrates were low.

Dagur turned a shade of red as this went on.

Gefn snapped, "Hroarr," and slammed them both with a blast of icy power because at some point Dagur wouldn't be able to speak through their furious brother's hold. The ruling God hissed out a breath and set Dagur down with force before turning his attention to her.

She understood Hroarr's fury hadn't gone its course, but if Dagur couldn't speak, it would be left to her to share what her reckless brother couldn't.

"Gefn, do not come between us in this," Hroarr snarled in her direction. His tone and the wild gusts of his fury spiked the flames in the big hearth, causing Spa and Velspar to rise, their dark scruffs lifting in warning as they paced to eye her rage-filled brother.

He growled, "Calm your beasts." The ancient Immortal creatures had been with her since birth. They were a sign of favor from her mother and father that had made most of her siblings hate her from the start. Hroarr had been given his own gifts and had never been jealous of hers. The beasts generally liked him, but they were loyal to her. Throughout the long centuries some of her more evil siblings had attempted to kill her beasts and paid the price. Not only were they incredibly powerful, her companions couldn't die, and they were deadly when challenged. Not even a God could withstand the force of their claws and teeth and not forever bear the scars. Which was why Dagur was eyeing them closely. Her more impulsive brother had always been wise enough to keep his distance.

"Talk," she demanded of her brothers. She wasn't happy with Dagur either, but she'd rather Hroarr heard the rest of what their reckless brother had to say. She sent a wave of love and calm through the unique bond with her beasts and they settled at her feet, still facing her brothers.

Hroarr turned his attention to their brother. "I'm aware that you captured a God with your reckless idiocy. And I was told that formidable warriors fought to protect him."

"Yes."

"How many of my warriors were lost?" Hroarr snarled, still forcing his brother to say the words that damned him in their world.

"Several dozen." She felt the ground shake under her feet as her brothers faced off and the harsh bite of so many losses hit them all.

"And you did not venture to this world before sending them to take the God?"

"No." Dagur at least had the intelligence to look completely repentant even though she could almost feel his teeth grinding. Thule had gone through much death throughout the centuries and birthrates were low.

"And you didn't go through *with* my warriors?" Hroarr was gaining in fury again.

"I did not."

"Why?"

Dagur's eyes darted around, looking trapped before answering. "I had already opened the portals, sending a messenger to you once. Weeks ago," her golden-eyed brother bit out. Dagur's jaw twitched. "You didn't come back, and I checked again to find the God gone."

"Gone?" Hroarr growled.

"Yes," Dagur snapped. "And I wasn't certain he'd return."

Gefn had been considering this since Dagur told her earlier. It seemed the God could portal out of his world, something they'd never seen from another world, or maybe he could mask his presence there. That was a question she wanted answers to.

Dagur continued, "I kept resending the spell to check the ethers for Creator blood for days after, and when the God returned, I didn't want to chance waiting, but after sending out so many messengers, I didn't have enough energy to keep a portal open from there." Dagur shot her a stony-faced look.

She nodded. It was still reckless, but she somewhat understood. Portals drained energy quickly, from all but Hroarr, and it took time to replenish strength.

"I wasn't at my palace when the messengers came," she admitted. Dagur had been left to make a choice, and it hadn't been the best.

Hroarr ignored her and kept at their brother. "You should have gone to the world first. Or waited." Hroarr's eyes were nearly glowing now with his fury. Gefn agreed, but she could easily guess why Dagur had done it.

Excitement.

Hope.

Fear that the God would disappear and never come back. That he'd have lost a monumental chance at taking a rare and needed God. The hard look in his golden eyes confirmed that.

"It's done," she bit out. She didn't like it, but now they needed to figure out the rest while they waited for Kara to arrive.

"Show me the God. I will know everything he knows about that world," Hroarr growled.

She suddenly felt an odd sensation in her stomach. A bad feeling?

And where was her errant sister? Kara should have arrived before Gefn.

Chapter 14

Sacha's Paris Home, Earth Realm

Hades rolled to his side, burning with lust. A groan slipped from his lips as he slid a hand over cool empty sheets. A growl followed as his eyes shot open before the initial worry hit. He sat up as he felt for her; had something brought on another memory? When he felt her emotional state, the worry slid away and he lay back in the tangle of blankets.

He hissed out a breath as he gripped his aching cock and groaned, but forced himself to move. A second later he was reforming in front of her. His hard cock pulsed against his stomach, unashamed. He wasn't alone in his desire, he felt it coming in equal measures from her, so why hadn't she woken him?

She gazed up at him, her deep chocolate eyes sparking with heat in the early morning light. She was fighting back the need. Or trying to.

Air hissed from his lungs at the image she made sitting at a small stone table, her delicate hands encasing a cup of something. Her shining dark hair edged over the pale robe she wore haphazardly tied. He barely paid any attention to the material. Not when his eyes were gliding down to see one gorgeous thigh peeking from beneath the covering.

She was the most gorgeous creature he'd ever seen. Not just her outer beauty, it was also the strength and depth of her soul that tantalized him. Its song still called to him, forcing him to fight the need to claim every sweet perfect inch inside and out.

The morning seemed to have come with new, harsher need. He attempted to lock up the sharp edge of that need as he watched her. But, fuck, it was difficult not to bend her over the stone table, rip the material from her beautiful body, and take her hard while the humans in the city below went about their lives.

The sound of her breath catching forced his thoughts back down.

Memories of her in the shower the night before came back with hard force. He still needed to be careful with her, and he was thinking things that were anything but.

"Why did you leave the bed?" he asked calmly as he dealt with his lack of control, all the while assessing their bond.

He felt her desire, there was no fear, but there was some hesitancy.

Her voice was a sultry cadence that added to his need. "I'm not afraid." She wasn't, but there was enough uncertainty that he didn't take her up on all that arousal. He caught her eyes taking in his cock and he felt as if she'd touched him. His muscles twitched in near agony.

"Why are you out here?"

"I take coffee out here most mornings," she admitted as she gripped the large cup in her small hands.

The low breeze wasn't cold enough to take the heat from his skin, and the nearly painful need wasn't easing. He glared at the offending mug in her grip. "Coffee?" It smelled bitter and unnecessary. "Why?"

He could feel the strength of her desire, but she wasn't acting on it for a reason. She was considering. And her emotions were all over the place.

*****

"Amusement... Habit?" Sacha replied. In truth she was out there because she hadn't known what to do with the God in her bed. Her breathing escalated, forcing her hard nipples against the material of her robe. Her skin was flushed and her body was primed for him already; it was her mind that stalled any progress.

His frown eased, eyes heating as he watched her. Through it all he spared another glance at her coffee cup as if the object had committed a crime.

She mentally sighed, part of her amused by his expression because she doubted he was aware of it. Another portion of her was incredibly aroused, yet the larger section of her mind was still focused on the problem she faced.

Her.

"Would you like some coffee?" she offered as her eyes moved over his body. She couldn't help from getting distracted at the sight of him even when her mind was all over the place. Hades was a being of pure sexual beauty. And she wanted to experience every single wicked pleasure she knew he could offer, but she hesitated in taking him up on what she felt him imagining. The triggers were messing with her mind, and she could almost feel the numbness waiting... That position had the potential for trouble, and she hated having to consider that, but last night in the shower he'd been just as effected and powerless to stop her reaction. If he bent her over the table or the balcony...

He growled low, and she looked up at him, wanting him to understand that she knew it wouldn't be the same. It wouldn't stop her from doing these things with him. She only needed him to understand that she might not be able to do it yet.

She breathed out. She'd spent the last half hour wet and aching as her skin tightened with each passing minute. Now that he was out there with her, his need was only amplifying her own. She ran a hand over her robe, and the silky material sliding over her naked flesh only excited her more.

She'd swear they were going through the frenzy, even though she knew he'd bypassed it by soul bonding them.

His eyes captured her as he slipped the warm cup from her hands. "The only way I want coffee is from your lips," he said huskily. She wasn't sure where he set the mug, but it wasn't in his hand anymore when he leaned down and touched his lips to hers. One hand slipped the tie free from her robe and the front opened to his questing hands. Warm fingers slid around her waist to pull her in. She groaned when the sizzling heat met her oversensitive skin. She dug her fingers into his hair, holding his lips to hers as he lifted her up. They devoured each other, her tongue gliding over his as she wrapped her legs around his perfect hips. He rode her up and down his hard cock, and her thoughts were lost, her ears buzzing as her hands snaked around his back and dug into the twitching muscle.

His mouth swallowed her moan. Her fingers trailed back to

scrape over his scruff-covered jaw. She couldn't get enough of how he kissed her. His jaw muscles worked under her palm as he continued to ride her up and down his shaft. Close. She was close to coming just like this.

He turned and started walking toward the door, and she smiled against his lips before porting them to the bed.

When she reformed straddling him, she was caught by the sight of the beautiful hungry God laid out in her bed. Hers. His heated gaze burned for her, and his hands were massaging her ass and back as he leveraged up to take a nipple into his mouth. She whimpered when he sucked her in. Her hands gripped his head, holding his hot mouth to her swollen flesh as pleasure sent shivers through her entire body.

It felt so good she didn't want it to end, but she needed something else. "I want all of you."

He sucked her nipple one more time before rubbing his stubbled cheek over it, abrading it before looking up at her, assessing her with the eyes of a God, seeing inside her.

At her nod he ported to stand at the side of the bed. She moaned when his wings released and expanded. The relief he felt bled into her and added to the beauty. It was a shot to the gut. She refused to let him hide anymore. And that was what he'd been trying to do to avoid her thinking of the past.

The black feathers shone in the light from the cloudy skies through the glass skylights. They were gorgeous.

He was gorgeous.

His hot gaze tracked her features as she took in the sight of him in all his glory.

Wings in general weren't unheard of. Brianne, as a Geraki, a race of half bird of prey, had wings, and dragons had their own leathery version. But both races had been created by Apollo's experimentation on the early Immortals.

Hades was the only God born with wings, and they were majestic. Her back flexed and arched in reaction to the way he moved them. At some point she'd moved closer, sidling up to the edge of the bed with her hands on his hips as she moved to rise up on her knees facing him.

Nothing about his wings triggered anything more than lust, and she made sure he felt that.

She cupped his neck, but his lips were already descending to hers. Her fingers explored his skin as his hands pulled her in. His skin was just as feverish as hers. He crushed her body tighter to his, letting her feel his pulsing cock at her stomach. Seconds later he lifted her higher, dragging her wet flesh over him.

She squirmed for more, trying to leverage higher with legs wrapped tight around his hips. She was wet beyond comprehension and she whimpered for more. He groaned into her mouth and finally lifted her up, impaling her hard. She broke the kiss to gasp for air, their harsh breathing and the scent of sex in the air made her dizzy, and she felt a wild scratching need in the deepest darkest recesses of her mind. She blocked it before rolling her hips. She was so damned full and she wanted more. She couldn't stop moving her hips as she gasped and moaned when he slammed her down harder and faster. She couldn't hear past the ringing in her ears or the sexy grunts and groans of her male.

His palms massaged her back and ass with every thrust, just as lost to the sensation. The loud pumping of their hearts matched beat for beat as her lips and tongue made their way to nip and taste his collarbone.

"Yes," he grunted. Neither could think, much less speak as he rode them through to the wild, bitter end. She cried out against his hot skin when he hit a spot that wrenched the climax straight from her soul.

He roared and she felt hot come jetting inside her before she split apart, flying... porting? Reforming in the shower. She felt pulled and nearly ripped apart as power slid from her lips, and she pulled his mouth down to hers in a daze. She was dizzy when he slowed the kiss. Steam slid over her sensitive skin as water rained down her back. He was still moving her up and down his cock, but it was a soothing pleasure.

When he finally broke the soft kiss and looked down at her, she had a hard time breathing. His eyes were full of emotions as he watched her, tuned to her at a level she'd never felt before. It was beautiful. He smiled down at her, and she felt her heart stutter in her chest.

His wings were cradled around her as water slid over them both. She pulled his lips down and kissed him again; she didn't know what to say. He hadn't given her a chance to feel his come between her thighs, and she knew that was his purpose in porting them there.

She closed her eyes and broke the kiss, grazing her fingers over his shoulders as she looked up at him. Her voice was low. "If it hits, I can deal with it." She could handle it all. She only needed him to understand that sometimes it might take her a minute to take care of whatever hit.

He stilled and his eyes sparked. "Just because you're capable of dealing with such things without me, doesn't mean you will..." he said silkily. His power was around them, licking at her skin and mingling with her own.

He lifted her up, sliding his cock free, but instead of putting her on her feet, he held her to him as he manipulated the water to wash away the evidence. He was determined, almost compelled to do it.

After a second of staring at each other, she shook her head. He thought she'd fight him, and in truth, a small part of her might have wanted to. Though something about the fact that they nearly had a power struggle over who washed away his come seemed ridiculous instead of annoying. When he was done, she raised an eyebrow. "Better?"

"Much, *thisavre mou*." The sexy, pleased grin on his face pulled a chuckle from her lips.

His eyes warmed as he smiled down at her.

And then things changed. She felt the wards trip.

Hades' packed muscles tensed and his features took on a powerful and deadly glint. Power licked out all around, and before she could stop him, he growled, "Stay here." And was gone.

She ported to her closet, drying in the process. She tossed a shirt over her head, reforming at the edge of her living room to take in the situation. She'd expected human thieves. She was already anticipating having to contain them and make arrangements for altering memories. The last thing the Guardians needed was humans seeing winged Gods materializing from thin air.

Had she been alone, this would have gone differently. Stealth obviously wasn't a consideration for her furious mate.

Instead of thieves, she found about a dozen demon-possessed held motionless by the power of her rage-filled male. Demons could only possess the most evil of humanity, and the ones currently held didn't appear to be any exception. She saw a variety of different races, builds and dress, but there was a hard edge to each one and a sickly shadowy soul slithering around the human host's slightly more solid version. She could actually see it all happening inside them. An ability that had to be coming from her connection to Hades.

Hades' sheer wild ability snaked out, holding them easily as his power slid inside, wrapping around the demon's souls and crushing them until unearthly cries rent the air. "Coming here was a mistake." His voice was deadly calm, and she wondered what his face looked like. His fury was all she could feel until the biggest of the possessed spoke.

One convulsed in a way she'd only expect to see in a horror movie. And then the eyes changed to flames, the male's lips turned up in a sickening sneer, and the scent of sulphur filled the room.

It was chilling when it spoke. "Release us." The voice reverberated with what she could only imagine was pure evil. It sent chills down her spine, and nothing did that. It wasn't a human tone or even anything she'd heard from a possessed, and it spurred her forward. She flexed her fingers as she moved to stand beside Hades. She sent a call to Drake and P with an image of what she was seeing. Hades didn't need help, as the other possessed were still shrieking, but the dragon needed to see what was happening here.

The flaming eyes narrowed at Hades as the male repeated the words in that eerie, echoing tone. Every word seemed to leech some of the color away from the host's skin. "Release us." The male's head turned and angled at her as its eyes slid to her and over her skin. "A pretty toy." She felt that gaze and wished she'd put more clothes on, but she didn't move or take her eyes off the possessed.

Hades unleashed a wave of power so wild it ripped the demons free of the remaining possessed and extinguished them to nothingness, destroyed as the bodies thudded to the ground, twitching and groaning. "You give your attention to me! You *only* stand because I allow it," Hades sneered back.

She felt the moment Drake and Pothos ported into the room, but didn't look at them. The possessed's eyes went back to Hades, and he whined in a creepy childlike voice that was chilled with eerie malice, "You need us!" The host's face had turned a creepy ashen as if the human was dead or very near death. The flames of the eyes danced brighter, and the male's lips curved in a twisted sickening sneer he directed back at Sacha. The demon had found a weakness to poke.

Her.

And it worked. Power pulsed from Hades as he snarled in fury, "No. I don't, Deimos." Her jaw slackened at confirmation that one of the Tria had used a demon as a conduit to speak to Hades. The building shook with the power Hades was unleashing, and air snapped all around them as he used it, twisting and crushing the shady demon soul until the mixed sound of repulsive laughter and harsh shrieks echoed in the room around them. Sacha touched the link to her mate to calm the raging storm of power, calm him, but it was too strong and she was too late. The flames of the possessed's eyes snuffed out, crushed into nothingness like the others. She heard the thud of the human host's body joining the other bodies littering her floor.

Heaps of barely alive humans writhed on her floor as she processed what just happened. Power and soothing emotion rolled from her into her raging male, instinctually working to calm him, but that only led to another problem. Desire. Completely inappropriate need flooded them both. This wasn't an adrenaline comedown, she was aching and wet while humans littered her floors as her brethren stood watching. She sucked in air, and even the sulphur didn't dissipate it.

Hades growled and pulled her into his naked body and kissed her; she moaned.

"What the fuck?" Drake demanded, and Sacha had almost forgotten he was there as she pulled from her male, but he hauled her back to his front and she felt wild desire riding them. She was flushed and dizzy as she fought it. He was just as confused. The fury was still an echo in his mind, and this was out of control.

She tried to answer her leader. "I don't know." The humans on the ground weren't a threat. Demon possession was a death sentence. The demon soul gave the human host a sharp burst of strength and speed, but it eventually killed the body who'd let it in.

Drake groaned. "I thought the Creators cursed all the Gods with the same shit as us. How the fuck can you harm humans? And what the hell is wrong with you two?"

She felt her mate's exasperation and irritation as he growled, "I didn't harm the humans, I relieved the bodies of demon souls."

"What'd you do with them?" Drake demanded, but Hades' head came down to her hair, both out of control. He was fighting the need as hard as she was. The desire had been getting progressively stronger with each time they had sex. Insatiable. But now? No, this wasn't right and they knew it.

"I destroyed them," Hades growled.

"And the one was Deimos using a demon soul or was it his soul?" Drake demanded of her mate and snapped her attention back as much as it could.

"Demon soul. And yes, it was Deimos," Hades growled.

"How was he here?" Smoke curled from Drake's lips.

Deimos was said to be the worst of the Tria, and he'd somehow communicated through a possessed on Earth. "He wasn't here. And he'll never get out of his fucking prison," Hades said with force as he held her to his warmth, against his pulsing cock.

P and Drake both looked down at the humans. The one who'd spoken was dead. Or looked it. The others were alive, but they were weak and seemed disoriented.

"I don't like it. Why come here? Why demand to be freed? They've never done that," Drake snarled.

"I wasn't here before," Hades bit out. "Now go."

"So that means they can track your power?" P asked.

Hades growled when she suddenly felt a pang in her stomach and grunted in surprise. He pulled her against him, ready to teleport her away, but she stopped him with a touch to the link.

"What the fuck is going on with you two?" the dragon snarled as his and P's faces showed confusion and discomfort.

She rushed out, "It feels like a mating frenzy."

"Shit. Get to the island in Tetartos. And have Sirena check you both later. That shouldn't be happening if you're already soul

138

bonded." Drake growled as he rubbed the bridge of his nose.

Her face heated as she nodded at the same time Hades ported them away.

Nothing about this need would be denied.

Chapter 15

Sacha's Paris Home, Earth Realm

"The walls to the Tria's prison haven't weakened," P growled while looking at the mess they'd been left with. His father had seemed pretty fucking sure the Tria weren't getting out, but that didn't stop P from mentally checking and now rechecking to ensure there really were no cracks.

That prison held a portion of P's life force, so he could sense it.

"It's holding," Drake ground out in agreement, but smoke was filtering from his lips up to the high ceilings. P felt just as uneasy and angered at the display they'd just witnessed.

Uri and Alex appeared, and P glanced over, knowing Drake would've called them there.

He ran a hand over his head, remembering Sacha and Hades' exit. That was one more thing that hadn't been right. Why would they go into a frenzy now? But she'd looked pained and his father seemed like a wild rutting beast. He could understand adrenaline burn-off, but that was not what they'd seen.

P wasn't sure what the hell that meant, but if he never saw his father's dick again, it would be too damned soon.

Uri's silver eyes swirled as he looked at the mess of damaged humans. As the only Aletheia Guardian, a race known for their mental abilities, he'd always handled memory extraction or alterations as needed. His Demi-Goddess mate added her own unique powers with their mating bond, so checking the humans' memories should be simple for the two. P wanted answers as to how or why Deimos decided to speak through a demon soul. He wasn't sure they'd learn anything from the humans' memories, but they had to attempt it.

Alex stood with her hands on her denim-clad hips. "What happened?"

"Hades happened," Drake growled.

Both silver and sapphire gazes shot up to Drake, but Uri was the first to speak. "Shit. He can fucking harm humans?"

Drake shook his head while explaining to the two what his father had said about ripping the demons souls free.

P glanced at the humans in disgust; only the worst of the race could be possessed. The mortals were in bad shape; the demon souls would have been pushing the bodies past their limits. Though he guessed the boosts in strength and speed were only part of it. The Guardians had no idea what the demon itself did to the host, only that possessed generally died within weeks of possession. Which still wasn't soon enough, in his fucking opinion.

Uri's other brow lifted. "If Hades can do that, then dealing with possessed just got a whole lot fucking easier." Uri was right. Guardians couldn't kill humans, so they were forced to contain possessed until they died. And the demon was released back to Hell for the Tria to send them all over again. It was never ending.

Neither P nor Drake answered, they only nodded. He wasn't so sure his father was in any shape to be useful at the moment.

"See if you can read anything from these assholes' memories," Drake bit out, but Uri and Alex were already heading to the first body. P felt the sheer strength and scale of their power sliding into the mortals' minds from ten feet away. The two had been getting stronger since the moment they'd mated.

He watched, waiting to see if there would be any clue as to the Tria's reasoning for sending possessed here. P wouldn't necessarily credit the evil triplets with being smart, but something had shifted in the past months. They'd always been intent on feeding off pain and destruction, and they enjoyed playing with their food. But P and the others always thought it had been a game for them. Up until the point they'd found a way to track Uri and almost drugged him. Now it looked as if they'd tracked his father's power to Sacha's. The question was, why?

"I don't want Sacha or Hades back here until I know what the fuck just happened and why she thinks they're in the middle of a mating frenzy," Drake growled as he looked around. P nodded his full agreement. Possessed were no match for his father or Sacha, but if the two were feeling compelled to screw, their attention wouldn't be what it should be. P would still bet on his father, but being cautious and sending the two to Tetartos wasn't going to kill anyone. The problem was figuring out why she thought they were in the frenzy. That particular phenomenon was for the sheer purpose of pushing a pair to complete a soul bond. That was what they'd always thought. And they were already soul bonded, so that meant something was wrong.

You told Sirena to check them out? P questioned Drake, because if the dragon hadn't, he would.

Sirena is going to give Sacha and Hades an hour, Drake answered.

P cringed at the mental image that brought up.

He looked around and noted a breeze coming from the open French doors that went out to Sacha's patio. The door was forced open. The special glass was fine, but the lock carved a hole in the wood. Sacha's sanctuary had been invaded, and he could only imagine how that felt. She'd just woken up and dealt with a mating to his father, and he knew that hadn't been easy for her. How long before his calm sister Guardian lost it?

They would fix everything here. He just hoped that something wasn't going wrong with the mating.

He clenched his fists. He was anxious, had been for days, and he didn't like the constant hold it had on him. It had been building since Apollo had been taken. And amped up after learning his mother was from another world. A world that was apparently dangerous to him.

Uri growled, drawing his attention. "Nothing. We aren't getting any memories and their minds are screwed. They don't have any clue where they are or that we're even here."

The male's Demi-Goddess mate glared down at the humans, and he could almost feel her desire to commit murder. "I'd kill them, but they don't deserve a quick death." Alex could be deadly and unforgiving. A trait she may have gotten from Athena, but she was a hell of a lot warmer than her mother.

Uri drew her into his side.

"We'll drop them somewhere and let the humans deal with their own trash," Drake gritted out.

143

"What were they doing here?" Uri asked, eyeing them.

Drake growled, "They were here so that Deimos could talk to Hades." The dragon added the details when Alex's and Uri's jaws dropped.

"Fuck." Uri held Alex a little tighter while violence whirled in his silver eyes. "They've never spoken through a possessed. For millennia... Is it a new ability, or is their prison weakening?"

"It's solid," P gritted out before telling them about the hordes of Hell creatures that had flocked to battle Hades the day before. His father's presence seemed to rile the Tria.

"The last fucking thing we need is them finding a way to get free," Uri growled. "Not unless we find a way to kill them." And his brother looked like he wanted that more than anything. But they'd been impossible to kill; that was why they'd been imprisoned all those fucking centuries ago.

"They wouldn't have demanded freedom if they could already escape," P pointed out to soothe the Aletheia.

"And they said Hades needed them? Why?" Alex's voice was hard.

Drake snarled, "I don't know... It could be that they felt when the portals to Thule opened. If we felt them open, they might have felt them too."

"Why track Hades? Why not just tell any of us at any time? We've had surges in possessed since that second portal opened," Alex asked, and P noticed how stiff she'd gotten. She was right, they'd been getting an influx of possessed in the days since they'd captured the Goddess Kara.

"I don't know," Drake ground out in answer to Alex's question. "It may be that he's a God and his power signature is even stronger now that he's soul bonded Sacha."

P nodded at that answer before adding, "He's not just a God, he also helped imprison them."

If the Tria were ever freed, it would be the second coming of Hell on Earth. Deimos, Phobos and Than were some of the sickest beings ever to walk the Earth, and nothing pleased them more than feeding off pain and suffering, torture.

He looked at Drake. P had always suspected that his father had put more into the spell than just a piece of his life force like the rest of them had. He rubbed his neck. What had Hades done, and did it matter? Was there a reason why the Tria thought Hades could free them? Scenarios kept popping up in his mind. None of them good.

I don't like being reminded that we don't know what will happen to that prison if something happens to my father. Or any of us, he sent to Drake.

The dragon nodded. This wasn't the first time either had considered it, but they hadn't had any better answers all those millennia ago than they had now. And he wouldn't be the one to mention it in front of Uri.

If things had been bad before, he had a feeling that things were about to get worse.

145

Chapter 16

Hades' Island, Tetartos Realm

Sacha reformed beside Hades on the beach outside the island home, out of control, wet and needy as hell.

It was a different time there; moonlight and starlight flickered along rolling waves. She'd needed fresh air, but now she knew it was useless. Her bare feet sank into the soft sand, and she barely caught a breath of the salt air before she felt a pang deep in her stomach.

Hades growled, furious that she was hurting, but the second he lifted her up with his hot palm on her bare ass beneath the shirt, she felt blinding relief. His lips found hers as power and need whirled around them in heavy gusts, churning the winds around them. She moaned, knowing she'd have to deal with getting answers to what was happening later.

Her entire attention focused on what he was doing to her mouth and how hot his skin was against hers. Every grind of his cock against her.

He was just as wild with the lust and the soul-biting need to ease her. His jaw worked as he devoured her mouth, and she loved the spicy sweet taste, the way he held her tight.

He growled against her lips when her shirt was in the way of his questing fingers. Within moments his power surged and the material disintegrated to be swept away in the winds whipping around them. The air was cooler, but nothing could take away this heat. Her fingers fisted in his hair as she leveraged and writhed against his big body, her swollen breasts gliding over his bare chest. His wings flared and flexed as she breathed in his scent and got dizzy from it.

All that mattered was getting him inside her. Her aching pussy was so damned wet.

Sacha leveraged up and shivered when his cock pulsed to her opening. With a soft groan she slid down, stretched so full it was perfect. Ecstasy didn't describe how every single nerve came to life and lit her up from the inside out. It blurred her vision as her legs pulled him tighter, wanting everything he could give her.

She wasn't alone in the need for more; he was caught up in the animalistic urge to mark her, claim her. Her stomach clenched as he lifted and slammed her down until her vision dotted with the sheer pleasure.

Thunder crashed around them and the skies opened up. Cool rain pelted down and she relished every drop on her bare skin. There hadn't been any clouds at all, and now water washed over them and he let it. They both needed it.

Anything to ease the heat.

His muscles were rock solid under her roving fingers. She caressed the straining tendons of his neck, trailing the water sliding down their bodies, slipping between them. He was barely holding a thread of control, still being careful not to hurt her even though he was losing his mind at the tight pull of her sucking him in.

She pulled from the kiss and was caught by his glowing blue gaze. He clamped his teeth down tight and his wings cradled her as he thrust before holding her down on his cock for long seconds before doing it all again. His breathing was harsh and she could feel the pounding of his heart against her chest. His head fell back and she couldn't resist the sight of his throat. She leaned in to lick and suck at the hard column as he growled. The vibration against her lips ripped a moan from her. His skin tasted just as good as his kiss. Her hips rolled, needing more, and she tried to leverage up to get him harder and faster, but he controlled every move. Even though his skin was on fire, his grip on her ass was immovable.

"Don't," he bit out, and she knew he had a tenuous grasp on the need driving him. He couldn't think, could barely speak through it.

"Come," he demanded. And she knew if it didn't happen soon, he'd lose control completely. He'd mark her. He'd do things he worried would trigger her past. She let go, her pussy pulsing around him as she cried out into the skies.

She gasped as more heat pooled and slid around him as he powered inside her, rolling his cock in a way that ran shivers of pleasure straight to her clit. Water slid down her lashes to her cheeks and she loved it. She licked the drops from her lips and his eyes caught on her tongue. It was so damned hot, but it was his soul-wrenching need and the internal war he waged that sent her back over the edge.

She came so hard she felt like she'd break apart. Like something was trying to split her in half, her muscles tensed so tight she knew she was yanking on his hair as she pulsed around him, trying to hold him deep.

He growled in pleasured relief, but continued to thrust harder and faster as his wings flexed and pulled her in. The wet feathers slid along her back.

She came again, this time biting into his neck. She didn't break the skin, but something about her teeth at his neck brought a roar from his throat as he slammed her down so hard on his cock. The warmth of his come and the way her clit pushed tight against him triggered another mind-blowing orgasm.

She gasped for air as power cracked around them, and she felt something pulling inside her, trying to break free. Something in a deep locked-away section of her mind. Ancient power trying to slam its way out until she beat it back along with the numbness she worried would come with it.

She didn't feel them move or port, but soon she was chest deep in cool ocean water. His wings were partially submerged and still cradling her to his chest, keeping the waves from sliding into her.

He sent soothing emotion through the link, and she dropped her head to his chest to listen to the pounding of his heart. She closed her eyes as she made sure the swell of her own ability wouldn't come back. It shocked her that it had even tried to rise. She hadn't thought about it since becoming a Guardian. Water gently swayed over her sensitive skin, and she wasn't sure how long they stayed there as she calmed.

"Tell me what you need, *thisavre mou*," he told her, and she felt his guilt that he'd been too rough. He hadn't.

"Just this," she said.

His fingers caressed her back gently as she evened back out.

She knew he was wondering what she'd held back. "I am," he

confirmed, their emotions giving their thoughts clarity.

She breathed him in before answering. "It's a part of me that I buried deep a long time ago. Old power that I didn't need."

He looked down at her. "What power? You know I would never allow anything to hurt you," he said with the certainty of a God. That arrogance should have turned her off. It should have done anything and everything but relax her. Warm her.

"I know."

"What is this power?" he asked again.

She shook her head, still vaguely shocked that it would be trying to break free after all this time, but it seemed her past refused to stay where it belonged.

She thought about his question, but wasn't sure what to call it. "I consider it a mutated version of teleportation."

"Why wouldn't it be useful?"

She felt her stomach clench when she spoke. "I've never needed it to kill Hell beasts or contain demon-possessed." That was the truth, the Creators had blessed her with all the power she needed, and it had allowed her to cage the ability she felt belonged in that old life.

He brought a hand up to touch her bottom lip.

She softened at the gentle touch. He was still considering her, but not pushing.

She needed to contact Sirena and figure out what had happened in her home. Drake would probably have questions, but first she needed to know if something was truly wrong with their mating. They shouldn't be going through the frenzy, but that was the only explanation for what they'd felt earlier.

He grunted. "Yes, call your healer."

And then she took a deep breath and ported them inside, making sure to use the air currents to dry them before reforming them in the first bedroom. There would be clothes there.

She stretched her neck, feeling the surge of power and ability running through her veins from mating with Hades. She'd need to figure out what it all encompassed and how to use it at some point.

She felt him at her back, his heat warming her, and tendrils of desires started to form again. And they'd just had sex. She'd come multiple times only minutes ago; this couldn't be normal.

"It's not," he growled, and she sucked in a breath at the wave of desire coming from him. She turned and saw his hungry gaze slide over her naked body before he spoke again, and he sounded frustrated. "I haven't even tasted you yet. And already I can't wait to get my cock back in you."

She sucked in much-needed air and then focused to get the images of him going down on her out of her mind. When he leaned down and kissed her neck, she moaned at the gooseflesh that came with his touch, his warm breath. She forced herself to move back a few steps.

"Not yet," she said through a haze. They definitely needed Sirena. Both were getting distracted way too easily. She couldn't live like this.

Sirena, we need blood tests, Sacha sent to her sister Guardian as she grabbed a robe. He moved out the door and reappeared seconds later wearing dark slacks.

She raised an eyebrow.

He grinned and answered, "This island is mine now. My things were moved from Pothos' home yesterday."

She couldn't focus on what he'd said because her mind short-circuited at the sight of the bulge against the fly of his pants. The material was useless to hide his hardening length, and the waistband hung low on his hips, showing the thin trail of hair disappearing beneath.

He needed underwear.

She swore she could actually see the ridge of his cock in the outline of the fabric, and the need to cover him up was strong. His chest was bare because his wings were out, so there wasn't much covering she could do there, but that bulge?

She knew he was grinning down at her; his amusement was slipping through the bond.

I'm here, Sirena announced, and Sacha curbed the urge to cover him up.

It didn't matter, Sirena wouldn't care or notice, but Sacha would know his cock was on display. She clenched her fists at her sides, mentally striving for some calm before porting into the living room and away from his sexy, knowing grin. His eyes and emotion told her how pleased her shot of possessiveness had made him.

She mentally shook her head. *You understand what it means if I'm possessive?* It meant that the "God Groupies" would never be making a return appearance. Not ever.

I do, thisavre mou. And there was a part of him that was definitely pleased under all the building desire to have her.

"What's happening?" the blonde demanded. "Drake said he thought something was wrong. He said you thought you were in the frenzy." Her violet eyes were serious, tinted with worry.

Sacha nodded. "There was pain, and it was like we were hit with a compulsion to have sex," Sacha said with an edge of discomfort.

Her sister turned to pull out a needle from a small bag.

She could already feel the desire burning a little hotter, having his body so near.

"And the need is already coming back," Sacha informed Sirena.

Her sister stared at her and nodded. The healer's brow furrowed, obviously considering it all as she took Sacha's arm. Hades didn't like the sight of a needle in her flesh. It didn't hurt and she let him know that even as another part of her warmed at his reaction.

Her sister spoke. "I'm not sure this will help. But I'll test the blood. If it looks the same as other mated pairs, then you should be past this point." Sirena turned her attention to Hades. "The soul bond is there, isn't it?"

"Yes," Hades confirmed, crossing his arms over his chest.

"And you have no idea what Athena and Aphrodite went through?" Sirena demanded of Hades.

"No," he growled, and Sacha could feel how much he hated that fact.

"You should be past this. The frenzy leads to sex, which leads to blood bonding to ease the way for the soul bond."

Sacha's heart chilled, worried that the healer would suggest starting at the beginning. Not having to blood bond was the one part she had been grateful for, the silver lining of not having someone see every dirty bit of her past. Hades didn't like the tone of her thoughts, but he forced back his worry and agitation to send her soothing energies instead.

She could feel his power fluctuating as his worry for her increased. Winds were whipping against the house, joining the thunder cracking outside while the lightning flashed over the seas beyond the big windows. She felt one of his wings curling around her, and she sent back her own soothing thoughts.

She looked up and caught the flashing of his eyes as he pulled her into his hold. She didn't fight it, he needed it, and that seemed to matter to her.

When she looked back at Sirena, she saw a hint of warmth and sadness in her sister's violet gaze before she had time to mask it. Sacha felt a distinct pang in her heart at the sight. She wouldn't voice it or draw attention to it, not with Hades there, but she sent a little prayer to the fates that Sirena wouldn't feel so alone. Wouldn't be alone.

A second later Sirena had Sacha's blood vial stored and was holding out another needle. Hades wasn't pleased, but he offered an arm. His stance was every bit the arrogant, annoyed God, and the twitching of his wing against her side brought a slight smile.

"It won't hurt, big guy," Sirena encouraged, her lips curving.

He growled, offended. "I know."

His next thought would have brought a laugh if desire wasn't distracting her. "Yes, Sirena knows you're a God."

Sirena laughed. "I see your arrogance is still alive and well under this suppressed, contained version of Hades."

Sirena's word use had her thinking. "Could suppressing power cause this?"

Sirena stared at her. "Tell me more."

She braced herself. Brianne and some of the others knew about her ability because they'd been caged on Apollo's island with her. She'd used her power to find ways through the palace, but she'd never spoken of it with the healer. She doubted anyone would have discussed it. They both needed to know if it was the problem.

She braced herself for what she was about to describe.

Chapter 17

Hroarr's Palace, World of Thule

Gefn stepped beside her brothers to look in the holding cell deep beneath the palace keep. The shimmering blue power at the door kept the God from ever gaining freedom.

This wasn't Gefn's first glimpse of the dark-haired male, but her reaction was the same. His short dark hair and the arrogant set to his lips stirred nothing. Not fear, sympathy or even the slightest hint of arousal, which sadly wasn't surprising. Nothing stirred the latter, but a small part of her had hoped.

She may have been unfazed, but she couldn't say the same for Spa and Velspar. The beasts didn't like him any more this time around than they had when Dagur had brought her down earlier.

She listened to her animals pace behind her with their scruffs raised. She stepped away from the hazy spell-covered doorway. She didn't need to look into the darkened room anymore. Hroarr would have their answers soon enough.

Velspar bumped her in the back, and she shot the beast a glare.

They were always so protective. She shook her head, but ended up scratching their ears while her brothers continued their silent assessment of the prisoner.

The God demanded in the old language, "Release me now."

Hroarr didn't bother to speak. He just studied the male, and she could tell from Hroarr's stance that the ruler of Thule found this God lacking.

"What do you want?" the male snapped.

Her brothers turned from him without answering. That seemed to infuriate the God if the slamming of something against the cell wall was any indication. She'd guess that was one of his fists since everything else was built into the room and unmovable. Hroarr wasn't as rash as Dagur. He would wait, allowing the God to stew over his fate, and then return to learn all he wanted to know. No one withheld from him. Hroarr was fierce and intelligent and capable of harsh cruelty when crossed. He led their world with the ruthless determination of a warrior.

She'd feel sorry for the captive, but in reality his fate wasn't all that terrible.

She may not have liked Dagur's way of handling it, but in reality she was grateful her brother had found a much-needed God. She'd assumed they'd never find any.

She turned and walked through the flame-lit corridor. Three guards slipped from the shadows to trail behind Spa and Velspar.

They moved through a doorway guarded by warriors, each bearing the golden staff of the dragon. Hroarr's insignia.

The three remained silent until they were in Hroarr's study.

The room was two stories high, containing walls filled with shelves of ancient artifacts and books they'd found in all of their thousands upon thousands of years of existence. The space was dark and masculine and fit her brother well.

The second the door shut behind them, Hroarr snarled, "I will learn his secrets later, and then I will see this world. Why is Kara not here?"

Gefn felt rising excitement at the idea of visiting a new world. As much as she hated that they'd lost so many warriors, she was curious to see those who'd been able to best them.

She shook off those thoughts to answer her brother. "Dagur and I both sent messengers to Kara." Her reckless brother was staying quiet, which was likely wise.

"When?"

Her teeth set at his demanding tone. "Mine left a few hours ago. Almost as soon as I arrived."

"I sent for her weeks ago, and the warrior returned days ago with word that she would be here within a day," Dagur growled.

"Maybe you need to learn how to send a summons," Hroarr bit out as he rubbed his hand over his bearded chin. She knew that meant he was considering everything.

Her golden-eyed brother's silence ended on a growl. "Or my siblings could actually come when I say they are *urgently* needed."

Gefn changed the subject when Hroarr's eyes hardened. "If Kara doesn't return in the next couple of days, I will go retrieve her myself." That would give Gefn the time to refuel the ability needed to open portals there and back, at least for her and her sister.

"Yes," Hroarr agreed as he turned his attention from her to Dagur. "Are the priestesses well?" The females would have been the ones to heal the wounded and release the dead.

"They are resting in the baths," Dagur growled, and if Gefn had to guess, she'd say the females were no doubt furious with Dagur as well.

Dozens dead when they had so few…

They needed the God, but that didn't ease the harsh pang of loss.

Gefn added, "Now that you're here, I will go see the priestesses. Inform me when you learn something from the God. We'll also need to make arrangements for the families of the fallen." She eyed her brothers as Hroarr nodded his agreement.

The second she slipped from the tension of the study, Laire matched pace at her side. The massive blond warrior had been with her for centuries, just as his father had before him. His broad muscled chest was bare but for the crisscrossing leather straps holding blades at his back. The leather of his kilt barely moved as he stalked at her side with all the grace of a beast instead of a mere mortal.

He was unfazed by Spa and Velspar. They'd long ago approved of him, and he knew it.

"We are going to see the priestesses." She turned to see a wicked grin form on his usually calm features. She shook her head and cocked a brow. "I'm not sure they will be in the mood for entertainment, Laire." But what did Gefn know? Her guard had always been favored by the females, and he might improve their spirits. She could only wish for the desire they had, it might improve

159

her own mood.

"Yes, my Goddess." She didn't miss the fact that his smile had fallen when he added, "Hroarr was in the middle of dealing with two warring clans. He would not return without knowing why, and then he demanded to know everything."

"I assumed as much." She nodded. The male was loyal to her, but she'd put him in a difficult position when sending him to Hroarr with instructions not to tell her brother about the losses. "I'm not angry." Hroarr was the ruling God of their world. You didn't go against him, assuming you were even capable.

They came to the end of the corridor, and two guards moved aside as she sent power to splay the doors wide. She stepped inside, feeling the warm steam immediately caress her skin. Bright light came through frosted glass all around them, and it glittered off the wet skin of the females standing in one of the pools.

Three sets of glittering eyes set on them as they stepped through and the doors shut quietly behind them.

Chapter 18

Hades' Island, Tetartos Realm

Hades waited with the healer as Sacha searched for the words to explain her suppressed ability. "I believe it's a mutation of teleportation, but the two are not linked." She paused. "I'm not sure what it would have become. I haven't used it since before I became a Guardian and then only in dire circumstances."

He saw Sirena nod and go behind the kitchen counter as she spoke calmly. "Brianne once told me that you'd been able to get into almost any part of Apollo's palace."

He felt Sacha's aversion to the memories that brought. He clenched his teeth tight but managed to keep a gentle hold on her hip while tamping down the hatred he felt for his brother. His fury wouldn't help her.

"Most any place," Sacha agreed. She was trying to find a way to minimize her explanation, and he knew this was going to gut him.

Sirena lifted a bottle of wine and some glasses as she considered her next words. They came as she uncorked and began pouring the deep red liquid. "You said you suppressed the ability?"

Sacha nodded and easily accepted the glass handed to her as if the two had done this a million times through the centuries.

He declined a glass with a shake of his head. He wasn't interested in wine; he was interested in what his female would say next.

"It just tried to break free… during sex."

Sirena nodded. "You don't need to tell me the rest unless you want to. I truly don't know if it could cause symptoms of a frenzy because I've never come across anything like this. But I will say that mated pairs always meld abilities from the start. I'd think if it's trying to get out, then you're going to need to let it." There was a hint of empathy in her violet eyes as she spoke, and she tilted her head, adding, "That brings up something else that could be a problem. Has your beast blood manifested its match in Hades?"

The healer's eyes settled on him. He hadn't considered her having a physical animal like his sister's consorts. "I don't feel a beast." He'd felt Era's beast halves and had been able to release them, but there was nothing like that in him. Nor did he see it in Sacha. "What kind of creature are we talking about?"

"Kairos are a race with the smallest amount of beast blood. It wouldn't feel separate, but it manifests in impulses. And to answer your question, the blood was from an ancient bird Apollo created. I was once told that he'd done it to make the Kairos stronger, smarter and quieter than the original teleporters without adding the temperaments that came with the shifting breeds."

"I felt an odd clawing when my power started trying to break free," Sacha admitted.

"But nothing before?"

"No. I've never felt anything from the animal blood," Sacha agreed, and his female hesitated a second before adding, "But if it's

162

impulses, I believe it has manifested in Hades."

He did a mental scan.

She turned to him. *You seem surprised by all the need to dominate and mark me. If that wasn't something you felt before, it seems to me that would be an impulse she's talking about.* Her bronze skin flushed beautifully with the mental words. She was imagining him pinning her down and fucking her hard. He gritted his teeth as his cock tented the dark slacks. She angled her body to cover the evidence of what her thoughts had done to him, and that amused him immensely.

"You may go," he commanded the healer, his gaze never leaving his female's.

Sacha narrowed her eyes at his dismissal of her friend and turned, making sure her body still hid his hard cock. He liked this side of his female.

He glanced over her head to the healer and, to appease his female, grinned. "Please." He leaned into her back and let her feel what she'd done to him, what she wanted to hide. He didn't need to hide anything.

He heard her gasp of breath and curved his hands around her small waist. The material couldn't hide the shiver that racked her frame.

He barely caught the healer's next words, but he didn't miss her twitching lips. "I'll go double-check the blood and let Drake know that you're still figuring things out. He wants you two to stay here until we understand what's going on."

He had no intention of taking his female back to her home until they were through whatever was happening to them. This island was secluded and secure. He mentally sighed before commanding, "Tell my nephew that we are only to be disturbed for two reasons. One, that the tests show something's wrong." Which he doubted now that they had other reasons for what was happening. He had a hard time believing for a minute that a beast or suppressed power could cause a compulsion like this in a God. But they would find out soon enough. "Or when the Goddess of Thule wakes." He said the last with a growl. He would have the location of Apollo and he would make him bleed for eternity for all he'd done.

Sacha sucked in a breath and he knew she felt his need to give her retribution. And he would. *My brother will suffer,* he assured her.

His thoughts were interrupted when Sirena sighed. "I'll let Drake know."

He heard the healer's telepathic words to Sacha. *I think it's going to take both of you letting go. Let him catch you. Call if you need me.*

The second the healer was gone, she turned to him. "You heard everything she said?"

"I did."

He could feel her displeasure at having more of her thoughts opened to him. She breathed out and he understood her frustration.

He pulled her against him and looked down into her eyes as she sighed. "You have links to all the Guardians now?"

"I do." He could see them in his mind's eye, and he'd tested his ability to block them already and was assured that it would work easily enough.

He waited as she let everything settle in her mind. She was strong and intelligent. Perfect.

Her eyes heated as she understood his emotion. "You are beautiful," he admitted before adding, "Bring your wine, *thisavre mou*. We need to discuss this for a moment," as he led her to the biggest bedroom.

With a thought, the flames roared to life in the hearth as he materialized a tie to contain his hair.

He had a feeling the healer was correct in her assumptions, though he still had trouble believing the small amount of beast blood could affect him at all. At the moment he was more concerned with Sacha letting go of the power she'd bottled up. This he could free her from, but he wouldn't harm her and he knew she'd instinctually latch onto it. She'd contained it for centuries, and he knew she was going to struggle with letting it free.

He gently slipped the glass from her hand and set it on the table beside the bed. A moment later he retracted his wings and smiled at her frown. "I don't like lying on them, and right now I want to lie with you and talk."

She cocked her head before nodding regally.

"Can you trust me to help you, *thisavre mou*?" He felt her sifting through his emotion to figure out where he was going with that, and it made him smile.

She considered that for a moment before nodding. "I do." And that surprised her, but her serene features didn't share any of that. She knew what he was thinking and that helped.

He lifted her to the bed and lay facing her, his head resting on one hand as his eyes slid over her beautiful face. She was wet for him, he could feel her desire, and his cock pulsed in answer. He was dying to be back inside her, but not yet. "You've fought off the horrors and numbness before." He fought back fury at that thought. "Can you let me deal with containing the power that comes out while you battle the memories?" He needed her to feel comfortable to just let it all go, no matter how powerful. He'd never let her fall. But she needed to release it when her instincts fought to hold on. He'd still be there to fight the memories with her, but if they put it into pieces, she might let go.

He could open it for her, but he wouldn't chance that hurting her. Not when she could let go.

"I'll try," she agreed huskily.

She looked small, yet she somehow projected the appearance of a Goddess even snuggled into a robe that was too big for her. And it wasn't only in how she looked, it was in the power sliding from her. He wanted to unwrap all that fluff and devour her, to hear her sultry cries. His eyes tracked back to hers. "Okay."

"It's not trust that's the problem," she replied softly. "It's just one part of a past I buried, and I'm not sure what will come with it." Her memories. "I'm prepared for it. Are you?" she asked while gliding her small hand over his rough cheek.

"I won't like anything that makes you hurt." He searched her eyes. "I can't take any of it away now. But the power I can control so we can deal with the rest. I only need you to tell me how the power works."

"So sure of yourself? I have no idea what it's going to be," she said with a raised brow.

"I'm sure I can deal with the power," he admitted easily. He was the most powerful of the Gods. That was the easy part of this.

She nodded and waited for long minutes. "It starts with a kiss."

He frowned. "Yet my kisses have never triggered the memories?"

She shook her head. "The power itself used to make me feel strong. It's what came after that left me numb. That's what I don't want to feel when I'm with you."

He took a deep breath and calmed the anger at the pang of shame he felt from her. "So the power won't hurt?"

"No."

"What did you use it to do?" It wasn't a hard guess to assume that his female would have had good reason to do something that caused her shame.

"To protect Sebastian," she said before adding, "And later to search for a way to free us all from Apollo and Hermes."

He lifted his hand to move her hair off her cheek. He needed to touch her skin, not because he wanted her, because he cared for her. Her lids lowered a fraction at the contact and he smiled as he confirmed, "Bastian?"

"Yes."

"How did he become your son?" He wanted her to relax, and he needed to know about her. She'd warmed at the thoughts of her son.

"When his mother, my sister, died, I promised to protect him."

"Yet everyone considers you his mother instead of an aunt."

"The moment Phedra forged a mental link between the two of us, he was mine," she said with fierce protectiveness and warmth. He was glad when she continued, "He was such a smart, caring child, but those were dangerous traits to have in the warrior camps. They could have gotten him killed." She shook her head and he felt the love she had for her son in every word. "He had to learn to mask it." He felt the regret in her words. "Those were lessons I wish I never had to teach him, but in the end he grew into an honorable and beautiful male. A Guardian." He was caught by the pride in her tone, in her heart.

She'd chosen to be a mother to a child she hadn't birthed; she'd done things that she'd hated to protect the boy. That made him feel things he'd never experienced. He already cared for her, but this... feeling was so much more. It was only one more reminder of how perfect she was.

"You humble me, *thisavre mou*." He breathed and couldn't stop touching her face. "There isn't a more perfect female in all the worlds." He leaned in and tilted her chin to accept his fleeting kiss. When he moved away, her fingers curled around his neck and pulled him back for more, and he wouldn't deny her. He knew at that moment, he would deny her nothing.

She took a longer taste that he couldn't help taking deeper. He slid his tongue along hers, slowly teasing them both, but he managed not to pull her hips against his aching cock.

Not yet.

When he finally broke the kiss and looked at her swollen lips, he groaned. "You distract me, *thisavre mou*."

She took a deep breath.

"What exactly does the power do? How did you use it?" he ground out. He needed to understand before deciding how to move forward.

"I would breathe it into their lips," she said, watching him for a reaction.

"Whose?" He braced for the answer.

"The guards to the warrior camp."

"And what would it do to them?"

"It jumbles the mind. It used to stun them in place," she admitted. "I'd slip through to the camps. By the time I returned and they came out of it, they wouldn't even know any time had lapsed."

He understood what she wasn't saying. She needed to seduce them to get close, and she would likely have needed to finish what she started so they wouldn't suspect. Or she might have been forced. He stifled a growl and heard the crackling thunder above the house. She caressed their bond and the thunder stopped.

He bit out, "I wish I'd have known you were there. That I would have freed you."

"I won't say I'd ever *want* to go back, but I do love who I am now. I love being a Guardian. And knowing what I do, I would have done those things a thousand times over to make sure Bastian was safe." She sent him some soothing energies and he calmed as she spoke. "I truly haven't given it a thought in centuries. I think that's why it was so shocking the first time the memories came." She sighed. "I hadn't considered what sex would be like now. By the time it was all a distant memory there were no males who appealed to me."

He felt the truth in her words, but it didn't ease his guilt, because this wasn't all she'd endured there. What she was sharing was only a small part of her horrors. This was the piece of hell she'd selflessly chosen to endure.

They stayed there for a moment, just staring at each other as the dark thoughts eased and desire started pulling at them.

She ran her thigh over his hip, drawing his cock against her hot pussy. She wanted him to forget. And she wanted to forget with him.

He rolled her to her back and commanded the kiss, feeling the desperation slowly melt away until the only thing left was pleasure. She sucked on his lower lip and he growled. She loved his lips and he planned to do so much more with his mouth.

You feel the pull to let the power free when you orgasm? he whispered through her mind.

Yes, she breathed.

He trailed his lips to her ear and nipped, and her gasp made him growl for more. *When the time comes, let it go for me. Let me take care of it. Of you.*

She moaned. "Yes. And you don't need to be so careful with me."

His dick pulsed against her. *One thing at a time, agapi mou.* The words stilled her, but she was his love and he smiled against the pulse beating at her throat. He laved her smooth skin and groaned, she tasted better than anything he'd ever had, but she was thinking too much.

He trailed his tongue down to her collarbone while sending mental images of all he wanted to do to her. Starting with getting his head between her beautiful thighs.

Her throaty moan was exactly what he wanted to hear, because he was going to take his time, no matter how much his dick ached.

The second her head fell back, he unwrapped her, sliding the tie from her robe and opening the sides to display her gorgeous curves. He leaned down and nuzzled the other side of her throat before trailing his lips and tongue over her soft skin. He was rewarded with her small tremors of pleasure.

The sweet scent of her wet pussy drove him on, but he didn't want to miss any part of her. And her full swollen breasts deserved special attention.

"I love these." He groaned as he pushed them together to kiss and suck as he enjoyed her throaty gasps and whimpers of pleasure. Her hips writhed against his stomach, and he bit back the ache to get inside her. They were a long way from that point. Her features were always set in a beautiful calm, but in his arms she didn't hide what she was feeling. She responded to every touch and kiss and he reveled in it. The robe disappeared and her hands slid over his burning skin. The soft touch of her fingers on his shoulders and face fanned the flames and made it harder for him to contain the arousal.

He released his wings, unable to keep them leashed. Her moans were destroying his control as much as that beast blood demanded he move faster, pin her down, and slide his cock deep until she couldn't remember anything but the feel of him giving her what she craved. He growled as he bit back the impulses, but not before hearing her whimper of need as her fingers gripped his head. He sent a slow slide of power to lick over her lips and neck as he nipped at her hard nipples. He wanted to touch her everywhere at once, wanted to give her all the pleasure a God had to offer, but he was forced to start small.

He tuned to her emotions, making sure nothing was overwhelming her, and she growled, "Stop being careful." The demand in her voice brought a smile to his lips.

Nothing would sway him from his course, but he'd take her at her word and give her more. With a thought, her wineglass was in his hand. Her eyes locked on the glass.

"You enjoy this wine?" he growled as he eyed her.

"Yes," she breathed out.

"Then I will taste it."

"From my lips?" It was as much a question as a plea. His female loved his lips on hers and that pleased him.

"Eventually," he said with a grin. At her harsh breath, his eyes were drawn to her beautiful swollen breasts, imagining all the things he wanted to do with them. For now he dribbled a drop of dark liquid on the tip of one and watched it slide down between them. He leaned down and captured it with his tongue and followed the trail back up as the sweetness slid down his throat.

She moaned and her hands were at the tie holding back his hair. "No, Sacha." And he sent power to gently remove her hands. She groaned but didn't fight the hold. She was lost in the promise of more pleasure. Her wet pussy was sliding over his stomach and making it hard not to speed the pace, but he wanted to draw it out as long as he could. He focused his attention back on giving her more; he trailed his tongue over the nub and then sucked. Her body rocked beneath him, she was close. He pulled back and gave the other a soft nip before moving lower. He'd never wanted to explore anything more than he wanted to learn every dip and curve of her body, inside and out.

His cock jerked, dying for its own exploration.

*****

Sacha moved her hips in invitation. "Not yet, *thisavre mou*. Now spread your pretty thighs wide for me." The noises she made only made him go slower, and she was dying for more.

Instead of opening for him, she pulled her hands from his telekinetic hold and slid her fingers over his shoulders and demanded, "No more teasing." She wanted his mouth on her, she wanted to know what that would feel like, but she almost needed to be filled more.

He grinned up at her. Power whipped around the room in waves as he held himself in check though she'd told him not to. Even now he held her hips down with his stomach, and his warm flesh against her aching pussy was too much and not enough all at once. Licks of power teased every inch of her skin as his lips tormented her.

"Spread for me, Sacha. And keep your hands by your head. I promise it'll be worth it, *thisavre mou*."

She felt his determination and mentally cursed him as she did as he asked.

He spilled another drop of the wine she loved. This time it pooled in her belly button, and her body arched into his lips as he licked and sucked it from her skin. She was on fire. He was holding back so much, yet she was coming apart. Splayed open and needing more. She wanted to torment him just as he was doing to her. She watched as his thick shoulders moved down her body.

"I'll make my body available for anything you want. Later," he promised, and she lay there burning up as she planned her attack.

He chuckled for a second before he slid back and gazed at her open and wet. If anything, his eyes blazed hotter as he looked at her.

She groaned, her pussy clenching in anticipation. "I can't take much more." She was willing to admit defeat. He couldn't just look at her and not touch.

She could feel how much he wanted to take her. A flash of her bare pussy filled her mind, he was sharing what he was seeing.

"Beautiful," he said reverently.

She could see her own juices, she was ready. And then he dribbled the wine and showed her as the silky liquid slid over her clit and down her lips all the way to her ass. She wasn't sure where the glass went, but his hand gripped her, holding her wide as he licked from her tiny back hole all the way back up, groaning as her hips jerked. She silently screamed as her vision blurred. His tongue slid inside her before moving to flick over her clit. She barely had time to breathe before his mouth wrapped around her sensitive nub and sucked.

The sheer pleasure rocked her hard enough that she almost broke apart. She could feel her cells trying to snap free. He held it back, grounding her on the bed with his power.

When he lifted away, it was only to suck on her lower lips. The look in his eyes when they met was searing. "The wine's not nearly as sweet as your pussy."

He lowered again as she gasped for air. He didn't do anything but look at her. His big hands still held her splayed for him.

"I'm thirsty, *thisavre mou*. Give me the wine I want," he growled as he gently set both thumbs to her clit, sending her the images of what he was seeing. Her thighs wide, her pussy and ass open to his gaze, to anything he wanted. His thumbs were driving her crazy.

She groaned, "What are you doing?"

"I'm watching your sweet pussy work. It wants to give me more sweet juices to lick up." He growled as he gently manipulated that nub until she watched a drop slip free and start sliding down to her ass. She could barely breathe through her own pleasure, but his was nearly as intense. He loved watching her get wet. She moaned as another followed. "That's good, Sacha. Give it all to me."

Her back bowed as her senses were taken over by the soft circles of his thumbs on her clit.

He trailed his tongue over the nerves of her ass and slowly made his way higher until her muscles were so tight she was sure she'd come the second his hot breath ran back over her clit.

He didn't do as she expected; instead he changed his grip and brought her pussy up to suck her clit as his eyes locked on hers.

She cried out when he lifted her up and thrust two fingers inside her and twisted his wrist as he moved back up her body. She came pulsing around thick fingers, sucking him in. His eyes flashed and then his lips were on hers, taking her screams as he pumped his fingers until her power slammed inside her mind.

175

Let it go. I've got you.

The taste of her desire and the sweet wine slid down her throat as he slipped his fingers free and let his bare cock ride over her aching clit until another blinding orgasm gripped her. She breathed him in as she let go of her iron grip on the power. The sheer force of it arched her back, but she held onto him, loving the soft feathers and bare skin against her calves. She had no idea where his pants went, but she was glad they were gone.

He grunted as his power slipped out to rein hers in. He never stopped kissing her, his cock grinding her pussy hard as she soared. Her power was captured by his and she felt him diffusing it as it came. It was wild and freeing as power unleashed from her into him and back out into the room. It was unleashing a hurricane all around them. The fire flared higher in the hearth, and the heat from their bodies almost burned.

When it finally calmed, he broke the kiss and groaned deep. Come jetted on her stomach and her breasts. His head fell back on his neck, his wings stretched out majestically, and it was the sexiest thing she'd ever seen. When the last warm stream of come pooled in her belly button, he gazed down at her with so much reverence and divine beauty that she was certain he was everything a God was meant to be.

Chapter 19

Guardian Manor, Tetartos Realm

P leaned back against the solid wood table in the war room. Soon the place would be filled with Guardians and their mates. For now P listened to Drake explain what had happened with Sacha to Bastian and his Tasha.

"He's attracting possessed? Why didn't anyone call me immediately?" Bastian, the usually calm Kairos, demanded.

He and Drake had dropped off the possessed in some dark alley while Uri and Alex dealt with the broken lock at Sacha's. After that Drake had called Bastian in because the male needed to hear what happened before the others did.

"We took care of it," Drake bit out. "Sacha and Hades need some time to deal with their mating. They're at the island."

Bastian's eyes hardened a fraction as he hissed out a breath. His mate inched closer to him. Bastian couldn't exactly be thrilled to hear about his mother's mating.

P pinched the bridge of his nose. This was fucked, he just hoped his father was doing right by Sacha, though a part of him knew Hades would. His father had always had a soft spot for females, but that wasn't exactly a selling point anyone wanted to mention at this

177

point.

Sirena came in a second later and listened to Drake finish. The healer was in her usual fifties-style dress, this time with glasses that she didn't need perched on her small nose. When Drake was finished with the details, she added, "The blood tests on Sacha and Hades came back fine. I'm sure they'll be through this getting-to-know-each-other part soon enough," she assured Bastian, adding, "He cares for her."

That was what the Kairos needed to hear, because his shoulders seemed to relax as he growled, "Good."

"She'll be fine. We just need to allow them some alone time," Tasha said, leaning into her male. Bastian tucked his beautiful female into his side, looking down at her with warmth. It felt like the two had forgotten they were even there, and P mentally sighed. This was the way of the mated.

Guardians and mates started filtering into the room, most talking as they entered. Conn came in with his female and all of her sisters and brothers. The Lykos clan was chatting boisterously with Brianne and Vane as they all walked in. Conn shook his head as he tucked his mate into a chair next to him. The male was in his usual flannel, his tattoos peeking from the rolled sleeves. Dacia's amber eyes flashed in annoyance at something one of her more outgoing sisters said, and P smiled.

The Guardian family had expanded a lot. Most of the wolves helped where they could here in Tetartos Realm. And some of the more technology minded were taking over corners in the war room on a daily basis in order to help Conn with some of the office shit. The Lykos and his brother-in-law, Hagen, argued often about investments of the Guardian money.

The females had mostly taken over the gym at the manor, as Alex, Ileana and some of the other warrior females were determined to teach all of the females how to fight.

Rain came in chatting with Alyssa. Dorian's and Gregoire's mates had been childhood friends. Something about all the chatter made P feel both happy and unsettled.

Sander entered and sauntered directly to P. The Phoenix had been his partner for centuries, even before they were Guardians. Sander and Jax had been the ones to help P search for the artifact that called the Creators back. They'd bonded then. The male's bronzed skin and bald head made his white tee shirt stand out. One look at the printed slogan sent a blast of laughter from P's lungs. In bold black letters it said TEAM NASTIA and below were slanted red letters that said "see proof below" with a black arrow pointed down at the Phoenix's dick. Which was exactly where Nastia ensured Sander was marked as her male. P had been at their mating ceremony and unfortunately witnessed that particular marking.

It was tradition for a mated male to be permanently tattooed with the symbol on their chest.

Sander bit out, "Fuck you." But Nastia was right behind him with a beaming smile on her gorgeous face. She was in leather pants and her white tee shirt made more laughter escape. In bold black were the words SANDER IS TEAM NASTIA and below in red letters were the words "see proof" with an arrow pointing to the left. It was ridiculous, but the Phoenix growled something about losing a bet. His brother Guardian's eyes lit with amusement as he grabbed his female and tucked her into his side.

P could only imagine what the bet could have been between the two. Sander shook his head as the remaining Guardians and mates piled into the room and sat while poking fun of Sander.

Family. P needed the reminder when everything seemed unknown.

Drake broke it up and quieted everyone. The room was filled with people.

P stood at the back of the room, with his arms crossed, and listened to the details of what happened at Sacha's for what felt like the fiftieth time. His mind trailed back to the lake where Hades had called the Goddess of Thule. P itched to get back there and stare into that cool mountain water in hopes that he'd learn its secrets. The waters stayed a deep glassy blue even as everything else froze around it.

"And Hades was able to rip the demon souls out without the pain rebounding back?" Jax bit out, the Ailouros, half cat, sat with his arm around his mate's chair, looking incredulously at the dragon.

"He said it didn't hurt them."

P felt his powers pulling at him as he drifted off, not paying attention anymore, as he was too busy focusing on getting his ability under control, which took some effort.

By the time all the questions about Sacha and Hades were answered, Drake bit out the other problem. "The Goddess of Thule isn't healing fast enough to wake up." Era was standing at the dragon's side, watchful and silent, but the connection between her and the dragon was intense. Their power sizzled in a room full of powerful beings. She was eerily beautiful and completely devoted to his cousin. The female was everything Drake needed. She was as powerful and strong as she was intelligent. And P respected and was grateful that she'd been helping Sirena with some of the healer's duties. Sirena never took downtime, and looking at his sister Guardian, he could see how exhausted she was. She may not want to take time off, but she needed it, and now they had someone else with healing power to ease that load.

P watched as Sirena spoke to the room at large. "The copper-lined room is draining the Goddess's strength and power, and she doesn't seem to be catching up."

"So take her out of the room and put her in another prison cell until she can heal," Brianne offered.

"That's what I plan to do," Drake ground out. "We need her awake." The dragon's attention went to the small blonde sitting next to Erik, Alex's sister-in-law. "Sam, can you forge shackles of copper?" She wasn't a Guardian or a fighter, but her mate, Erik, was the Demi-God son of Athena, and they both helped anywhere they could since the Guardians helped rescue Sam from their old enemy.

"Yes," the blonde agreed, and P smiled at the sparkle in her eyes. She had a rare ability with metal. In fact, she'd been the one Conn used to line the cells the second Hades told them that copper weakened those from Thule.

"Good. I want her awake, but not to be strong enough to open a portal out of the damned cell. We're not exactly sure how readily she can use that skill, or if our spells and ward will be enough. Not since she managed to hide damned warriors in plain sight all the while keeping one of those portals open and battling Hades. She's powerful," Drake bit out.

The voices of his brethren drifted off to the background as P's concentration ended. His hidden ability slipped free of its hold, and he noticed Gregoire's eyes shift to him. The big Hippeus, half warhorse, was sitting in a chair at the back of the room with his tiny pregnant mate cuddled on his lap.

What's going on? his brother asked. Alyssa's child had given her a powerful shield right before the first portal opened and Apollo was taken. No one but Gregoire could touch her or get too close to her, and that suited his brother Guardian's wildly possessive tendencies, but that didn't take the worry off the hulking warhorse's bearded face.

I'm fine, he assured the male. Alyssa's pale green eyes slid to him at the same time and she smiled warmly. It was easy enough to assume that she'd heard their telepathic conversation.

Gregoire narrowed his eyes on P. *I know this shit is fucked for you. Hades is a pain in the ass, but he wouldn't get you benched for no good reason.* Gregoire assumed it was agitation at being left out of the fight that was making his power slip free, and P hoped that was the case.

They couldn't afford any more problems than were already on their plates.

Chapter 20

Hades' Island, Tetartos Realm

Hades retracted his wings and turned to lie beside Sacha, braced on a forearm so he could see his come marking his female's flat stomach and round breasts. The sight pleased him far more than it should. His thumb slid into it, massaging it into her heated skin. Her beautiful bronze curves stood out against the white bed linens, and he found he loved the sight of her dewy skin in firelight.

When her fingers came up to dip into the evidence of his pleasure, he couldn't take his eyes away. As she lifted the small digit to her lips, he felt his blood heating, and when her pink tongue darted out to taste, his cock twitched to life.

Her eyelids lowered and he was taken in by the way her slim throat worked and the burst of pleasure he felt in the link. He groaned, but couldn't take his eyes off of her. He'd never get enough of this; her taste was still on his tongue. Fuck, he wanted to watch her get off a thousand times over. It had been the most enthralling thing he'd ever seen.

"I don't think it worked." She breathed out as her eyes closed. The desire to have her was still there, and he knew that was exactly what she was worrying about. Her pent-up power hadn't been what had caused this driving compulsion to have each other. That left them at a place he struggled with, he didn't want her memories coming back if he did the things the beast blood wanted. He forced the thoughts back, wanting to enjoy taking in the sight of her soft flushed skin carrying his mark.

"I know," he agreed as a small towel he'd seen in the kitchen made its way into his hand. He gently ran the cloth over her supple skin, cleaning her even though a part of him wanted to leave it while another needed to take care of her. The desires were intense, maybe even greater than his need to have her again. "How do you feel, *thisavre mou*?"

"Aside from aroused?" She breathed out.

He grinned wickedly. "Yes." He'd meant her power and she knew it. He wanted the answer from her lips and to see if she fully understood the scope of the ability they'd uncovered. It was strong. The overturned furniture around them proved that. It was evidence that he'd underestimated the extent of what his female was capable of locking up inside her small frame.

*****

Sacha shouldn't have tasted him. He had tasted too good on her tongue, and now she was forced to block the desire that was already building again. She took a deep breath, and that was another mistake. The scent of sex filled the room. She mentally pushed it back to answer his question. "I feel good." In truth it felt like an immense weight had been lifted away. She felt a mix of things; relief was only the most prominent.

"What happened?" The real question she was asking was what had he done when she released the ability.

He gazed down from his raised position, and a wicked grin formed on his perfect lips. "I contained and filtered it out. Right before I came all over you."

He searched her eyes, growing more serious. "Can you let it out now?"

"You want me to use it on you?"

He raised a brow and his smile brightened all over again. "It won't harm me. I want to see if you can call it back easily. You need to feel it, understand it. The ability is a part of you."

She let her mind wrap around it, inspecting all that she'd held back for centuries. It was different than she remembered. Stronger. Her mind's eyes trailed over and around it. Her eyes shot to his, because this was far from what she'd wielded before. This was much more intricate.

He nodded.

Her mind spun at the scope. "Is this because of you?"

He considered it for a moment. "I imagine that's part of it."

She hadn't used the power since her slave cuffs were removed by the Creators. Those bracelets had suffocated all of her other abilities except that one.

"It's so much more than I thought."

"Yes," he agreed easily, searching her eyes. He was waiting for her to fully understand what her ability was capable of.

"You can feel how it works?" A question. More a confirmation,

185

she supposed.

"I can."

He nodded and assessed her. "You're essentially able to break apart anything in slow motion like you'd done before. Among other things."

"I feel like I can call to anything." Could she paralyze anything with a thought?

"Yes," he answered easily.

She wouldn't need to get close like she had before. What could this mean for killing Hell beasts and dealing with possessed? That thought led to a pang of regret at not having let that part of her out sooner. As a powerful Guardian Kairos, she'd always been able to port large amounts of things or people. She could even get through metal, a limitation for those of her race. She'd never struggled in battle; her teleportation and blade had always been true, until that creature from Thule poisoned her.

This ability was entirely different. She almost felt like she'd be able to teleport a Hell creature's beating heart into her hands.

"It would be messy, but possible," he pointed out with a raised eyebrow, and a hint of his amusement filtered into the bond.

She didn't have a moment to appreciate how gruesome that image had been. Her mind was too busy studying every intricate part of what lived inside her.

He caressed the curve of her waist, waiting patiently as she assessed everything. Giving her time to work it out on her own, to learn every minute detail of everything that had changed inside her

186

mind and body.

Her eyes focused back on him. "You can wield it now too?" Their powers had blended stronger than even before. There was so much power running inside her that hadn't been there before, and she could feel the signs of more to come. The trickling of his soul power was what stilled her next. Would she be able to do what he'd done to the possessed?

"I believe you will be able to use it the way I can." He nodded, and she felt him sorting out his own thoughts on that particular fact. She was almost his equal in power already, and that was staggering. What he was mulling over was the fact that she would also have an ability he hadn't even passed to his son.

She reached out and touched the hand that was drawing circles on her skin, the instinctual need to comfort him was strong. "I'm not sure I understand half of it," she admitted. She'd need his help in figuring it all out.

"I will," he assured her with a soft smile. "As far as the soul ability goes, I don't generally destroy them. There is a great deal of responsibility when dealing with souls," he added seriously. "There needs to be balance in the world. But those deserved destruction."

She watched his eyes grow hard at the thought of the possessed in her space. Under the building desire was Hades' anger that one of the Tria had so much as looked at her.

She ached for him, and since suppressing her power hadn't been the problem, that left them one other option. That he'd have to stop holding back the need to dominate her. A wave of need sent shivers through her at the thought. Her beast responding? Or did she truly want him like that? Was it the wild power running in her veins that made her desire him at a baser level?

He growled, but she could feel him warring with the need. He didn't want to trigger her memories. That meant she was going to have to force him to truly let go when the time came to set his beast free. For now something else was pulling her more than desire.

She wanted to know more about the God. Knowing him on an emotional level was only making her more curious about who he'd been and why. They wouldn't have long before the need got too out of control, but they could take a few minutes to talk. Humans dated to get to know their partner; Immortals went through a frenzy and blood bonding that left them completely aware of the other on a deeper level through their pasts. She and Hades seemed to be going through some middle ground of both.

She liked him... cared for him, but she only knew what she felt and what she'd been told. She needed more.

His eyes sparked with amusement and heat. "What would you like to know, *thisavre mou*?"

"You were close with Aphrodite and Athena?"

He smiled. "With Aphrodite. No one could be close to Athena, she was a warrior completely lacking in a sense of humor, but we were allies."

"Did you spend a lot of time with Aphrodite and her mate?"

"By the time they mated, there was a lot going on, but we did meet as often as possible. We made sure that Draken and Pothos had time together." It had been important to him that his son have a companion that understood him. Sacha knew that Drake and P had been close as cousins, but something about his emotion and the

188

words brought fond images of young Demi-Gods at play. Hades hadn't just worried about his son being a warrior.

"His power wasn't questionable. And I did teach him to fight, there were always wars, but I didn't want his life to be filled with duty and darkness. I wanted him to embrace and appreciate the pleasures that life had to offer." He shook his head, a touch of a smile on his lips. "Aphrodite and I tried, but those two were still fairly serious."

"They were the same age?"

"Draken was a few years older," he admitted.

"How did you come to raise Pothos? Brianne said that his mother was a priestess of Thule."

He eyed her for long minutes. He wasn't used to discussing his life, and he hesitated. He finally spoke. "She was. Eir was an emissary of sorts for a God named Agnarr."

He was hedging. Not wanting to upset her with talk of other females, but it only made her more curious. "Did you care for her?"

"I didn't know her well," he admitted. "She was a strong female who wasn't opposed to..." She felt him searching for any way out of admitting to having had sex with P's mother. She didn't want to think of him with another female, but she really didn't want to think that he'd cared for Pothos' mother and lost his love. Sacha didn't like the idea that she'd feel like she was in some competition with a dead female.

He brought her hand up to his lips, and the warmth of his breath made her skin flush and desire slide down the length of her body. His eyes were serious when he spoke. "She bore my son and I'm grateful,

189

but there is no comparing my experiences with her or anyone else to *this*." She felt the truth of his words.

"When did you learn about Pothos?" Sacha was curious about the whole situation.

"After he was born. She found a way back during one of Agnarr's visits. I think she may have been the one to convince the God to come. That was the first day I laid eyes on my son," he said with remembered awe. The sheer joy he'd had in seeing his son was there for her to feel all the way to her soul. "He was perfect and most definitely mine. He had the smallest wings, and I could feel the telepathic bond the second I set eyes on him. It was the most incredible feeling I'd ever had."

"You didn't know she was pregnant before that?"

"No." He shook his head. "She told me that she'd hidden her pregnancy and Pothos from everyone in Thule. I have no idea how she would have done that, but I believed her when she said it. She was frantic."

"Did she explain why she was scared for him?" Sacha couldn't imagine being so worried for her child she'd feel it was safer to send him away. That would be a hell all in itself.

"She said that the Gods of her world would consider Pothos dangerous. That they'd try to kill him," Hades ground out in fury at just the thought of someone harming his child. "There had been a few Gods who'd gone mad like so many of my siblings. They were killing priestesses and Gods alike. She said if they didn't kill him, they'd attempt to imprison him there, and she couldn't protect him."

She'd already heard some of this. About how Agnarr had sought out allies to stop his warring siblings.

"Why kill the priestesses? How were they a threat to the Gods? Or had it just been for the pleasure of killing?" The majority of the Earth Gods had fed off the energies of death and torment, demanding sacrifices in their honor. Those energies addicted and drove them into deeper depravities. Hades and his sisters were the only ones who'd only fed off Earth's pure energies.

"It had to do with the way their world was set up. Instead of nine Immortals with various powers for each God, the Creators of Thule made three priestesses for each of their Gods. Eir was more powerful than the average Immortal here. I'd say they were closer to the strength of your Guardian powers in that aspect. They were immune to the Gods' powers and had their own abilities to use against the Gods."

If the priestesses could wield power against the Gods, it made sense that they would consider a priestess's son a threat. "So she left him with you?"

"Yes. I tried to get her to stay," he admitted, and that made her think even better of him. He shook it off. "I knew that some of their Gods had died already and so had a lot of priestesses, but she said she had to go back. Then she made me promise to never let a God of Thule see him."

"What happened then?" She knew P's mother was dead.

He nodded absently. "I got the news of her death on one of Agnarr's trips to discuss the alliance."

She furrowed her brow as she considered the time line. "Why did it take so long?" she asked. P was more than grown by the time they found the artifact that called the Creators back.

Her questions were bringing him back to the fact that she'd

191

been a slave during that same time. She stopped him. "This isn't about that." There was no going back to change anything even if she'd wanted to, and dwelling on it wouldn't do him any good.

"Agnarr was creating a special prison for the other Gods in his world. Something he assured me was almost finished *every* time we spoke for decades," Hades gritted out.

"You were able to imprison the Tria in Hell. Why couldn't they do the same?"

She felt his hesitation; he wasn't used to sharing. "What we did couldn't be done again. It was dangerous, and he couldn't have contained the four Gods of Thule who'd banded together to destroy everything in their world."

"Why?" But she understood more as soon as the word was out.

"We used a portion of our own life forces in the creation of that prison. Even if we'd been able to get a hold on the others, we couldn't have done it again." Using a life force was strong power. The mating spell was created when Charybdis used a portion of her life force to stop Apollo from using the Immortals to create his army. The female had been an Immortal breeder, one Sacha had known. She'd known that giving away her children to the warrior camps, to the Gods, had driven Charybdis slightly mad. Sacha had been lucky enough not to have suffered that fate. In order to make the spell eternally binding, she'd used her own life force and become nothing more than a shell of a being after that.

"So you understand why it took me as well as Aphrodite, Athena and my sisters' consorts to add a portion." He clenched his teeth. "Even Drake and Pothos added a small piece of themselves to it." She could feel that he'd not been pleased by that when he added, "There hadn't been a choice. It would have been better to make individual prisons, but it wasn't possible and we were losing our hold on the demon spawn."

"You caught them when they brutalized Alex in Athena's palace." She nodded, knowing the story. Uri's mate could have died along with her brothers, Vane and Erik, who'd tried to save their sister.

"Yes," he growled. She knew he was seeing the carnage and the need to kill was strong. "And that meant we couldn't afford to let them get away. It was Ares' and Artemis' doing. They'd sent their demented sons out to create havoc and torment Athena. And they would have done it again. They could have sent them to harm Pothos next." He growled.

She could feel his hatred for his depraved siblings. It was their incestuous coupling that had spawned the Tria. And the evil triplets were driven by their need to feed off the pain and suffering they caused.

She ran her fingers over his, which were again moving absently on her skin. The need was building, but the simple desire to touch him was nearly as strong.

"Why do you think Deimos came to you?"

"I'm a God," he mused as if that was answer enough, but she could feel his mind working. "I assume they felt my power reawakened, and maybe they hope I'll free them using the tether I put on their souls."

Sacha's fingers stilled along with her heart as she stared over at him. He was still on his side with his head in his hand as if his words hadn't been disturbing. "What do you mean by tether?"

He raised a brow. "A means to call them to me."

She could feel how his answers seemed to make perfect sense to him. "But that means they're linked to you." Linked to her? She felt vaguely sick at the thought of that evil anywhere near either of them. She mentally sought it out, but couldn't find any kind of link to Hell.

He came up over her, bracing on his forearms with his heat and weight settling her into the bed. "It's nothing more than a tag inside them that I can use to call them out of Hell. They aren't physically attached to either of us." He growled, "I would never allow them to touch you. You will always be safe."

Desire hummed at the feel of him on top of her, but she couldn't succumb after his revelation. She needed to know more, even if the weight of his cock between her legs was making her body pliant with want. "Why did you do that?" she asked. "Why have a way to get them out of their prison?"

"As a precaution. If the walls ever weakened, I'd rather be able to pull one out at a time and deal with him. It would be easier than dealing with all three," he explained even though he wasn't pleased at having to consider the possibility of the prison ever coming down.

She nodded and found that his answer made him all that more attractive to her.

His grin was beautifully devilish. "I hope my brilliance isn't the only thing you find attractive."

She mentally sighed before cocking a brow. He was definitely arrogant, but if anything, she found it amusing. "I don't believe brilliance was in my stream of thoughts."

"It was inferred." He sighed and rolled to his back, pulling her into him so that her cheek rested against his chest. "Ask your other questions, *thisavre mou.*" He understood her need to know him and was allowing it when all he really wanted was to have her again. Her lips twitched against his warm skin, relishing the moment of closeness she needed with him, but they wouldn't have a lot of time.

He stopped massaging her back long enough to give her shoulder a soft squeeze, and she knew should check in with Sirena before it wasn't an option. She could feel his hard cock at her side and knew the time for holding back was nearly at an end.

She needed some confirmation that their blood hadn't been the problem.

Chapter 21

Hades' Island, Tetartos Realm

Sacha felt for the link to Sirena and asked, *What did the blood work say?*

The healer's voice came through a second later. *You are both fully mated and powerful as hell. Did you try the things we spoke of?*

One. My power is free.

And?

We still feel it.

Then you know what to do. If it doesn't work, I promise we'll figure this out, the healer assured her.

Thank you.

I'm only a call away. No matter what. Sacha felt her sister's warmth through the bond. The Guardians had been a family of sorts from the moment the Creators linked their minds. They fought together and amused each other, but through it all they loved one another as blood siblings would.

She sent her gratitude through the link and dropped the

connection as she took a deep breath, inhaling his scent and the sex in the room.

"Blood doesn't always mean love and loyalty," he said thoughtfully. "You really have forged something special."

Those traits had definitely been lacking in his relationship with his siblings. She could feel it along with the heat burning under his skin; that need didn't stop her from asking, "Did you spend time with all of your brothers and sisters when you were a child?" She wondered at the young boy Hades had been. And had the other Gods always been evil? Not that it mattered, but she was curious. Was it only caused by feeding off dark energies, or were they already prone to evil?

Sacha knew that Brianne was one of the Immortals created fully formed by the Creators to care for their children when they left the world. Her sister Guardian had been assigned to a young Hades and spoke fondly of the young hellion he'd been.

He grunted and she felt the action against her cheek and rubbed her face against it without thought. "We had separate palaces, but we were brought together often. And, no, they weren't all evil as young, but they were always assholes, which was the reason they started taking in dark energies to begin with." She could feel his disgust before he added, "Aphrodite and I were close from the start, always getting into mischief together." He took a deep breath before continuing, "And it wasn't as if our mother and father wanted to leave. This world couldn't hold them, and we wouldn't have survived with them if they'd attempted to take us."

Hades and P both had mothers that were forced to leave them behind. Sacha liked to think that she would have found another way. But reality wasn't always kind.

She couldn't help the direction her mind trailed to from there. Could a baby be in her future? She'd never birthed a child; it was part of why Apollo and Hermes considered her a failed experiment.

"Would you want one?" he asked, and she felt his attention focused on her answer.

It wasn't an easy or simple question. Immortals were able to have young, usually about a decade after mating. Birth rates were much lower than they had been before the mating curse. But Gregoire had conceived with his mate the night of their mating ceremony, so things might be changing.

She took a deep breath before answering, "Want?... Yes." Very much, actually, but she added, "But it's complicated."

She lifted up to look at him. "I have a duty to the Realms." She saw he was about to speak and shook her head. "I'm not mated to a Guardian, Hades. I *am* a Guardian. I'm a warrior as well as a diplomat. I protect. A pregnant Guardian out dealing with possessed and killing Hell beasts? That wouldn't happen."

She saw his eyes go hard at that, but she sighed and went on, "Having a child isn't a choice we get to make, there are no forms of Immortal birth control, but it's something that will likely be difficult for me no matter how much I'd love it."

She was snared by the heat sparking in his eyes and the way he gazed down at her stomach with longing. That look made her nipples ache and her skin pull tight. He didn't even need to touch her for her to feel him against her skin.

She needed to finish this conversation so that he understood. "There are four Realms to patrol. We do have more help now, with all the powerful mates helping. And Alex has been teaching some of

198

them how to fight. Her sister-in-law, Sam, is powerful and learning, as well as the others like Dorian's and Conn's mates, who weren't raised as warriors, but that will take some time. And there is a lot going on right now. We have a God loose and a Goddess from another world imprisoned. Not to mention the Tria causing trouble and now communicating with you. I'm needed."

And as soon as they worked out the key to easing their constant need, she would be out there fighting beside her brethren as she was meant to. "If you thought you were getting a mate that would stay in your bed day and night, that's not the case."

He growled, "I will deal with the possessed and the Goddess of Thule. I can also dispose of more Hell creatures." It was said with the arrogance of a God, but much as she frowned down at him, she couldn't argue the fact that he'd dispatched a dozen possessed in her home with a mere thought. His help would be valuable, and according to Brianne's memories, it was technically part of the deal he'd worked out with her brethren so they wouldn't return him to stasis after getting his help to find Apollo.

She could feel him disregarding all her worries as something he would take care of, and she mentally sighed. She wouldn't argue with him; he would learn soon enough what it meant to be a Guardian. She had a bad feeling he would be unbearable if she did get pregnant.

"I may not even be able to have a baby," she warned, and a part of her stilled, awaiting his answer to that. Who knew what the future held.

He finally calmed and pulled her down for a kiss. *I'd love another child. But I don't need anything more than you and my son.* She could feel his mind working. *I suppose Bastian is mine now as well. That means I have two sons, so if we don't have more children, we still have a family.*

She broke the kiss as laughter bubbled free at the image that came with his mental words. He'd been dead serious, and she couldn't contain the amusement that mixed with the swelling of her heart. Bastian was a fully grown male, and her relationship with her son had grown to a loving friendship, even if she'd always be his mother. To imagine Hades trying to be a father to him was as touching as it was amusing. She could almost imagine the look on Bastian's face if Hades ever said such a thing.

When she took in his expression, she expected matching amusement, but what she saw sucked the air from her lungs and made her forget her amusement. There wasn't a good description for it, other than maybe "awe."

"Your laughter." His eyes traced over her lips with a smile. "I didn't think you could be more beautiful, but this..." He touched her lips. "This is enthralling, *agapi mou*." His love.

Everything changed in that moment. Their need finally boiled over and all thought of talk was gone.

Hades pulled her back down for his kiss, and she got lost in the pleasure somewhere in between the slow glide of his mouth against hers and his hands on her burning skin.

He sucked on her tongue and it pulled a moan from deep within her. She straddled his cock and rolled her hips, getting him slick with her desire. She could already feel him holding back, and she was going to enjoy making him lose all that control. The animal needed to be set free if they had any hope of getting through life without screwing every fifteen minutes. You'd think her beast was a damned rabbit instead of some ancient bird.

He groaned as she grabbed his wrists and lifted his hands from her hips to push them down to the sides of his head. His amusement was short lived when she pulled power until it was like soft licks were trailing over his neck... chest... his thick thighs. All the while she continued kissing him and preventing him from touching her.

This is as close to an orgy as you'll ever get again, she whispered the warning into his mind. She knew his proclivities and she was about to show him the error in his ways.

Is it? he taunted silkily. *I have no desire to feel another female's hands, but I wouldn't mind seeing a female make you come. The sight and sounds of your pleasure are addictive, thisavre mou.* And her dirty God meant every word. He'd get off hard watching her come, and she found something incredibly sexy about that.

She moaned. She wasn't interested in ever feeling anyone else's touch, but she could fantasize and allow him to do the same. She sent him wicked images, the ones he'd sent as he watched her juices slip from her pussy. At his groan she manipulated the picture to add a masked female bent over lapping up the juices.

He lifted up to her as he grinded his cock against her clit. He'd broken her hold to bring them chest to chest as she let the images change; soon there were delicate fingers slipping into Sacha's pussy. Her body writhed, pushing her pussy into the imagined touch along with his very real cock.

He growled. *Show me the juices slicking her fingers. There's nothing more beautiful than your sweet wet pussy.*

She was getting so hot she gasped against him, as affected by her own dirty seduction as he was. He lifted her up higher to impale her on his cock as he watched her play the images he demanded. *Now grip her head and make her bury her face in your cunt. Let me see you grind your pussy against her and then show me your beautiful face as you come.*

She was caught up in their play when he slammed her down on his cock. She'd been so close that the second he powered inside, she came hard around him. He growled, breathing hard, but the animal demanded more than he was giving it. She broke free of his hold and eyed him as she turned around to her hands and knees.

"No," he growled. She bent lower so that her head was in soft bedding, but he was struggling because of what she'd said before about being bent over things. He was fighting it even as she widened her thighs so he could see just how wet she was.

Nothing about it brought anything negative. She was in there in the room with her male, nowhere else, and the slight hesitation slipped away. The past something far from her.

He still didn't move, but a glance back showed his wings rippling out in the wild firelight. He still needed convincing, his control was barely holding, but he refused to let it go. Worried for her no matter that she canted her hips in invitation.

She moved her fingers over her clit and up into the come that slid from her body, the same liquid that marked his cock. He hissed out a breath, and when she dipped her fingers inside her pussy, moaning, she knew he was close.

He bit off a curse as thunder shook the walls and flashes of lightning flickered. She angled her body so she could look back at him as she touched herself. His eyes were focused on her fingers, and she felt the battle waging inside him. He wanted her, wanted to pound into her relentlessly. He needed to hold her down and fuck her hard. His eyes glowed with the sheer force he was expending in holding the instincts back. When she brought her fingers up to lick, she watched his eyes shutter, but he still didn't move. The beast's focus was caught between her pussy and her lips.

"If I let go now, I'm not going to be able to stop," he bit out. She sent the licking sensation over his hard cock and bent lower, pushing the slickness from her pussy to her ass and circling until she heard wild gusts of winds slam into the home as rain pelted the roof.

She pushed that single digit until it slipped through the tight muscles of her ass, making her groan.

That was all it took to snap his hold. His power lashed out until her hands were planted on the bed. Her hips were lifted higher as he slammed deep and hard on a harsh roar. She gasped at being filled so fast and then moaned as he shafted her, thrusting inside her over and over as his own power caressed her breasts and clit. She cried out, coming hard in an instant, but he didn't stop. His hips battered against her ass, and his power held her down, the beast forcing its dominance. Making her take every inch until she was dizzy with the pleasure of it. Her own beast fluttered inside her as she tried to push back for more. He wouldn't let her.

He grunted, almost completely taken over by the animalistic needs. "Take it, Sacha. Take every fucking inch."

"Yes."

"Damn it, Sacha," he growled, "I'm going to come hard. And I want you to take it all. Grip my cock when I come, hold it deep so not a drop spills free."

She swallowed and nodded, because she was about to come

again and words were beyond her at that moment. She was gone, loving every minute.

"Fuck. The things I want to do to you," he bit out.

She moaned, "Do it." He was ruling her body with his power, his cock, and when she felt his thumb circling her ass, she came hard, her pussy clamping around him. She turned her head to bite the blankets as he thrust harder and deeper, and then, holding her hips tight to his body, his cock as deep as it would go, he roared to the ceiling, emptying inside her.

Hot jets filled her up, and something deep inside her preened and stretched to life. She felt incredible, no memories, never had she been anywhere else but with Hades. It had been wild, freeing... incredible.

She smiled when he ported them into the ocean. Rain fell for only a moment as the clouds moved away until moonlight spilled over his hard, beautiful features. He wrapped her legs around his hips in the cool water and held her jaw as he kissed her softly. Their tongues tangled as his wings circled her in their embrace. *Are you okay, agapi mou?*

More than okay. Perfect, she sent and instantly felt his muscles relax under her hands. His palms moved down her body to caress her back and hold her breasts against his chest as the water rocked against her cooling skin. She leaned her head back, looking up at the stars, and felt a sense of wonder and excitement for the world that she'd never truly felt. Power thrummed in her veins and his soul cradled hers.

She looked into his eyes and saw his beautiful smile.

The memories were in the past and he was her future.

Chapter 22

Sacha's Paris Home, Earth Realm

Hades watched Sacha glance around her home the second they reformed in Paris. His female was frowning as she looked at her floors where the bodies of the possessed had fallen.

He knew she was remembering the invasion, and he took the smallest sense of satisfaction in having destroyed the demons' souls. It had been worth it. He would kill anyone or anything that posed a threat to Sacha.

She stalked through the living area, watchful as she moved to her bedroom. The bedcovers were still messy from use, and in that moment he wished they were staying.

"We can't stay in bed all the time." She sighed.

Whatever they'd been going through seemed to be subsiding. He wouldn't say it had passed completely, because he had a feeling the beasts weren't done with them. The beast might not be trying to rule him now, but the attraction still buzzed between them just from being close. Her scent was intoxicating.

"I disagree," he groused in answer to her comment. "My nephew is more than capable of waiting until we're ready to see him."

She turned to him with a perfectly cocked brow. "You don't need to go with me."

He growled. She'd said the same thing at the island and it had done something to him. He had a strong aversion to letting her out of his sight. He wasn't sure why that was, but it was powerful. That meant he was forced to deal with his nephew on Sacha's time frame.

"Don't," he growled. "If you go, I go."

She only nodded. "Okay. After we're done at the manor, I want to enter Hell Realm to test my ability."

What she suggested was smart. His female was a warrior and he couldn't fault her reasoning, that didn't mean he had to like being taken from their bed to do it.

"Yes, *thisavre mou*." He would wield it as well. He'd been powerful before, but was even more so now that they'd soul bonded, and he needed to test the new boundaries of it.

She nodded before turning to her closet.

He felt her amusement as he followed. She tossed the robe aside, and her plaited hair trailed along the delicate curve of her bare back. He stood with his arms crossed as he watched her slip on undergarments that appeared too tiny to be useful in doing anything but making him suffer. He wanted to rip them off with his fucking teeth. She glanced back with a laugh and his cock shot to life at the sound.

He moved to haul her into his arms without a second thought. His lips met hers as he leaned down and kissed her to the point of breathlessness.

When they broke apart, she groaned and glared up at him as she sucked in air. "Why don't you go get some of P's fighting leathers? They're spelled against Hell beast blood."

He growled as he felt her determination to do this meeting and test their need to see if it would escalate again the way it had before.

"I wouldn't care if the leather was spelled with the magic of a thousand Gods, I will not wear them." He felt his cock ache just imagining its captivity in those tight pants.

Her laughter filled the closet, but she'd already turned to pull on black leather pants that hugged her ass in a way that he knew was meant to make him lose his sanity.

He bit back a low groan, and she turned and shook her head.

A second later she was zipping the matching shirt over her big tits, and he cursed the prison she'd wrapped them in. A halter sheath was the next addition, and his cock felt like it would break when she slid a blade inside.

Her eyes sparkled when they landed on his. "If you get through this, I'll give you a reward." He'd just pulled her into his arms when she ported them away, and he was disgruntled as hell when they reformed outside of his son's home so that he could get a blade suitable to his size. Hers were small.

His cock twitched, making its own annoyance known.

"We wouldn't have left if we'd started," she said, and he could feel she wasn't exactly happy about delaying their pleasure, but she'd already contacted Draken and was anxious to get there. He didn't care.

He stepped over to a massive cabinet and opened it wide to display his son's collection of blades. He pulled one out, thinking that he really needed Pothos to go into the storage and get Hades' old blades. Pothos had stored most of the items he'd salvaged from Hades' old palace, but that also meant he needed to know where they'd end up living.

"I like my home, Hades," she pointed out, and he turned to her. There was a hint of curiosity as to whether he'd demand to live in a place of his own.

He eyed her for a moment and then nodded. "I'll have Pothos make arrangements to buy the building. I like space," he added before asking, "Will that work, *agapi mou*?"

She smiled up at him, and it would have been worth living in a shack to see that look on her face. He pulled her into his chest for a moment, because he was finding it difficult not to touch her all the time.

A second later she asked, "What if everyone doesn't want to sell?"

"They're human. If they can't be bought, we would only have a matter of decades to wait for them to die, and can buy it from their heirs," he said with a smile.

Problem solved.

She choked out a laugh and he swore he'd never get used to the beauty of her smile and the way her dark eyes lit from within. "This pleases you?" he asked.

"Yes," she breathed. "I would like that," she agreed.

"Good. Now let's go deal with my nephew and test your powers so that I can have my reward." There were many dirty possibilities with his female, and he couldn't wait.

She grinned up at him. "Yes."

They ported away to the Guardian manor in Tetartos Realm, moving through the wards and protections as if they didn't exist, reforming in front of a big table where Draken and Pothos awaited them.

They barely had time to get settled before his nephew started spouting questions about what had happened with the possessed. Hades wasn't sure how minutes could feel like hours, but they did.

His wing curled to touch her arm. He didn't pull her into his side, feeling her discomfort at showing affection in front of others. He'd ease her into it, because he planned to touch her anytime he could, no matter where they were.

Drake growled, "You're telling me you marked the Tria's souls?"

"Yes," Hades bit out even though he was just repeating himself at this point.

"It was to prepare in case the prison ever weakened?" his son asked.

Hades crossed his arms over his chest, waiting. "I did. I had no idea what would happen if one of us died."

Drake and Pothos nodded, apparently considering things before Drake asked, "Are you two okay now?"

Hades was ready to say yes, but Sacha spoke first. "Mostly," his female said with a nod as she eyed him. It was true that neither felt certain it was over. She added, "We're fine for the moment."

His son and Drake were both watching them closely, but it was Pothos who finally spoke. "Good." His eyes warmed when he looked at Sacha, pleasing Hades greatly.

Hades knew Sacha felt his affection for his son. Good, because when he finally got her pregnant, he wanted her to remember what a loving father he was. Her gaze shot to him and he grinned wickedly, counting on her knowing exactly what he'd been thinking.

She shook her head, but he saw her pouty lips twitching. They were nearly done here. He had a question of his own before they went to Hell Realm. He was getting irritated at not having any information on Thule. Shifting his eyes to his nephew, he ground out, "You still haven't gotten any information from Kara's warriors?"

Drake's eyes hardened and he answered, "No."

Hades would go question them himself as soon as he was done in Hell Realm.

"Don't think you can get more," Drake bit out. "They don't speak the language of the Creators. They speak something else. And they're only mortal warriors. We need Kara to wake up. She's the only way we're getting to Apollo or finding out why and who has him. I didn't like the look on her face when you questioned her about their weapons and who had one with a dragon insignia. She didn't know Apollo was there until we told her."

Hades' wings flexed in agitation. He would still see what information he could glean from the warriors, but Draken was right, Kara needed to wake up. "Learn the language," he commanded.

His nephew growled, "We're working on it."

"Is Kara improving?"

"Sirena said yes, but only in small fractions. I'm not sure how much the copper room is impeding her ability to heal from the battle." Hades had been the one to inform them about those from Thule being adversely affected by copper. It was something Pothos' mother had shared when leaving his son in his care. Immortals and Gods of Earth felt the same effect from nearly all metal.

Hades bit out, "Kara expended a lot of energy keeping the portal from Thule open and fighting me. Add in the draining effects of the copper coating the room and she may be unconscious for a while yet." Frustration was eating at him. They had a lot to learn and very little to do with the Goddess being unconscious. "Take her out of the room for a while."

Smoke filtered from the dragon's lips in his irritation. "We're in the process of preparing another room now."

Hades noted his son's tense muscles and the hard set of his jaw. "You're not to be anywhere near her," he commanded.

"He won't be," Drake growled. "But stop being an asshole and tell him why."

Hades' wings flexed. "I haven't hidden anything. His mother said that he would be a threat to the other Gods of Thule. That priestesses are immune to their God's power and they have their own abilities that can affect the Gods in Thule."

"So I'm the perfect one to interrogate Kara," P growled.

Hades' muscles pulled tight as he growled, "No! Your mother

211

made me promise you would never get near a God of Thule." The rains were back, a storm flaring back to life outside the walls. "She planned to tell me more, but when they came back, Agnarr said one of his brothers had killed her. I believed her worry for you. You. Will. Not. Go near that Goddess." The building shook under his feet as Sacha sent soothing energies.

He was still staring at his son. "Draken?" he snarled, wanting confirmation that his nephew would ensure Pothos was not a part of this.

"Hades, he's not stupid and neither am I. Pothos hasn't gone near her or the warriors, so calm the fuck down."

Sacha's fingers slid into his, calming him. It took long moments, but the fierce look on his nephew's face appeased him some. But he didn't like the look on his son's face as Pothos' muscles finally relaxed.

Draken, I'm trusting you to make sure he's far from this, he sent to the dragon.

I'll keep him away from them.

Hades' wings relaxed for a moment. His son and Draken had been more like brothers than cousins since they were young. And Hades' nephew wasn't a boy anymore, but that didn't completely ease his worry for his son. That would be there until they resolved the issue of Thule. That meant the Goddess needed to wake, and when that happened, he would find out why Apollo was taken and get his ass back.

Hades' frustration was biting; he didn't like not knowing what secrets his bastard brother could be sharing. Hades wanted the bastard back, and once that happened, he would make the male bleed. The need was nearly consuming in its strength. He could feel his power slipping free as he pictured the agony on Apollo's face.

He barely heard the dragon's snarled words, "Get it together, Hades."

He could feel Sacha's displeasure at the strength of his desire to hurt the male who'd dared enslave and harm her. Who'd dared touch her. He growled and she stepped into his arms. Soothing energies and the warmth of her body against his tense frame started to ease the rage.

When Sacha spoke, it was directed at the dragon, but she was looking up at Hades. "It's fine, Drake."

Hades nodded down at her, but added definitively, "I'm fine, but Apollo. Is. Mine."

He stayed looking down into her eyes as she moved through her own emotions until she finally made a decision and spoke. *After all these centuries I truly care less about him suffering than I do about allowing him to affect what we have. I don't want the past to find its way into our future any more than it has. You can put him in the sleeping unit in pieces if that's what you need, but the only thing that I need is to have him put away and forgotten.*

They stayed like that for long moments as he watched her, loving her all the more for her strength.

*****

Something brought Sacha's attention back to reality, though for a moment it felt like she and Hades were the only two people in the world. She slipped from his embrace, but he didn't let her get too far, tucking her into his side with a wing curled to cradle her there. She didn't fight his need to hold her even though public displays of affection were still very new and a hint uncomfortable for her.

"One more thing." She breathed out as her mind and eyes refocused on their audience.

When she faced Drake, she lost her train of thought. The dragon was smiling; it lit all the way to his emerald eyes as he gazed at her and then moved to Hades. Pothos' lips were curved as well, but it was the dragon that caught her off guard. Her heart warmed, realizing how happy Drake must be, because she couldn't remember ever having seen him smile. Especially not when they had so much happening in the Realms. It made her very curious to see Drake's female, Era.

Era is very possessive and incredibly powerful. Volatile, Hades warned, sending Sacha images of a female with black cherry hair and wild golden eyes standing in front of Hades. Sacha could almost feel Hades' skin singing with the power Era had wielded against Sacha's mate. There wasn't a doubt in her mind that Era felt she was protecting Drake, her sisters had told her that the dragon's mate was protective, but seeing it made her mentally smile. Hades was playfully disgruntled that she hadn't worried for his safety.

You were fine. And she knew he had been. Hades at his most wild was still controlled. More than anyone probably understood. He could have harmed Era, but he'd chosen not to. She saw him so clearly and she knew that mental assessment pleased him, but she felt the need to add, *Drake spent the last several millennia caring for everyone. His life was completely about duty. Even more than Sirena. He didn't take any time for himself. So seeing his mate's need to protect him and care for him makes my heart swell.*

That was for another time. Now she had to get to work. She'd been off duty for far too long, but she needed to make sure she was comfortable with all the powers flowing inside her. A warrior didn't wield a blade without it feeling like a part of their body. It was the same with power.

"We're going to Hell Realm so I can test some of the new ability," she informed Drake.

The dragon eyed her for a moment before looking to Hades and nodding. "I'll go with you."

"So will I," P added.

She nodded, knowing they would likely want to see what she was capable of, and Hell was the best place to do it.

Hades shook his head at the two, but didn't say anything. He wanted them to see... she could actually feel his pride in her ability and it warmed her.

P eyed the blade Hades had with him and added, "I'll go get another blade and meet you there."

SETTA JAY

Chapter 23

Hades' Island, Tetartos Realm

Sacha reformed with her mate in the shower. The scratching need to get the Hell beast blood off her male was crawling under her skin. Clothes were ported away until they were naked under the warm water, and she completely submerged him in the spray as she silently washed his skin.

"I'm fine, Sacha." Hades smiled down at her with warmth and love, but she could feel his amusement. It didn't penetrate the driving desire to clean the poisonous stench from his skin. They'd only spent hours in Hell, but in that time hordes had come flooding from the caverns that led to the Tria's prison in the very bowels of the Realm.

She gritted her teeth, remembering every time his bare chest had been spattered with the acid blood of the beasts. The fury of it had driven her harder... added a more lethal cut to her blade.

They'd even been swarmed by rare Hell dragons, and Drake had shifted into his own beast to tear into them with claws and fangs. She'd never needed wings; balance and agility sufficed when porting onto the backs of the soaring creatures. Others crashed into the enflamed trees or fell into more thundering beasts below when she'd used her power to remove their hearts.

What should have been a quick test of her ability had turned into a war. The creatures had been everywhere. She'd never seen anything like it in all her patrols in that Realm.

"It's okay. I'm okay," he assured her, and she breathed out as Hades tried to soothe her with energies. He'd pulled the tie from her hair and sent water over her face and into the heavy mass he'd freed before massaging in the shampoo and soap. He didn't speak much as he allowed her to remove the blood from his skin.

She felt the comedown of the adrenaline rush. The second he was clean, she planned to burn off all the rest with his body.

"I'm happy to be of service, *agapi mou*," he said with a sexy grin as his fingers trailed over her skin, making sure all the small spatters of the acid were removed from her hair and face.

Her eyes tracked over his massive body and didn't see any marks, but she was having a tough time getting rid of the images of his sizzling skin.

"I'm fine," he said with a pleased smile as she cleaned him. "I'm a God, Sacha. Any bit of damage healed nearly the second it was inflicted."

She closed her eyes, knowing full well that the beast blood inside her had taken hold. Logically she'd known he was fine. She hadn't felt any pain through the bond, but... "You need to wear more clothes into battle." She sighed. "For my sanity."

He grunted in amusement.

The Hell beast population had been severely diminished, so that was something she tried to justify in her mind. "I've never seen so many."

217

"There are now less beasts for them to send to Heaven and Tetartos Realms," he pointed out to ease her.

"Yes, but the Tria must truly want your attention. Or they hate you."

He laughed. "Likely both."

That was why she'd ported them here and not to her home in Earth Realm. She'd been too agitated to deal with the potential of possessed breaking another door.

Sacha was happy for the size of the shower, because his wings were enormous. She slipped behind him and gently caressed the feathers to clean off any hints of the blood that remained. She took her time. They were beautiful and intact, but what caught her was the way the feathers twitched and flared at her touch. "Sensitive?"

"They are now." He groaned, and something about that pleased her immensely. They were truly incredible, with thick black feathers nearly touching the ground. She eased a little as she decided to start from the top and work her way down. She wanted to explore them; they were always curling around her and twitching or flexing in his agitation. They were a part of her majestic male and she didn't want to miss any of him.

He grunted, but she heard his deep intake of breath and smiled as she lifted up on her toes. Her fingers found the tie in his hair and slowly pulled it free. He growled. "I am cutting it tomorrow."

She smiled and breathed out. "I'll do it for you." It was beautiful, but she'd rather it be a length that she could run her fingers through.

He groaned in pure pleasure as she took her time washing his hair and cleaning his wings. The desire was strong, the adrenaline trying to move them faster, but she held back. This wasn't the compulsion it had been, and she was grateful. This was something more. Her big powerful God was nearly mesmerized by her touch, and she felt warmed and empowered all at once.

"Don't mistake me, *agapi mou*. I'm caught up imagining all the things I want to do to you when you finish making sure I'm whole after that little bit of beast blood." His words held a hint of a smile, and one tilted her lips as well. She'd never smiled or laughed so much. Brianne had always managed to amuse her through the centuries, but this was different. She wasn't sure if it was because she didn't have all the power pent up inside of her, or if it was because she was truly happy for the first time, ever. She guessed it was from the latter.

He turned and bent to kiss her as water streamed all around them. She lifted up and cupped his neck, holding him to her as she fell into his kiss.

It was perfect, but she wasn't done. Her soapy fingers slid down his chest and stomach as he growled against her lips. His cock pulsed against her stomach, and she slid her fingers around it, cleaning him as she pumped. He broke the kiss on a deep groan. "Do I get to choose my reward?"

She smiled that he remembered what she'd said before they'd gone to meet Drake and P. She raised an eyebrow, curious which of all his dirty musings he'd choose. "Tell me."

"It involves more soap," he said with a wicked grin.

And with that she knew what he was thinking. She smiled up at him before turning to the soap and lathering up her hands, but his were already there. "Let me." His grin only grew wider. "I want you in

219

every way possible, but I can't pass up fucking your beautiful soapy tits right now."

Her pussy clenched at the image he projected into her mind. "Sit up on your knees on the bench," he demanded, and her breath caught as her animal preened in pleasure. The bench was deep enough for a big male to sit on, so kneeling there wouldn't be a problem, and she knew he was doing it for height. A towel appeared on the hard marble before she could get up there. When she turned to face him, she caught sight of the hard glint in his eyes.

That dominant look made her take a deep breath because it wasn't only her beast that loved him like this. Even now he was holding himself at bay, but only by a small thread. She couldn't wait for the day when he didn't feel the need to hold back. She understood, but it would be a beautiful thing to know she'd freed him just as much as he'd freed her of the remnants of her past. But, more, he'd given her back a part of herself. The power she'd wielded today was hers. Stronger because of her bond with him, but she'd felt complete and hadn't realized she'd been so cut off.

She felt the swell of his love for her, and she smiled, but looking up, she could see he'd lost his hard edge at her thoughts.

That wasn't what she wanted.

She reached out and gripped his cock and ran it over her cheek, and then she slid the head over her mouth. When he groaned, her lips curved.

His big palms soaped her swollen breasts, pinching her nipples and making her gasp as pleasure shot all the way to her toes.

"Spread your thighs wide," he commanded, and she groaned deep as she sat on her knees with her legs spread.

220

"Good."

She couldn't help bringing his cock to her lips to take a taste of the pre-come on the head. It tasted like sweet male heat and she wanted more.

"I want that sweet mouth, but first I'll mark your beautiful tits." His gaze was intent on her heavy mounds, and her head fell back when he grazed her hard nipples again.

Steam filled the room and slid over her flushed cheeks.

"Are you going to let me fuck these?"

"Yes." His hands were driving her wild, and she wondered if she could come with him playing with her hard nipples alone.

"You'll come, *thisavre mou*," he gritted out as a promise.

He moved closer, and she took one more lick of his cock before he gripped it in his hand and guided it into the valley of her breasts. It slid between them, and his palms pushed the heavy mounds together so his hot cock was cradled there as his thumbs toyed with her aching nipples.

"So damned beautiful." He groaned as he watched his cock thrust. "Arch your neck and put your arms behind you," he commanded, and she could feel the beast driving his need for her submission.

As soon as she did, his power spilled free to toy with her pussy. It probed and invaded, sucked until she was a writhing mess of need. It was like fingers and tongues were gliding over her entire body... inside her pussy. Her ass. He was everywhere at once as he thrust slowly between her breasts, and a muscle in his hard jaw twitched as he watched the slide of his cock. His thrusts grew faster and she was already close.

"Now come," he growled while his power worked her pussy as he pinched her nipples harder. She gasped and came, pulsing around invisible fingers.

She was still dizzy from it when he roared his pleasure. Warm jets of come marked her neck and breasts as he slid down between them, milking his cock with her aching flesh.

She was a limp mass when she finally came down. There were no words to say how exhausted she finally felt as he gently cleaned her skin.

She didn't even remember getting into bed moments later, but that was where she was. He'd wrapped her in the blankets and was massaging her back as her head lay against his chest. She felt replete, snuggled and happy against his warm body. He leaned down and kissed her head.

"Sleep," he whispered.

She didn't argue; her eyes slid closed as she listened to his heartbeat lulling her under.

Chapter 24

Hroarr's Palace, World of Thule

Gefn strode silently through the firelit halls of the palace toward her brother's study. Laire moved from the shadows to walk at her side. She cocked a brow at the male. He couldn't have gotten much rest, but she couldn't miss the hint of a smirk on his face. "I trust that the priestesses are in brighter moods as well." He'd spent every free moment of their stay with them.

His smile widened. "I believe so, my Goddess."

She shook her head. "And Kara still hasn't arrived?"

"No." His grin fell with a shake of his head. "Are we going to retrieve her?"

"Yes," she answered.

He nodded, but her warrior was eyeing the shadows, equally unsettled by Kara's continued absence.

Unease and something else trickled over her spine. Something wasn't right, though she could not pinpoint the exact sensation. It had started with Dagur's summons, slowly growing and changing in the last days. She wasn't sure if it was caused by the presence of their prisoner or the fact that her sister hadn't arrived as she'd indicated she would, but this morning Gefn even felt something from her beasts. They'd been more watchful and alert, and in a way she'd never felt from them.

As they neared the doorway to her brother's study, the guards swept the massive doors wide for her and her beasts. Laire halted outside the doors as she entered.

Hroarr was going through tomes as she came to stand in front of his carved wood desk.

"Is there news?" she asked.

He glanced up with a furrowed brow, obviously annoyed at whatever he'd been reading. "Nothing for you to deal with," her brother growled.

Hroarr ruled with ruthless determination and cunning unmatched in their world. That didn't mean his responsibilities were always pleasant. The burden was heavy.

"Did you find out anything from the God?" she asked, knowing he'd been in with the male several times.

Hroarr shook his head in utter disgust. "His arrogance is his own enemy."

"So he told you what you wanted to know?"

"Some. He will tell me more as the days pass," he ground out, looking less than pleased at having to deal with a male he'd already deemed weak. A rare God who hadn't deserved to reign in his world. It was written on her brother's face.

Gefn trusted her brother's instincts. The otherworldly God

didn't stand a chance against Hroarr's tactics. "What has he said thus far?"

Her brother's eyes sparked with interest as he spoke. "He thinks his people will come for him. And he said the warriors were powerful Immortals he calls Guardians."

Hroarr leaned back in his chair thoughtfully before rising.

They'd never encountered others with the ability to open portals. And if these "Guardians" had been capable of such things, they would have already come. Even if she and her brothers hadn't felt that kind of disturbance, Spa and Velspar would have.

But Immortal warriors... She was incredibly interested to see these Guardians. She was still sickened to have lost so many of their own in the battle, but she firmed her lips because they'd have been trying to protect their arrogant God. She had to see them.

Their only Immortals were the priestesses. It had been incredibly rare to find a God, much less Immortals of other worlds. At least not since before the great wars of their world so many millennia ago.

"I want to go there," she said.

"As do I," he said with a hard glint of interest in his emerald eyes before he growled, "I'm going to see what more he tells me today. You're going to retrieve Kara?"

She nodded thoughtfully. "Yes. I'm going to her palace now."

He nodded. "Good. As soon as she's here, we will see this world."

Hroarr sent power to open the doors and they strode through together. Gefn paused when Hroarr turned in the direction of their prisoner.

She took a deep breath as anticipation licked at her soul.

Chapter 25

Sacha's Paris Home, Earth Realm

Sacha and Hades reformed on the moonlit roof garden of her home. She breathed in the night air and was pleased to hear the soft sounds of the city below. This was her home, one she'd loved for years, and it was good to be back there even though she and Hades were both alert for the potential arrival of possessed. If the Tria's demons could track Hades' power, then the probability of them doing it again was strong no matter where they were in Earth Realm. And that was why they were here. It was time to test her skills with Hades' soul ability.

Bastian's voice slid into her mind. *Tasha and I will meet you at your place as soon as we can.* She'd asked to see them after patrols were over. And that meant she and Hades were doing a patrol of their own, waiting to see if the possessed would return. Drake was waiting for her call when and if that happened.

She looked down at the streetlights below before turning to her mate.

The second she did, Hades pulled her into his arms, and when she glanced up, she was taken again with how beautiful he was. She'd cut his hair, not as short as P's, because she wanted to be able to run her fingers through it. When he smiled down at her, he looked sexier than ever in his dress clothes.

His eyes took on a wicked glint as he growled, "I hope my hair grows quickly so you can cut it again."

Visions of her straddling his naked lap played in her mind. It hadn't turned out exactly the way she'd imagined the haircut would go:

"Sit on my cock, agapi mou," he commanded as he pulled her nude body between his spread thighs. She groaned when his lips captured a nipple and sucked, sending shivers over her heated skin.

"I wouldn't do that when I have scissors in my hand," she breathed. She'd barely snipped the long mass away before he had her again. He was incorrigible and she grew wetter when he moved to the other nipple, sucking it hard as his palms wandered over her back and down to her ass. She'd never manage to finish this if he didn't stop hauling her into his arms whenever she moved around him.

"I want my cock deep while you do this." His pleasure at having her care for him like this was something she'd never expected. It felt warm. Loving. And her male definitely loved having her hands on him. It seemed like a constant need to touch, to be touched, and something about it made her feel... cherished. Coveted instead of suffocated, which seemed impossible to her.

She started to smile, but his fingers slipped into her pussy from behind and she jolted with pleasure. She held the scissors away, but barely. "You need to stop unless you want to bleed. Or look ridiculous."

"Impossible," he whispered into her mind with all the arrogance she'd learned to love. "I'll stop when you spread that pussy and sit nice and still on my lap as you care for me." The words were fuzzy as her mind focused on the fingers pumping demandingly inside her as

he continued sucking on her nipple. She moaned, knowing she was going to come any second. It turned into a groan when he stopped and looked up at her with a devious smile.

She growled, "Why are you torturing me?"

"I want my hair cut while my cock's all warm and slick."

She sucked in air and glared down at his wicked grin. He was going to kill her, because she knew he was determined.

She moved to straddle him on the stool, and the second she slid down his shaft, pleasure sent shivers over her skin. Her hips moved, rocking of their own accord until he clasped them in his palms and stilled her. She glared into his mischief-filled eyes. "Stop teasing."

"You can fuck me just as soon as you've made my hair the way you want it."

Eternity. He would torment and tease her for eternity, she was sure of that now. She sucked in a breath and hoped he wasn't bald in the end, because she needed this over quickly because she was too stuffed full and aching for release.

When she finally tossed the scissors aside and slid her fingers into his hair to shake it free of the strands she'd cut, he groaned and tilted his head. And the moment he looked down, heat was burning in his eyes and then they were rocking. It was a slow build, as he never let go of her gaze. Not even when he slammed her hips up and down his cock hard and fast. The entire time he watched her with an intensity that nearly brought her to her knees. She came hard, still ensnared in his gaze.

There were so many layers to him, and she found she loved them all.

She bit back a moan when she pulled away from his arms, willing the desire away along with the images. Sacha growled at her dirty male, "Bastian will be here any moment."

He grinned wickedly. "You love me dirty."

She sighed, but avoided admitting it. She turned and looked anywhere but at him as she fought back her desire. She inhaled the scents of the expensive restaurants below and focused on that.

"I'll play nice," her male said as he tucked her under his arm.

Sacha felt the second that her son and Tasha arrived, and they turned to greet them. Tasha moved in and hugged her, and Sacha accepted the warm welcome with a smile on her face. "It's good to have you back," Tasha whispered in her ear.

"I'm happy to be back," Sacha said, feeling guilty at not seeing them sooner, but she'd needed to deal with the newness of Hades and all the arousal before seeing her son. Though apparently the arousal would never be gone, she thought as she said, "I wish it could have been sooner."

"I understand," Tasha whispered as she broke their hug and winked. Sacha shook her head and turned to her son, who she'd heard say Hades' name as a greeting.

Bastian pulled her into his arms and she was a little surprised, but immensely pleased. She circled his back and squeezed before they moved apart. "I'm glad you're okay," Bastian said. She'd been unconscious for weeks and then mated a God. She imagined Bastian had been worried even though she'd spoken to him through their bond.

"I am. I only needed some time," she said without elaborating.

As it was, her son was eyeing Hades, seeming less than pleased. When his gaze turned to her, she spoke. "I'm going to show Tasha the koi ponds inside."

She felt like they needed a moment to get over their own awkwardness. She sent her love through the link to her son. *I know it's uncomfortable for you, but I'm happy. I love you.*

She felt Bastian's mental sigh. *I love you too. We'll be fine.*

She knew Hades heard it all, and he winked at her before she turned. Everything would work out.

*****

"You're going to stay here?" Bastian bit out.

"Your mother loves it here," Hades said, cocking his brow.

"The Tria know about it now," the Kairos said without asking anything. The male was assessing him.

"And we'll see what they do next," Hades pointed out. "They tracked my power here; they could track it anywhere."

"So why not live in Tetartos Realm? They can only send Hell beasts."

"We'll stay between both." Possessed weren't anything more than pests, they might be faster and stronger, but they couldn't do anything spectacular. And a part of him was curious as to what Deimos would say they needed the Tria for. He was sure it had to do with the bastards having felt the portals open from Thule, but he wanted Deimos to say that.

231

He focused back on his female's son, allowing him to know their plans. He didn't want the male to worry for Sacha. "I'm going to have Pothos buy this building and start renovations. I plan to make this place a fortress."

Bastian eyed him. "Do I need to make threats?"

Hades grinned. "You're welcome to... I appreciate the sentiment, but I'm guessing you know it's unnecessary."

"How do I know it's unnecessary?" the Kairos calmly pointed out, his big arms crossed over his chest.

"I love her," Hades said easily. "I'd never allow anything to harm her."

The tension seemed to ease from the male. "Good. She deserves the world. She should be cherished."

He understood where the boy was coming from. He and his mother had been slaves to a God. Hades wondered if the male knew all the things his mother had done to protect him when he was young. The look in Bastian's dark eyes said he did. At least more than he should have known. More than his mother would want him to.

Hades nodded. "She is cherished. And Apollo will suffer before going back in his box," he assured the male with a hard glint in his eye.

"As long as he goes in the box after I've had my own bit of blood," Bastian said, seeming calm, but the flexing in his shoulders told another story.

The male eyed him for a moment longer and then nodded.

Hades' instincts told him that he'd been carefully assessed and that he'd been deemed at least mostly worthy of Sacha.

Chapter 26

Guardian Manor, Tetartos Realm

"Any improvement with the Goddess yet?" P asked as he strode into Drake's office. P knew that Drake had Sander and Nastia watching over Kara's recovery. It made sense because the Phoenix had proven immune to the energy power of Thule's weapons during battle. Energy power that the Goddess had apparently wielded from the palms of her hands. Sander was annoyed as hell when P saw him. They had no idea how long it would take for the Goddess to wake up, and the Phoenix hated sitting around.

"Yes," Drake growled. "Sirena says it's been significant in the last few hours."

P narrowed his eyes on the dragon. What wasn't he saying? "Is she improving too quickly, then?" They had no idea how powerful she was.

"That's the fucking question and the reason you'll be the one to see how Sacha wields that soul power of your father's. I need to be here."

P nodded while his jaw hardened. Drake was sending him to babysit his father because he was trying to keep P away from the Goddess. Hades hadn't needed any help with possessed before, and if Sacha was able to wield the same power, that meant they had shit more than covered. Not to mention they were doing nothing more than waiting for possessed to come, testing how long it would take. They could easily call P when that happened.

He eyed the dragon. "I said I wouldn't try to talk to the Goddess."

Drake eyed him. "But you want to."

"Of course I fucking do," P admitted. "But wanting and doing are two different things. You don't need to keep sending me on bullshit tasks. I'm playing nice." He didn't like it. His father and Drake were both treating him like a child. He was a millennia-old Demi-God and he'd been generally calm and intelligent for all those thousands of years. He may want to get to the bottom of this shit, but he didn't plan on doing it. Not now. That might change if Drake didn't get some fucking answers soon.

"Are you?" Drake challenged.

He crossed his arms over his chest and stared down his cousin.

Drake sighed.

"I will take your bullshit task. I will have Sacha's back because I want to see her power. But also because there's nothing else to fucking do," P growled. The Tria had been quiet since the last bloodbath in Hell Realm, and the Guardians had a lot of people patrolling even with Gregoire off with his pregnant mate. They were in a kind of anxious limbo.

Drake growled, "Fine."

He narrowed his eyes at his cousin. "What's going on?"

235

Smoke lifted from the dragon's lips. "Alyssa's pregnancy has progressed quickly in the last few days."

P stilled, not liking the sound of that. The pregnancy was supposed to last some long-assed amount of time for a Hippeus, half warhorse. "Is she okay?"

Drake growled, "Sirena says yes, but Gregoire is losing his mind. He's worried as shit for her and being a demanding motherfucker right now, and I can't blame him. I'd be a fucking asshole too. Era's double-checking all the blood tests Sirena did in order to calm G while Sirena checks the Goddess again."

"But the baby's healthy?"

"Yes. Sirena and Era both confirmed it. I called you here because I want you to let the others know without calling a meeting or blasting it through the Guardian link." He couldn't resent messenger duty; everyone needed to know this.

"What's the difference in time frame? She didn't look like she was getting bigger," P pointed out. He'd just seen her at the meeting a couple days ago and she seemed fine.

"The bump's not that big," Drake growled, his eyes sparking. P could only imagine Gregoire right now. The male hadn't been able to keep his hands off Alyssa's flat stomach before, now that there was a difference, it was probably making the male insane.

"If it's not big, there's still time," P pointed out, relaxing a little.

Drake ran a hand over his neck as he gritted out, "Her sixteen-month pregnancy just progressed to eight months. That's faster than even a human pregnancy." And she was already at least a couple months into it, if P calculated correctly.

"Shit," P said, running a hand over his head. "Do we know the sex yet?"

"Girl," Drake said with a glint in his emerald eyes. The dragon's lips twitched until he shook his head.

P smiled a little. They were about to have a baby girl Guardian. "That's going to be screwed."

"Yes, it will."

"How's Alyssa mentally dealing with everything?"

"She's strong, but worried, maybe shocked. I won't be surprised if she rips Gregoire to pieces by the end of this. She was trying to soothe him when I left. She did add that she's been getting more energy jolts in the last day."

"Son of a bitch. What happens now?" And the last time Alyssa had these energy spikes, the babe had given her a personal shield. And the young had blown up a sitting room of the manor in the process.

More smoke lifted from the dragon's lips as he growled, "Fuck if I know. It's one more thing we don't have any damned control over, and I fucking hate that. Add in the fact that I have to go pick up Adras and Ava when we're done, and I'm not sure any of us will make it through this."

Sweet fuck. Alyssa's parents? Gregoire and Adras in the same place for an extended period of time while Gregoire was losing his shit? Adras and Gregoire had been friends until G met Alyssa as a babe and knew she would someday be his. They definitely weren't close now.

"And they're all staying here at the manor?"

"Yes. Gregoire wants to be close to Sirena, and Ava and Adras insisted on being near their daughter." It was a good fucking thing Drake had built the manor so big. There were a ton of people living there now. Shit, the Lykos alone took up an entire floor.

"Are Adras and Ava having someone take over their watch in Lofodes?" The mated pair were in charge of the Immortal warriors who guarded the city of Lofodes in Tetartos Realm.

"They're making arrangements now."

P groaned. "I don't envy Alyssa or Gregoire at this point." Or Drake, for that matter.

The dragon grunted. "Neither do I."

Drake eyed him for a second. "Now, why the hell do you keep going to that lake? Do you feel something there?"

"I already told you that I don't," P ground out, knowing that Drake had been mentally stalking him. "I don't know why I go there, because it doesn't do anything but make me question why my father needed to use that lake to call Kara?" His frustration started to peak. That water felt like one more mystery in his existence.

His power licked out, and Drake's eyes narrowed when the thrall came close to the dragon. "Are you having problems with your ability?"

"Yes and no," P bit out and then added, "It's a little harder to control, but I've also never been so fucking agitated in my life."

"Have Sirena check it out," Drake demanded.

"Don't you think she has enough to do?" P bit out.

Drake glared at him. "Have her check it the fuck out."

P ran both hands over his shorn hair. "Fine."

Drake nodded and P didn't miss the hard glint in his cousin's eyes. "I know you want answers. But you already know who you are. The Creators wouldn't have made you a Guardian if they didn't see a worthy male meant to protect this world. And you're not just a Guardian... you're my brother." Drake waited for P's nod before continuing, "You had my back when I was losing my hold on the dragon because of Era. Let me have yours in this." The dragon eyed him as he added, "I'll get your answers." It was a promise.

P blew out a breath and calmed the hell down. Family. Only half of him was from this world, but that didn't mean it wasn't his true home.

"Let's go see Sirena. I need to make sure Gregoire's okay. It's only a matter of time before one of the females knocks him out for his own good." Drake sighed. "And then I'll pick up his in-laws." P knew it was an excuse, but he wasn't going to call the dragon out. Gregoire needed backup either way.

Chapter 27

Sacha's Paris Home, Earth Realm

"They'll be fine," Tasha mused as she and Sacha walked toward the patio doors, leaving Bastian and Hades to talk.

She smiled at her new daughter-in-law. "I know." And she did. She could feel exactly what Hades was doing.

Tasha's eyes twinkled when she glanced over. "You're happy." It wasn't a question.

"Yes," she said easily before asking a question of her own. "Are you doing better now that Nastia's settled?" Nastia, Tasha's twin, and Sander had still been fighting their mating when Sacha had been poisoned.

"It's a relief, but it hasn't been without its challenges." Tasha grinned. Tasha was the calmer of the two and constantly worried for her sister. It had shown in her eyes when Sacha spent time with Tasha before her mating ceremony with Bastian.

She led the female to a sitting area with a view of the door and windows showcasing a view of their males. The two were talking, and she didn't feel anything off from Hades. It would work out. Her son was calm and logical like she'd always been.

240

"I need to get to the manor to see everyone." She'd been in her own world, bonding with her mate and trying to figure out her power. But she'd also needed that time to get comfortable with herself as a mated female and how it blended with the warrior and mother she was.

"No one faults you for taking time to bond and get to understand the power inside you. Trust me. We all know what a mating means and how awkward it is. But, yes, now that it's all calmed and you're comfortable, Nastia and everyone else are itching to see you. Nastia's mostly dying to see Hades downed by a mating. She's threatened to snoop in his mind for sappiness she can call him out on."

Sacha groaned. Nastia's mental ability really was incredibly intrusive.

Hades turned and pinned her with his gaze through the window before sending, *Mental ability?*

She mentally cringed. Brianne had explained that Hades hadn't known Nastia was ferreting information from Hades' mind before he told the Guardians about Thule.

He growled, *She was in my head?*

Sacha closed her eyes and sent calming thoughts to him. He was furious and she understood, but her brethren had needed to know what he was hiding.

But she managed to get into my head?!

Yes.

She and that fucking Phoenix... He snarled. He was already

241

assessing his mental shields as a whole as well as mentally planning a punishment for all the guilty parties who'd been involved.

"Did you tell him?" Tasha cringed as they both gazed out the windows to where Hades glared furiously.

Sacha mentally cursed. "No. But we get each other's thoughts. In a way."

"Is he out for blood?" Her daughter-in-law eyed Hades. The twins were created as assassins of Gods, so while Tasha didn't look worried, she was definitely watchful.

Hades was pissed. *They're family,* she said. *You can't harm them.* He didn't seem to agree. Sacha mentally sighed, but she had no doubt she could calm him down later. His eyes shot back to hers through the glass, and she felt the spark there that took away a lot of his rage.

Not now, she sent with a raised brow. *And you're standing next to my son. So stop.*

Sacha shook her head and focused back on Tasha. "It'll be fine, but tell her *never* to do it again," she added with a cocked brow.

Tasha smiled warmly. "I will. And she really won't. She likes you too much."

Sacha smiled at that. "I like her too. Very much. She's happy?"

"So happy. I can't believe how perfect she and Sander are together. I thought they'd kill each other in the beginning, but he did it all right. He was patient when she needed it. Then he carried her out of battle when she was injured and won my heart for that. Sander challenges her. And I've never seen this side of her."

Sacha had known the two were perfect from the start, but she'd expected fireworks. The beginnings of matings weren't always pretty, but the endings could be beautiful. She knew that to be true for her son and all the other Guardians who'd found their mates. And now she loved a God. It was the last thing she'd ever imagined, but it felt incredibly right. She felt his warm touch on their link and looked out the window to see his glittering blue gaze on hers, a beautiful cocky smile on his lips.

"I'm glad you found your happily ever after," Tasha mused with a laugh before sighing. "I only wish we knew more about what was happening in our world."

"So do I." Sacha nodded and they both grew thoughtful for a moment.

It wasn't long before she felt a hint of something and stilled. "I think we have company." She and Tasha moved from the sofa out to the patio. Hades had felt it too and was immediately at her side. They'd both moved ahead of Bastian and Tasha. It wasn't that she didn't think they could handle possessed. It was that she didn't like the Tria's eyes on her children.

Hades sent her warmth, understanding her feelings.

They watched as one by one the tainted beings climbed up the fire escape to the patio. It was the same this time as the last. The nearly dozen males ranged from wearing dirty grimy clothes with big stomachs to slickly dressed businessmen. Evil wasn't limited to one station of those in the human Realm. The largest one had long blond hair slicked with grease. As he prowled forward, she could feel the sickening power as the stench of sulphur emanated from his skin. His black eyes were filled with flames.

243

She sent a mental call to P and Drake, knowing they'd want to see this.

P materialized a second later as tension filled the air.

"What do you want Deimos?" Hades demanded, sounding intentionally bored.

"Release us. You need us." The words hissed out in an eerie echoing voice. The flames in its eyes weren't as disturbing as the way the human host's skin grew more ashen as the moments passed.

When the fiend's head cocked to leer at Sacha, she felt Hades' fury ramp up, and she touched their bond to calm him.

He's doing it to get to you, she sent.

They needed Deimos to talk. But she felt Hades' need to rip away the soul and crush it in his power.

He growled, "Look. At. Me. Or I end this."

The male's eyes tracked to Hades and he sneered until Hades growled, "Speak! Why would I need you, Deimos?"

"You need all of us." This time there were the echoes of three separate voices reverberating into the skies.

All the Tria speaking at once?

It seems so, Hades ground out in their mental link.

That possessed convulsed, and then another lurched and stalked forward while the first fell. Flames licked in the new host's eyes.

The Tria were now switching bodies as one host died? Sacha

spared a glance at the downed male, his skin was paper white with blue veins showing beneath, the eyes were wide, unseeing. Dead.

She focused on the new male as Hades growled, "Doubtful. Why would I ever need you?"

They roared in fury, and Hades' lips lifted in a slight curve.

"Something is coming." The glee and maniacal laughter that slipped from foaming lips was a sound she never wanted to hear again. It seemed the other possessed were there only as conduits because they stood still as another body landed and one more stepped forward. This one wore tight leather over his drug-riddled frame.

"You're boring me, Deimos," Hades said with a bite before adding, "If you don't tell me something useful, I'll end your little playtime."

"Darkness is coming." A demented smile curved its lips, but the eyes only made it creepier. "Death is coming." It seemed all three were determined to talk at the same time.

"And that's a reason to let you out? I don't see it," her mate said, crossing his arms over his wide chest.

"We will help." The voices were determined and childlike, and that truly gave her a sick sensation in the pit of her stomach. Hades sent her energies. *I would never allow them to hurt you.*

I'm not scared. I'm disgusted.

"Why do you think something is coming?" Hades commanded, more than tired of the Tria's game.

245

Another body fell and they were running out of conduits. "We told you," they snapped.

"You told me nothing," Hades growled.

"Darkness calls. You will know soon enough. And you will free us." That sinister laughter seemed to echo out into the world as that body dropped and two possessed were left standing. No more flaming eyes. They lunged and she felt Hades mentally guiding her through how to slide the power free and into the bodies. She used it to grip the smoky black sickness beneath, and then she tore it free with a wild rending that dropped the hosts to the ground. Shrieks filled the air as Hades helped ease the hold and let the sickness go. The blackness was sucked back to Hell Realm.

She gazed up at Hades, shocked and pleased at how easy that had been, while sickened that her power had touched something so noxious.

Hades smiled down at her with pride and sent her warmth as he pulled her into his arms. She forgot for a split second that they had company.

"Father," P snapped before they kissed, and she flushed as they moved apart and faced Bastian, Tasha and P.

Tasha's eyes were twinkling, but both males looked uncomfortable until P bit out, "What the hell does darkness mean?"

*****

"I don't know," Hades growled. "If they had something real to say, they could have. Either they mean Thule, or they were playing a fucking game. I don't feel anything coming." Because the only thing left was what the Creators had cryptically warned him about. That he and the other Gods would one day be needed to protect the world.

They told you that too? Sacha asked.

Yes. But they said there would be many warnings. And that the Guardians would know to wake the Gods from sleep, and that we would know how to protect the world when the time came. They didn't say anything about releasing the Tria. So unless you feel something, Sacha, everything is fine. Could be fine for years or centuries yet.

He felt her worry and he hated it. He tucked her into his side.

We've known the same thing, but I don't like it. The Guardians have been finding their mates in quick succession and gaining power. It has to be for something, Sacha said.

Don't worry, agapi mou. If something comes, I'll take care of it.

She sighed. *You're not saying this out loud because you don't want to worry our children.*

Yes, he growled, hating that he hadn't been able to hide these thoughts from her as well. They didn't do any good. The Tria would not be aware of something he wasn't. Hades was only frustrated his parents had refused to say more.

He mentally growled, *All the Guardians have the same information, love. If the Tria felt something big, I promise you that either Drake would feel it, as the leader of the Guardians, or I would.*

They were taken out of their mental conversation when Bastian spoke. "I don't know," Bastian said. "Yes, the Tria love games, but I don't know if that's what this is." Hades noticed her son didn't say more.

Tasha shook her head. "I'm with Hades. If the Tria thought they had a shot at getting out, why not give details? Unless they're bluffing."

She's right, agapi mou. He tried to soothe her. Worrying about it wouldn't help anything.

I know, she sent.

P growled, "I'm going to tell Drake what happened, and we'll go from there."

"Why wasn't he here?" Hades demanded.

"Because Alyssa's pregnancy is progressing extremely fast. He's at the manor."

Sacha stilled before asking, "Is she okay?"

"Yes. She's fine and so is the baby. Everyone is healthy." P nodded.

Hades knew his female couldn't get the thoughts of "darkness coming" out of her mind as Pothos explained the rest about the pregnant female.

By the time the others left, he was dying to ease her worry.

Chapter 28

Hroarr's Palace, World of Thule

Gefn pulled power from deep inside her soul, and the watery portal opened before them. She breathed deep of the mountain air coming through from the other side. No one else would scent or feel the breeze on their skin, but she could, and it was always freeing.

"Give me a moment, my Goddess," Laire said as he stepped ahead of her. Her warrior never allowed her to enter a portal ahead of him. It didn't matter to her guard that Spa and Velspar held vast powers and instincts that would never allow her to step into danger.

She smiled to herself at Laire's behavior and felt a pang in her heart. One day he would leave her just as all his ancestors had before him. It was cold comfort that his line had at least survived to this point, but of them all, she valued Laire's friendship the most.

She shook off the morose thoughts. They'd been coming more often since Dagur had condemned so many of Hroarr's warriors to death.

Spa and Velspar yowled, and she frowned at the rare noise from the cats as they stepped ahead of her through the open portal. She glided behind them through the thick air to the other side. Her booted feet landed on stepping stones set just inside in the mountain lake that lay in front of the ivy-covered palace of her sister. The second the portal closed, she knew something wasn't right.

One of her sister's female servants rushed to the edge of the water where Laire was awaiting Gefn's presence. With a thought she was there, becoming one with the winds to stand in front of the frantic female. "What is it?" she asked Trima. The female's bright blue eyes were wide and the freckles on her nose and cheeks stood out against her pale skin. "Our Goddess Kara and her warriors went through a portal and have not returned."

Gefn's heart stilled. "When?"

Trima took a deep breath before answering. "Over a week ago. I sent messengers to Hroarr's palace on the fastest steeds."

Gefn cursed under her breath. The riders likely wouldn't make it to her brother's home for days yet.

The female ran a hand over her wild curls. Gefn had never seen her anything but calm and collected, but a week of worrying over her mistress would have made for sleepless nights. "Did she give any indication where she was going?"

"No, my lady. But she handed me her ring before going through and said to give it to you or your brothers if she wasn't back within the hour." The female slipped a shaky hand into a pocket of the long dress and lifted out the bulky ring set with a blue stone. A long gold chain dangled from the familiar jewelry. Kara had never taken it off, had always worn it against her chest. Her cold sibling had once said that the ring had been Agnarr's, one of their long-dead brothers. Gefn knew that the two had been close until his death, but what did any of that mean now? Why take off the necklace before opening a portal? And why take her warriors unless she'd had cause to be worried?

Gefn balled her fists, cursing her sister for not telling Trima what she'd been doing. If she'd taken off the ring, she'd done it for a reason. Her sister was too damned arrogant.

She was sure that Kara and Dagur would one day drive her mad.

She needed to get back to Hroarr's palace. If the ring had the answers to her sister's location, Dagur would figure it out. He was the most skilled in spells.

Other servants flowed from the palace keep, all bearing worried faces. "I will find her," she assured her as she stepped back to pull her power in anticipation of opening another portal.

Spa and Velspar yowled again before prowling in the opposite direction. Both creatures shot golden glances back at her, and she knew they wanted her to follow. She hoped they'd lead her to a clue to finding her sister. Gefn set off behind them as the stone warmed against her palm. "Stay here," she commanded the servants. "I will be back."

Laire moved to follow, and the cats turned in unison to hiss at her warrior.

"My Goddess?" Laire queried, surprised. They'd never done anything like that to Laire, they liked the warrior. Whatever they wanted her to see, it was to be done alone.

"I will be right back. Make sure the servants are okay." She gave him a look and then assured him, "I'm not helpless, Laire, and you know they'd never allow me to come to harm. I'll be back in a moment." She added a smile and headed in the direction of the massive garden maze behind her beasts.

251

Chapter 29

Hades' Island, Tetartos Realm

Hades pulled his naked female into his arms. Her skin was still warm and supple from the shower. "Better, *agapi mou*?" He'd done his best to ease her worry about the fate of the world, but he knew it was still in her mind.

"I know you're right. Something could happen in days or centuries," she agreed.

"And nothing ever said the world would end. The Creators only said that the Gods would be needed."

She seemed to ease at that. "And if these are my last days, I plan to make them all special," she said with determination.

"They're not the last. I promise I will keep the world safe. I'll keep you safe," he growled before leaning down to nuzzle her neck.

"You always smell edible," he growled.

Her hands lifted to his hair, and without a thought he moved his head into her tunneling fingers, closing his eyes at the pleasure of her touch.

Aphrodite had been right, having a soul bond seemed to make

everything more incredible, more intense. Each touch was more powerful than anything before. And the desire to care for and please his female gave him more joy than anything he'd ever experienced. Their bond was addictive. And nothing could take it from him. He would make sure the world was protected when he was needed.

He lifted her up into his arms and carried her toward the patio doors.

Her arms slipped around his neck and held him as she smiled. "Where are we going?"

"To talk, *agapi mou.*"

"Outside?" she asked as he sent a thought out to span the doors wide.

He smiled. "Yes." They'd come back to the island because both wanted some quiet after dealing with the possessed. But he knew his female liked open spaces, so he would talk with her as the sun set over the water.

He retracted his wings and sat beside the table out there with her snuggled in his lap, her legs over the arm of the chair as his other held her back. Her dark eyes twinkled as she watched him.

"What is it?" she asked.

He grinned down into her beautiful face. "I want to know if you'd like a mating ceremony, *thisavre mou?*"

*****

So that was what Hades and Bastian had been talking about before the possessed arrived. Sacha had been trying hard not to focus on his emotions, thoughts, while speaking to Tasha. She wondered if her son worried that she'd been cheated out of something. That made her smile. Her male would never allow her to feel as if she'd missed anything.

With a soft smile she answered simply, "No." She wouldn't want her sisters fussing with her, and she'd never enjoyed being made the center of attention. None of that was comfortable for her.

He assessed her closely, and her heart truly felt like it would swell out of her chest. He loved her so deeply that it was there inside their connected souls. It was beautiful. And she planned to live her life enjoying every moment with him.

"The world is yours for the asking, Sacha. You realize that?"

She did and let out a soft sigh as she gazed at the beauty of her male. He was everything a male should be: sexy, immensely strong, amusing, and unapologetically loving.

His grin widened. "As much as I love that you see all of my colossal attributes, our sharing of emotions will always make it difficult to surprise you, *agapi mou*."

"I'm not overly fond of surprises," she said with a cocked brow. And she wasn't. It seemed her son had filled his mind with the notion that she needed more than what they had. She was happy and she couldn't think of anything else she'd want.

"What about marking my chest in your tradition?"

She'd known it was coming, but that didn't prepare her for the impact of the words from his lips. "You would want that?" Hades rarely wore a shirt, and if he took the traditional mark of a mated male, it would be visible for all to see.

"This surprises you?" he said, grinning wickedly.

She couldn't help returning the smile. He brought a finger up to graze the corner of her lips. "I like this," he growled.

Her smile widened before she nipped at his thumb. "You know the mark would cover your entire chest?" she pointed out, but she didn't know why she asked because she didn't want him to be marked like that.

"You don't?" he said with a raised brow.

"No." She thought as she eyed him. Yes, a part of her wanted the world to know he was hers, but at the same time, she didn't want him to bear the same mark as so many others.

"What mark would you like, *agapi mou*?" He was serious.

She considered it for long moments as the horizon lit with pink and orange.

Her mind turned it over, and she kept picturing the tattooed wings on Brianne's back. They were done to mostly match her very real wings. Sacha had always thought them stunning.

And since Hades had so easily chosen to live in the human Realm with her, he'd have to hide his wings most of the time. Same for patrolling possessed anywhere in Earth Realm. That meant at least part of the time that sexy part of him would be secreted away. If he was willing to take a mark on his body, she'd want him to have black wings on his back with the mating symbol secreted there for her to know.

He growled, "I like this." His eyes flashed a beautiful bright sapphire.

Now that she was considering it, she very much wanted some of her own. Black like his real wings. She'd never have a set of her own. It was something Hades had been born with, not a beast half to manifest; it was a part of him. She pictured them. Hers more delicate than what his would be.

Taking the mark would be an erotic experience, and that sent her thoughts to what he'd been doing to her body in the hours they'd been home.

Her pussy slicked at the sound of his growl and brought shivers over her skin. She remembered that sound vibrating through her entire body as he'd growled against her shoulder blades. She groaned as images of him sliding into her from behind replayed in her mind. She'd had him every possible way, and her skin flushed at how he couldn't seem to get enough. When he'd fitted that massive cock into her ass, it was like he'd sent them both to another level of wild pleasure. He'd been so animalistic at the idea of having taken every inch of her body.

His fingers slid between her thighs. "I like these thoughts."

The second he slid a finger inside, she nearly came. They might not be in a frenzy of lust, but there was no way either would ever get enough of this.

"Never," he growled. "I think we need a replay of my haircut."

A gasp escaped as she spread her thighs wider over the chair. She bowed against his strong forearm as she grinded her pussy on his fingers, loving the slide as he invaded her. She clamped down in bliss.

"That's it. Come all over my fingers before I make you sit nice and still and mark my skin."

"How?" she groaned, meaning the marking. A mating mark was made with healing power so that it was truly permanent. A normal tattoo would be gone if the skin was ever damaged and the new flesh regenerated.

He sent power to toy with her nipples and clit so his pumping fingers weren't the only things tormenting her. She cried out into the darkening sky, and when she opened her eyes, she saw him staring down at her with hunger in his eyes. "I'll never tire of watching you come. It's fucking perfect."

She groaned when his fingers slipped free and he brought them to her lips. "This is ambrosia, *agapi mou*. There is nothing sweeter."

She licked his fingers as he growled. Less than a second later they were seated on the same stool she'd used to cut his hair.

"Healing is not my strongest ability, but it is sufficient for this," he ground out. She felt the extent of his need, not only in the throbbing of his cock, but in her entire being. "Now spread wide and take your God."

She groaned because she couldn't wait. With a thought she was straddling his hips and sliding down his hot shaft.

"Now sit still. I want it to come out the way you like, *agapi mou*." He took her lips in a fleeting kiss as he wrapped her hands around his back. When he broke the kiss, he gazed into her eyes and spoke the vows of a mated male in the old language. She couldn't breathe at the sound of his voice in her mind and on her lips as he promised to love and cherish her through all eternity. He hadn't added the word about it being in blood because they'd never need to blood bond, but she still felt something beautiful open up inside her at the words.

Now mark me as you will, he said in her mind as he showed her how to channel the power. When it flowed out from her palms, it wrenched a deep groan from his lips. She used her mind's eye and the dips of his body to guide her hands and the power she pulled to make black sweeping marks. A tribal drawing of his wings that led to his ass.

She wasn't sure how long it was taking as his muscles twitched and the blinding pleasure of the act made his cock pulse and throb inside her. Gasps left her lips as her heart pounded in her chest. She was panting by the time she slid her palms back up to add a small mark of a mated male in white along the thick black lines forming the tops of the wings. The twin serpents, attached by tails in the sideways eight that symbolized their dual eternities.

She sucked in a deep breath when it was done, but it was like something unleashed inside him. He was wild with need when his wings erupted from his back and they soared into the skies. She gasped as she cupped his neck and gripped his hips with her thighs. She heard the gusts created by his wings thrashing through the air to take them high. Shocking pleasure set her body on fire as her male slammed her up and down his cock with a fierceness she'd yet to see from him. Her lips met his neck, but the movements were too wild. She glanced at the moonlit sea below as her stomach fluttered at flying with him. He tilted his head back for her, and the tendons of his neck stretched and she couldn't help but nip his skin as he drove them on. He was hitting her so deep in a spot that made her dizzy. "Take all of me. Every ounce of come, *thisavre mou.*"

She moaned in agreement.

"You rule me, Sacha." He growled as she kissed his neck again. All the noise of his powerful wings taking them higher drowned out the sounds of her wet pussy smacking harder on his cock. Her hard nipples were raking down his chest every time he slammed her down as he possessed her. He grunted and growled as he took her hard, and she whimpered at how good it was. Wind whipped over her heated skin, but nothing could cool her.

"Come. I want your juices running down my thighs." He growled and she cried out as she clenched and throbbed. He roared his pleasure to the skies and she felt the hot come pump deep inside her. Her head fell against his chest and she realized that they'd evened out. His powerful wings held them at the same distance in the air even as his breathing evened out. He kissed her head and she peered up at his beautiful face before looking down at the island seemingly miles below.

She gazed at him in awe. The world was so incredibly beautiful this high in the sky. "Coming and flying at the same time?" she mused. That seemed incredibly impressive. She felt his chest rock against her breasts as he chuckled.

"You've only seen some of my talents, Sacha."

She shook her head. "The real test of skill will be to see if you can mark my back with the same wings while we're up here," she said in challenge.

His eyes flashed and she felt his cock twitch. "I'll give you anything you ask for."

She warmed with happiness as she gazed up at him and whispered, "I love you."

She felt his pleasure at her words as he uttered ones of his own, "And I you."

Chapter 30

Mountain Lake, Earth Realm

P ran a hand over his head as he gazed out to the moonlit
water. He'd needed a moment of quiet and calm after
informing Drake about what happened with the possessed. Drake
hadn't been happy when he'd shared what the Tria had said, and he
felt the dragon's agitation. It hadn't sat well with P either. There
seemed to be nothing but unknowns, and they were forced to wait
for things to play out.

That wasn't the only reason for his tension. He knew that at any
moment the Goddess could awaken. If Sander was still on guard
duty, the Phoenix would tell him immediately, but he was still...
waiting.

P, Sirena sent through his mind.

Is everything okay? he asked the healer, automatically alert.

*Yes. I just forgot to tell you that your blood work didn't show
anything out of sorts. Everything shows as it always has, including
your power levels.* The healer sounded exhausted. He must be as well
if he'd forgotten she'd even taken his blood. So much had happened
in the last hours.

Are you okay? he asked her.

I'm fine. Era's helping, but there's a lot going on. I'm checking the Goddess now. She paused for a second before adding, *She's not awake, so you can relax.*

Is there any more news on Alyssa?

No, but her parents are here, and she just snapped at both her father and Gregoire to "Get the hell over their bullshit." Sirena mentally chuckled. *When she cracked the whip on their brooding and sniping, I'm not sure her father knew what to say. They're all tense and worried, and I know it doesn't help that I don't have any answers for them. The only good part is the baby seems perfectly healthy... powerful as hell, but healthy.*

If you need me to play referee, just call. His ability might be of use calming them all. They'd be angry afterward, but he'd do it to help ease Alyssa's mind.

Adras calmed way down when I explained that it wasn't good for the baby to upset Alyssa. We should be okay for a while. She sighed.

Good. When was the last time you slept and refueled your energies?

Don't start, P, she growled. *How are you doing?*

Nice subject change, he countered. He and Drake had always tried to get her to rest, but in the last months it had been impossible. Now that she had help, he hoped she'd actually use it.

I'm going to get energies right now, she snapped, and her irritation at being forced from her domain was in each word. He shook his head.

Okay. And please try to let Era help more. She needs to help as much as you need a break.

Noted. But you know as well as I do that this is the worst possible time for any breaks, she growled. It was, but even having Era cover her for a few hours would be worth it, and he was just about to say as much when she snapped, *Your turn.*

He sighed. *I'm fine. Only frustrated.*

I understand. You know you can talk to me.

I do. And I would if I had anything to say. She'd been a sister to him and Drake since well before they'd all become Guardians. *Now get some energy and let me know if I can help with anything.*

I will. She sent a wave of affection that warmed him before the connection was cut.

He rolled his neck and took a breath of the cool mountain air. He needed to think of anything other than the answers he hoped Drake would learn from the Goddess.

His mind went back to the possessed. The entire display had been eerie, and the scent of sulphur was still in his lungs. Neither he nor Drake knew what to do about it. They could buy into what his father thought about it being something to do with Thule or some game, but in the end it was one more unknown.

The Creators had cryptically told them that the Gods would one day be needed on this world. With all the shit happening with Thule, they still weren't certain if *this* was that time or if something else was coming.

A flash of something near the water caught his eye. He frowned and ported to the edge to see what was there. The surface wasn't smooth for the first time. Ripples moved over the usually glassy waters, and when he looked down, he saw a lighter blue liquid shimmering along the surface.

Before he could truly focus, his entire body was being sucked down through something watery but not wet. He violently attempted to teleport through the thick air, but it held him for long seconds before he was dropped onto hard stone in a crouch. His wings had erupted from his body in the process and he breathed out as he scanned his surroundings. Ivy-covered stone and a fountain caught his eyes before they landed on brown leather boots and pants that hugged long feminine legs.

His eyes shot up as he stood to his full height, sucking in a deep breath. He growled deep.

That scent. It was sweet and sultry.

Female.

His.

Brilliant emerald eyes were set into the most beautiful face he'd ever seen. Soft pouty lips were open, and long pale hair whispered through the winds. The only thing stopping him from moving forward were the two giant black lynx staring at him with intelligent golden eyes.

The vibrations of their loud purrs dulled out almost everything but the hard thumping of his heart. The only other thing to make it through the thrall was the rush of her shocked breathing as she glanced at the animals who'd stepped back from her side.

Two moons were dim against the bright blue skies. The warrior in him assessed that they were the only two people there, but his eyes never truly left hers. He couldn't tear them away, and he felt his body move and couldn't seem to control the pull to her.

Was this how a mating frenzy truly started? Because there was no doubt in his mind that she belonged to him. His cock beat against the zipper of his jeans.

He was in Thule, he felt it in his soul, and he had no doubt in his mind that the powerful female before him was a Goddess. Not just a Goddess.

His Goddess.

He growled again, trying to fight the thrall or he'd end up fucking mauled. At the moment he wondered if one touch wouldn't be worth it.

He still had enough thought to feel for the connections to Drake and the others. His father. They were all there, but he didn't reach out. Not yet.

"Did you call me here?" He spoke in the old language of the Creators, and she sucked in a breath.

Power weaved all around her. Elemental and beautiful. Enthralling.

*****

Gefn was faced by the impossible. She couldn't speak nor think as her eyes trailed over the beautiful male before her. He was bare to the waist, and his chest and stomach seemed chiseled by the Creators themselves. Massive ebony wings flexed from his back, outstretched and entrancing. His pure barbaric beauty called to every

264

cell in her being and made her ache in ways she'd never expected to feel. Her nipples ached against her confining leather shirt. Liquid heated between her thighs as she glanced at the hard shaft pushing against his leggings. Her own leathers felt too confining. She wanted them off. She should be on guard, but her beasts had brought him to her and they'd moved back. He wasn't a threat to her safety. The ring in her hands nearly burned now and she didn't care as she took in the rest of him. There were black things in his ears, and his thick muscled arms had markings over them. His black hair was nearly shaved off, and she wondered what it would feel like under her palms.

He stared at her with eyes the brightest of blue, and when he growled, it sent shivers racing through her body.

Though it was the purring of her beasts that shocked her. They'd never done such a thing. Winds gusted around her and her power surged uncontrollably as she was whirled away in the currents until she found herself caught up in those massive arms.

She moaned at the feel of his chest against her.

*****

The second the Goddess landed in his arms, he was lost. He growled deep at her scent, and nothing could stop him from tasting her lips, not when she'd ended up in his arms. Not even the fucking potential of a mauling. Her small hands were on his chest, and every muscle constricted in pleasure so wild he was caught up in it.

P took his female's lips like a male starved. He wanted to claim so much more and he would. He mentally snarled "mine" in his mind over and over as he tasted the sweetness of her lips. Her mouth opened on a gasp, and his tongue delved in to plunder as his hands

265

trailed over her small body and hauled her flush against his hard cock. She softened against him, and he could feel her heartbeat and smell the sweet scent of her getting slick. His fingers fisted in her hair as his other hand palmed her ass. It was intoxicating. He couldn't get her close enough. His mind was gone as he lifted her up. Her legs wrapped around his waist and he rode her heat up and down his denim-clad cock.

He felt something try to break through, a feeling. Nothing mattered but the soft female in his arms. His father and Drake called to him, but it felt far away, unreal. He inhaled her scent and reveled in her soft touch. One of her hands was fisted on his chest as the other roamed all over his face and shoulders as she kissed him back with the need sucking them both under.

The warning sound of the cats hissing and a male's voice invaded his mind, and he reacted. Pulled from his thrall, he spun her behind him and growled at the newcomer. A blond male with long hair and wearing a kilt was holding a golden energy staff pointed at him.

The cats grew louder as his female spoke behind him. It was another language, but the words seemed to move and form in his mind until he understood their meaning. She was telling the male to stand down. This male was her warrior.

And then he heard his father's voice a little clearer. He felt power pulling at his soul, trying to take him away. Something was happening.

He was jarred at the possibility of danger to the Realms.

He felt the call to his world and was ripped into the air. Porting away against his will.

266

Chapter 31

Hades' Island, Tetartos Realm

Sacha and Hades were getting back to the ground when she felt a wave of something. Unease? Premonition? She looked up at Hades, knowing that he'd been hit with it too. His blue eyes narrowed, and she knew he was searching out his connection to P. The Guardian's location wasn't showing. Why would P hide where he was? Sacha searched for Sander, who she'd heard was guarding the Goddess of Thule, as Hades demanded, *Pothos, where are you?*

Everyone get the hell to the manor now, Drake snarled through the Guardian link, and she rushed to get dressed. Both ported to the war room a second later as Hades growled again through the link to his son.

There was no answer for strained moments as she searched the room. Guardians and mates were everywhere. No P. And Sander, Nastia, Sirena and Alyssa and Gregoire were all missing as well, but that made sense. Era was standing beside the dragon, and this first sight showed Sacha the wild power the female leashed behind those golden eyes.

"Drake, where is my son?" Hades bit out, and she watched Drake look off and knew he was doing what Hades already had: he was searching for P.

Sacha's breathing stilled as she waited tense seconds before Drake snarled to the room at large. "P's not fucking answering, and he's off grid. Does anyone know where he is?" Drake demanded as Hades concentrated, and she could feel her mate's worry as he pulled power to search out his son's soul.

Drake growled at Hades, "We're about to have fucking company. I can feel it. We need to get to that fucking lake, P was there not long ago."

There was a flurry of movement as Drake commanded everyone. "Tasha and Bastian in mist. Vane and Brianne with me, Era, Hades, and Sacha. The rest of you stay back."

Sacha trailed her mate to the lake Drake was talking about. It was a rippling deep blue in the northern lands of Earth Realm. They were high in the mountains, and she breathed in the cool midday air as snow flurries fluttered to the ground. She was lending power to her mate. Searching for P's soul through the Realms and outward, he continued to demand his son speak as worry thrummed through him and into her. P was a powerful warrior. "His link is still there. He's okay," she assured her male.

Chapter 32

Mountain Lake, Earth Realm

P felt like he was falling through a void and it kept going. By the time he reformed, his head pounded and his limbs were like fucking Jell-O. And he was back at the lake on Earth Realm. He sucked in the mountain air as his heart slammed into his chest. He'd just ported from another world.

At least the pain killed the edge of his arousal. But it was still fucking intense. His cock hurt and he still had her taste in his mouth. His body was on fire with his need for his mate and he didn't even know her name.

"Where were you?" his father demanded above him. He was crouched on the ground? He tried to breathe, still unable to understand up from down. "What's wrong?" His father gripped his arm, helping him up with worried eyes. Hades' power slid over him, assessing him for damage as he had when P had been but a boy.

"I'm fine." He swore under his breath. He was anything but fine. He felt ripped apart and he was trying to get it together, but they needed to know what happened. "I was pulled into Thule."

His father's growl of fury was the only sound on the tense lakefront. P stood and faced his father's anger. "I didn't intend it." He took another breath. "But I just met my mate there, and I'm going

269

back for her, so we need to figure this shit out."

P was acutely aware of Drake, Era, Sacha, Brianne and Vane. He even felt Bastian and Tasha. It was almost as if he could feel the air molecules themselves. As if they were something he could manipulate in a way that he'd never done before. Power surged through him, but he clenched his teeth, because he *needed*.

"You will never return there!" His father's voice boomed with the power flooding the area around them. His wings were extended and flexing.

Before P could do or say anything, the air charged and he knew.

A portal was opening.

*****

The second the air charged, warning them of a portal being opened, Hades sent a furious wave of power that forcibly ported his powerful Guardian son to the island in Tetartos. Sacha felt the sheer storm of power her mate had unleashed to get his son safely away. And he hadn't just sent P there, Hades was caging P, confining the male in the other Realm.

Her heart felt as if it would break for them both. If P had found his mate in Thule, there was no stopping it.

Yes, there is, Hades growled in the link.

"What the fuck just happened?" Drake snarled.

"I sent him to the island. Which is where he'll stay." The sheer amount of power the furious mated God could release would have been frightening if Sacha hadn't known it was coming from the immense strength of a father's love and fear.

Brianne started to talk, and Sacha shook her head. He wouldn't hear it. She knew that. They all faced the portal as P bit out, *Father, do not make me fucking fight you.* He flashed an image of a beautiful blonde female. *She is mine. Now let the fuck go.*

She sent calming energies to her male. *If he has a mate, this could hurt him.*

Hades snapped, *If his female is from Thule, she WILL hurt him.*

"Drake?" Sacha sent the dragon the image of P's female as golden staffs of the dragon started through the watery air and she assessed any powers she could use to contain the newcomers.

The dragon growled. "Fuck. We will remove their weapons. Contain, don't kill," he commanded the others.

P released a burst of his unique thrall-like ability through the bond, and Sacha and Hades jolted. It was enough to relax Hades' iron hold on his son. Her male roared, but it was too late. Already P was standing in front of them, unleashing his hidden ability to calm while placing himself in front of the portal with his wings outstretched.

Everything happened in the blink of an eye.

Era and Drake expelled a barrage of power that ripped away the warriors' weapons before they'd fully stepped through.

Three incredibly powerful beings and two ancient-looking giant black lynx were between the warriors, and Sacha felt the combined power whipping the elements to near hurricane force.

They stood over the rippling water of the lake. P's beautiful female stood beside two males. One massive bare-chested one in a kilt with golden eyes and brown hair, and the other, the most powerful of the three, stood in the center. The center male had Hades' height and bulk, with wavy black hair pulled back and a short dark beard. His green eyes were hard and commanding. He reminded her of a darker version of Drake.

Before anything else could happen, the two black lynx prowled ahead of them and rent the skies with a wild earsplitting roar. It wasn't just noise, it was filled with a power so strong and pure it rocked the ground beneath their feet. It was enough to drop Bastian and Tasha from mist as it left them all immobile. And she was furious and worry filled at the sight of her son vulnerable to whatever they were facing.

Hades roared his fury as his wings flexed as he fought to break the hold.

The new warriors had dropped to their knees as if by compulsion. And Sacha felt the same pull, but she'd never kneel. She and Hades fought to move, and fear rocked her for a moment before easing away as the cats' golden gaze set on hers. There was something she couldn't place, but it was ancient and intelligent. The female's wide eyes settled on P without leaving as the other males stared at the beasts they'd brought through.

The dark male eyed the cats.

Both sides seemed to have been equally caught, but the others weren't fighting it like the Guardians and Hades were.

She watched as the felines separated, one moving to sit directly in front of P and the other prowling in front of the Goddess, and only then did the power holding them finally ease some. The dark male eyed the beast in front of P before looking up at Hades' son, assessing them before he snarled a command in the old language of the Creators, "It's time we speak instead of fight."

Chapter 33

Tria's Prison, Hell Realm

"He has no idea." Than's sinister cackle echoed off the dank cavern walls of their prison.

Anguished cries of the dead filled Deimos' soul with such supreme pleasure his cock hardened, but the vision of Hades' furious face only made it stiffen more. Ah, the God's female, he smacked his lips, she would know the sweet agony of their cocks soon enough.

"No. He doesn't feel it." He laughed as he faced his brothers, both identical versions of himself. Their pale almost gray skin and black eyes lit with flames. He rolled his massive shoulders and tilted his head back to enjoy the scent of pain and suffering. It was like mother's milk to them, and he fed deeply on it as his brothers fucked their toys ruthlessly. The screeches and anguished cries of the violated creatures only drove them on and filled their dark souls with energy, topping up the power they would be using soon enough.

"He is weak. They will have no choice but to free us!" Phobos' glee-filled tone made Deimos smile.

Hades, Aphrodite and Athena couldn't have given them a more perfect prison. Their power had only strengthened and adapted to new extremes in the last millennia. A few decades had been all it had taken to force the flow of dark souls directly into their space. They now had a never-ending fountain of pain to feed from after they'd learned just what they could do with those souls.

And now pure beautiful darkness was coming for this world. His lips stretched into a terrifying rictus of a smile.

Hades would free them whether he wanted to or not. When the darkness finally came and the other Gods were released, it would only require one death… Hades, Aphrodite or Athena would fall, and one crack to their prison was all it would take to reign supreme in the world.

Soon.

A creature screamed in pain as Deimos lashed out, grabbing it by its throat.

But first, he would feast.

Series Glossary of Terms and Characters - For Reference:

Agnarr – God of the world Thule, long ago ally of Hades

Ailouros – Immortal race of half felines, known as the warrior class, strong and fast

Akanthodis – Hell creature with spines all over its body and four eyes

Aletheia – Immortal race with enhanced mental abilities and power within their fluids, can take blood memories, strong telepathy, the race that spawned the vampire myth

Alex – AKA Alexandra, Demi-Goddess daughter of Athena, sister to Vane and Erik, mate to Uri

Alyssa – Hippeus (half warhorse), daughter of Adras and Ava, mate to Gregoire

Aphrodite – Sleeping Goddess, one of the three good Deities, mother to Drake

Apollo – God who experimented with the Immortal races, adding animal DNA to create the perfect army against his siblings

Ares – Sleeping God and father of the Tria

Artemis – Sleeping Goddess and mother of the Tria

Astrid – Kairos, friend of Ileana's dead parents, business partner to Rain and Alyssa

Athena – Sleeping Goddess – One of only three Gods that were good and didn't feed off dark energies and become mad, mother of Alex, Vane and Erik, mate to Niall

Bastian – AKA Sebastian, Kairos (teleporter), Guardian of the Realms, diplomat for the Guardians within Tetartos Realm, mated to Natasha (Tasha)

Brianne – Geraki (half ancient bird of prey), Guardian of the Realms, hybrid, mated to Vane

Brigitte – Mageia who managed Natasha and Nastia erotic club in Earth Realm

Charybdis – Immortal abused by Poseidon and then sold and experimented on in Apollo's labs, she gave a portion of her life force to create the mating spell, aka mating curse, so that no Immortal could breed with any other than their destined mate.

Conn – Lykos (half wolf), Guardian of the Realms, mated to Dacia

Creators – The two almighty beings that birthed the Gods, created the Immortals and planted the seeds of humanity

Cyril – Demi-God son of Apollo, Siren/healer, dead bad guy

Dacia – Lykos, mated to Conn

Deleastis Rod – A spelled artifact that was used by Apollo to lure Immortals to him

Demeter – Sleeping Goddess

Demi-Gods or Goddesses – Those born to a God or Goddess

Dorian – Nereid, Guardian of the Realms, mated to Rain

Drake – AKA Draken, Demi-God dragon, leader of the Guardians of the Realms, son of Aphrodite and her Immortal dragon mate Ladon

Efcharistisi – City in Tetartos Realm

Eir – Long dead priestess of Thule, P's mother

Elizabeth – Aletheia – evil female who found a way to free Apollo

Emfanisi – Yearly, week-long event where Immortals and Mageia of age go to find mates

Era – AKA Delia, powerful female experimented on by Cyril, mated to Drake

Erik – Demi-God son of Athena, Ailouros (half-lion), Vane's twin, Alex's younger brother, mated to Sam

Geraki – Immortal race of half bird of prey, power with air

Gregoire – Hippeus (half warhorse), Guardian of the Realms, mate to Alyssa

Guardians – Twelve warriors of different Immortal races chosen by the Creators to watch over the four Realms of the world.

Hades – One of the three good Gods, father to P (Pothos)

Hagen – Lykos, Dacia's eldest brother

Havoc – Uri and Alex's pet hellhound that was rescued as a pup and bonded to Uri

Healers – AKA Sirens, Immortal race, power over the body, ability with their voices

Hellhounds – Black hounds blood bonded to the Tria in Hell Realm

Hephaistos – Sleeping God

Hera – Sleeping Goddess

Hermes – Sleeping God and Apollo's partner in the experimentation and breeding of Immortals for their army

Hippeus – Immortal race of half warhorses, power over earth

Ileana – Ailouros (liger), Jax's mate

Jax – AKA Ajax, Ailouros (half tiger), Guardian of the Realms

Kairos – Immortal race whose primary power is teleportation

Kara – Goddess of Thule, imprisoned by the Guardians after her attempt to take Hades

Ladon – Immortal dragon, mate to Aphrodite, father of Drake, friend of Jax

Limni – City in Tetartos Realm

Lofodes – City in Tetartos Realm

Lykos – Immortal half wolf with the power of telekinesis

Mageia – Evolved humans, mortals compatible to be an Immortal's mate, have abilities with one of the four elements; air, fire, water, or earth.

Mates – Each Immortal has a rare and destined mate, their powers meld and they become stronger pairs that are able to procreate, usually after a decade.

Mating Curse – A spell cast in Apollo's Immortal breeding labs that ensured the God wouldn't be able to use them to continue creating his army. Charybdis cast the spell using a portion of her life force and now Immortals can only procreate with their destined mates.

Mating Frenzy – Starts when an Immortal comes into contact with their destined mate, a sexual frenzy that continues through to the bonding/mating ceremonies.

Mia – Dacia's sister, Lykos

Nastia – AKA Chaos, Immortal created by Apollo, twin to Natasha

Natasha – AKA Tasha and Nemesis, Immortal created by Apollo, Nastia's twin

Nereid – Immortal race of mercreatures, power over water

Ofioeidis – Huge serpent hell beasts, hardest to kill out of all the hell creatures

Ophiotaurus – Hell beast with the head of a bull and tail of a snake

Ouranos – City in Tetartos Realm

P – AKA Pothos, Guardian of the Realms, Son of Hades, second to Drake

Phoenix – Immortal race with ability over fire

Poseidon – Sleeping God

Rain – Mageia, destined mate to Dorian, best friend of Alyssa

Realms – Four Realms of Earth; Earth - where humanity exists, Heaven - where good and neutral souls go to be reincarnated, Hell - where the Tria were banished and evil souls are sent, Tetartos – Realm of beasts – where the Immortals were exiled by the Creators

Sacha – Kairos (teleporter), Guardian of the Realms, diplomat for the Guardians within Tetartos Realm, Bastian's mother

Sam – AKA Samantha Palmer, mated to Erik, power over metal, Mageia/Ailouros

Sander – Phoenix, Guardian of the Realms

Sirena – Siren (healer), Guardian of the Realms, primarily works to find mates for Immortals in Tetartos

Tetartos Realm – The Immortal exile Realm, once known as the Realm of Beasts

Thalassa – City in Tetartos Realm, where the Lykos clans live

Thule – Once thought a mythical land to the north, it is a world where Hades long ago found allies in God's birthed by different Creators

Tria – Evil Triplets spawned from incestuous coupling of Ares and Artemis; Deimos, Phobos and Than

Tsouximo – Hell beast resembling a giant scorpion

Uri – AKA Urian, Aletheia, interrogator, Guardian of the Realms, mate to Alex

Vane – Demi-God son of Athena, Ailouros (half-lion), Erik's twin, Alex's younger brother, Brianne's mate

Zeus – Sleeping God

COMING SOON!

New Releases

Subscribe to Setta Jay's newsletter for:

book release dates

exclusive excerpts

giveaways

http://www.settajay.com/

About The Author:

Setta Jay is the author of the popular Guardians of the Realms Series. She's garnered attention and rave reviews in the paranormal romance world for writing smart, slightly innocent heroines and intense alpha males. She loves writing stories that incorporate a strong plot with a heavy dose of heat. Her influences include Judith McNaught who she feels writes a smart heroine to perfection, Gena Showalter, Maya Banks and Lora Leigh. You can often find her writing compared to JR Ward, but if you are a fan of the Black Dagger Brotherhood be warned that Setta Jay's novels are more erotic in nature.

Born a California girl, she currently resides in Idaho with her husband of ten plus years who she describes as incredibly sexy and supportive.

She loves to hear from readers so feel free to ask her questions on social media or send her an email, she will happily reply.

Where you can find her:

http://www.settajay.com/

https://www.facebook.com/settajayauthor

https://twitter.com/SETTAJAY_

https://www.goodreads.com/author/show/7778856.Setta_Jay

CPSIA information can be obtained
at www.ICGtesting.com
Printed in the USA
FSHW02n2016140818
51449FS

9 781530 057214